MW01137945

Same Time, Next Christmas

Victoria Alexander

This ebook is licensed to you for your personal enjoyment only.
This ebook may not be sold, shared, or given away.
This is a work of fiction. Names, characters, places, and incidents are either products of the writer's imagination or are used fictitiously and are not to be construed as real. Any resemblance to actual events, locales, organizations, or persons, living or dead, is entirely coincidental.
Same Time, Next Christmas
Copyright © 2015 by Victoria Alexander
ISBN: 9781533117021
ALL RIGHTS RESERVED.

No part of this work may be used, reproduced, or transmitted in any form or by any means, electronic or mechanical, without prior permission in writing from the publisher, except in the case of brief quotations embodied in critical articles or reviews.
NYLA Publishing
350 7th Avenue, Suite 2003, NY 10001, New York.
http://www.nyliterary.com

This book is for my family who is always behind
me even in the midst of my Christmas meltdowns,
And for my friends, those women in my life who
truly are the sisters of my soul. Like the Muppets say
"Wherever you find love it feels like Christmas."
Thank you for brining me Christmas all year round.

Part One

Christmas 1885

1

Why Didn't I Pay more Attention to the Study of Italian?

Thati was the first thing that popped into my head, which was, in hindsight, completely absurd. One would have thought an eminently proper woman like myself would have first been shocked by the sight of a naked man swimming off the boulder-strewn, pebbled beach—*the private beach*—that was part of the property that had been reserved for me for Christmas, and two weeks beyond, on the coast of southern Italy. Certainly I could see no more than a head bobbing in the water, but given the stack of neatly folded clothing on the beach—*my beach*—it was obvious the man was no longer wearing anything of substance. Or anything at all.

It wasn't as if I'd never seen a naked man before, although it had been some time, as my husband, David, Lord Redwell, had died three years ago. Nor had David been prone to complete nudity even if, on occasion, it could not be avoided. Not that I had wished to see my husband naked, of course. That would have been highly improper and far too, well, adventurous. Adventure was not in my nature, although admittedly I was embarking upon what would be my first adventure of any kind. It was all rather exciting, and I am still proud of myself that I stood my ground and went through with it.

Nonetheless, I had not expected said adventure to include a naked man swimming in the waters off the beach, which for Christmas, and two weeks beyond, was for all intents and purposes my property. And I, Portia, Lady Redwell, did not intend to stand for it.

"Mi scusi, signore," I called.

He ignored me, or perhaps didn't hear me, and continued, his naked arms flashing in and out of the water with a relentless precision. Which did seem to indicate he swam more for the purposes of physical exertion rather than to delight in the rich blue-green waters of the Tyrrhenian Sea. I myself fully intended to venture into the sea during my stay, perhaps even as far as my knees, and had acquired a bathing dress for that very purpose. I did not know how to swim, and it had never seemed that lack of knowledge was a great void in my education. Still, at the moment, with the balmy breeze and beckoning waters, I did rather regret that deficit in my education, as it would have been quite delightful to fling my clothes aside and leap into the water. The weather, however, was far cooler than I had expected, although not nearly as cold as London in December. I had it in my head that this region of Italy would be more temperate, even tropical, and that was not the case. I was fairly certain the sea was not as welcoming as it appeared. Not that I would ever have done such a thing anyway.

My trespasser swam parallel to the beach in a southerly direction. It was probably too much to hope that he would continue on in that direction forever and I should not have to confront him and inform him in as firm a manner as possible that for Christmas, and two weeks beyond, he was not welcome to use my beach as an embarkation point for his aquatic activities. But, given he had left his clothes here, he obviously meant to return.

I tried again, raising my voice in a most unladylike manner. "Mi scusi!"

Again, he paid no notice, and as he was now a considerable distance down the shore, it was futile to continue to attempt to attract his attention. Besides, after *Mi scusi, signore*, I had no idea how to say what needed to be said. My French was adequate, my Spanish acceptable, but with the exception of a few pertinent phrases, my Italian was almost nonexistent. Unfortunately, languages did not come easily to me, and I spent a great deal of time during my school years avoiding the study of them. Which was foolish, as who did not hope to one day visit all those countries beyond France and Spain? I was exceptionally shortsighted in my youth, a trait I feared lingered today.

The gentleman's head was now little more than a speck in the distance. I heaved a resigned sigh, then carefully sat on one of the many boulders dotting the small beach to wait for my intruder to return. It was surprisingly comfortable. I could have climbed back up the treacherous little path that wound its way down the cliff from the villa and sent a servant to deal with the man, which would have been the proper thing to do, but I wasn't quite ready to face the climb. It was awkward enough to make my way down here in my navy blue-and-white striped walking dress. I had never before questioned the current fashion that dictated the necessity of a bustle, but that path was enough to turn anyone away from the latest style. Besides, this tiny beach, with boulders arranged as if by an expert gardener for the best possible scenic effect, and the sea beyond so vivid in color it was very nearly unimaginable, was entirely too enchanting to abandon. I had arrived a scant half an hour ago after spending the last week traveling from England to what I had begun to see as my sanctuary. I was not about to let some man intrude on my private adventure.

My gaze drifted off toward the horizon and the fishing boats far in the distance. Not that this had started out to be either an adventure or private. My Aunt Helena and I were to come to Italy together for Christmas, as most of the family was otherwise occupied. I also knew Aunt Helena's efforts to find me a new husband would only intensify during the festivities surrounding Christmas, and I was cowardly enough not to wish to face that. I was, as well, weary of it all. I sorely needed a holiday away from expectations and well-meaning intentions. Not that I didn't wish to marry again—I did— but I preferred to find a husband myself rather than have one thrust upon me.

However, the moment I said I planned to spend Christmas in Italy, my aunt announced, with a fair amount of satisfied glee, that she too had always wanted to spend Christmas on foreign shores and wasn't it too perfect that her dear friend Lady Wickelsworth had a villa to let on the outskirts of the small town of Sorrento across the bay from Naples? *Perfect* was not the word I would have used. Furthermore, I had it in my head to go much farther south, perhaps to Palermo. Without warning, my escape became Aunt Helena's holiday, and she took over the arrangements with unbridled enthusiasm.

But when we stopped in Paris, we encountered an acquaintance who wasted no time in telling us she had heard one of Aunt Helena's sons, my cousin Sebastian, had taken a wife. I could have told her, and perhaps I should have, that it was utter nonsense, but it was not my story to tell. My aunt and late uncle raised me, along with their seven children, after my parents died, and I believed this was the first time in my entire life that I shocked my aunt by doing what was not merely unexpected, but not entirely proper. I firmly informed her that she was certainly welcome to return to England, but I would not. I had planned to spend Christmas in Italy, and Italy was where I intended to be. Imagine a woman traveling to a foreign country accompanied only by her maid. Up until a few days ago, I certainly couldn't.

I credited, or blamed, the influence and example of my two dearest friends for my momentary aberration of throwing caution to the winds. They had always been far more adventurous than I. Julia, the new Lady Mountdale, had been forced to take drastic and potentially scandalous steps when her finances reached a deplorable level, although one might have also called her courageous. Of course, Julia really had little choice, in contrast to Veronica, Lady Smithson, who nearly always sacrificed the appearance of propriety to do exactly as she wished. Veronica believed women should be independent if they so desire. They should not be prohibited from joining organizations where similarly qualified gentlemen were granted membership, and they should absolutely be given the vote. She also felt women, particularly those of independent means, should marry only if they so wished and not because society expected it of them. She saw nothing wrong with a woman choosing to be a mistress rather than a wife, which I found appalling. Veronica's views about the relationships between women and men were truly scandalous, and as her dear friend, it was my responsibility to keep her opinions to myself. I had no idea how she came to her outrageous way of thinking. Nor did I have any idea how three such disparate women became the closest of friends. Yet we did, and I was grateful. They were the sisters of my soul, if you will, and I cherished them.

"Chiedo, signoro, perdono," a male voice called, and my attention snapped back to the swimmer. While my mind had wandered, he had turned back toward my beach and now trod water no more than twenty feet or so from the shore.

The sea around him sparkled with the light of the late afternoon sun. He was too far away to distinctly make out his features, but his wet hair appeared dark, and I had, of course, noticed his well-muscled arms. If I was a fanciful sort, I would have likened him to a Roman god emerging from the seas. But I am not usually fanciful, and he was not, thank God, emerging.

"Questo è imbarazzante, ma io sono nudo in questo momento," he continued. "Se vuoi essere così gentile da prendere il vostro permesso, vorrei venire fuori dall'acqua e recuperare i miei vestiti."

Oh lovely. I had hoped, given his folded clothes were more Saville Row than rustic Italian, that he would be from one of those countries whose language I could, however vaguely, comprehend. I had absolutely no idea what he had just said. I had an Italian phrase book precisely for moments like this that I had intended never to be without, but I had completely forgotten it in my eagerness to come down to the beach. I had even abandoned Margaret, my maid, in my haste, assuring her that someone would see her to our rooms. One would think I'd never seen the water before. But this was different. This was Italy, and I was, for the first time, an independent woman. An independent woman who had not expected to encounter anyone.

"Mi hai sentito, signora?" he called again. "Vorrei uscire dal acqua e recuperare i miei vestiti. Vi avverto, farò esattamente questo in un minuto." Irritation rang in his voice, as well as a certain amount of arrogance. But then, Roman gods did tend to be arrogant, or so I'd read.

Nonetheless, it was most annoying. He had no reason to be either arrogant or irritated, as I was in the right. He was no more than an intruder, a trespasser. One of those sorts who came to a party uninvited.

I rose to my feet and ran through my limited Italian vocabulary. Neither *How much?*, *Where is the train station?* nor *I would prefer tea, thank you* was appropriate. There was nothing to be done then but try to muddle through as best I could.

"Signore," I began. "This, questo. . ." I stretched my arms out in an overly dramatic gesture to indicate the beach, feeling somewhat grand as I did so. He might be a god, but I was a subject of Her Majesty, Queen Victoria, and not about to be intimidated. "Is, è, private, privato propertyo." Understand? "Comprehende?"

"Privato propertyo?" The swimmer stared. "Privato propertyo?"

Apparently, he did not understand Italian. I disregarded the thought that it wasn't the language he didn't understand so much as my version of it.

"Therefore. . ." I indicated the pile of clothes. "You may collect, collecto, your. . ." How did one say *clothes*? "Your. . ."

"Il vestiario or il abbigliamento," he said. "Either are correct."

"You speak English!" The momentary relief that I did not have to continue to flounder in the uncharted waters of Italian was swept aside by the realization that my trespasser was every bit as much a subject of Her Majesty as I. "And you're British!"

"And I'm cold!" he shouted.

"You should have thought of that before you trespassed on my beach, tore off your clothes and flung yourself into the water," I said in my loftiest manner.

He paused, and while he was still not close enough to be seen properly, I would have wagered a great deal that he was clenching his jaw and counting to ten in that way men had of trying to control their annoyance.

"I did not tear off my clothes, nor do I fling." His tone was restrained, as if he were trying to keep his voice level. It must have been most difficult while speaking loud enough to be heard. Knowing I had annoyed him struck me as a tiny victory. "And while I was swimming, I did not notice the cold. Now, however, it is most uncomfortable, and I would like to get out of the water."

"Then you should certainly do so, but not here. This," I said firmly, "is a private beach."

"Madam." He had the sound of a man nearing the end of his patience. "Forgive me for being overly direct, but I am freezing portions of my body which should never be this cold, and I should like to get out of the water before I turn completely blue. Unfortunately, I cannot do so with you standing there, as I have no clothes on."

I shrugged. "You should have thought of that too."

"Probably." He started toward the shore, his bare shoulders emerging from the water. "You might prefer to turn around, in the interest of propriety—"

"I daresay you abandoned propriety along with your clothes." I sniffed, although he did earn credit for folding them.

"As you said, it is a private beach." He continued to make his way toward the shore, the water now halfway down his chest. The oddest frisson of excitement shivered through me, which was absurd. I had grown up with four male cousins, and men, regardless of age, being the kind of creatures they were, were never as completely discreet as one would hope. Besides, I had been married. I had seen a bare chest before. Admittedly, I had never seen a stranger's finely chiseled bare chest before. He must do a great deal of swimming.

"I would suggest you stop at once." I picked up his pile of clothing, and he paused, the water now lapping at his waist. "I shall throw these to you, and you may dress where you are."

"That may well be one of the stupidest ideas I have ever heard," he said sharply. "First of all, I doubt that you can throw anything, let alone something with no real heft to it, this far and certainly not with any accuracy."

"You may have a point." I'd never been particularly good at throwing or athletics of any kind.

"Secondly, when you throw my clothes and they fail to reach me and sink to the bottom of the bay, I will still need to get out of the water." His eyes narrowed. "And I will still be naked."

Yet another point. "Very well, then." I placed his clothes on a large rock on the edge of the tiny beach, then returned to the boulder I'd been sitting on. I turned away from him and crossed my arms over my chest. "You may come out now."

"I already have," he said, his voice considerably closer than I expected. I heard his footsteps behind me moving toward where I'd left his clothes.

It struck me that it might have been unwise to wish to confront this stranger myself. After all, he could have been a murderer or kidnapper, or worse. But he was an Englishman, and even at nothing more than a glance, one could tell his clothes were of excellent quality, so he was more than likely a gentleman. I didn't feel the least bit apprehensive, although I probably should have. Indignation apparently bolstered one's courage.

"Privato propertyo," he muttered amidst the rustling of his clothes. "Was that your attempt at Italian?"

I could have lied, but it seemed pointless. "I am not well versed in Italian."

"Obviously." He snorted.

"I don't know why everyone can't simply speak English."

"As convenient as that might be for you, the rest of the world would not agree. What were you trying to say anyway?"

I blew a resigned breath. "I was trying to say this beach is private property."

The rustling stopped for a moment, then he laughed.

"You do realize Italian is not as simple as just adding a vowel to the end of the word?"

"Apparently not."

"Private property would be proprietà privata."

"Thank you. Now I know how to tell you this is private property—proprietà privata—and you are trespassing."

He laughed again. It was a nice enough laugh, I suppose, and yet it set my teeth on edge.

"Exactly what in my statement do you find so amusing?" I asked as coldly as I could.

"Only the fact that you are at once right and so very wrong." Amusement lingered in his voice.

"Oh?"

"You're right in that this is indeed private property, but I am not the one trespassing." I could hear the grin in his voice. The self-righteous, triumphant, smug grin. "You are."

2

It was all I could do to keep my mouth from dropping open in disbelief. I adopted my frostiest tone. "I beg your pardon?"

"Chiedo scusa?"

"What?"

"I said, *I beg your pardon*." A chastising note sounded in his voice. "If you're going to stay in a country, you should know at least a smattering of the language. It's rude not to."

"I do know a smattering of the language, and I am never rude."

"I doubt that."

I ignored him. "And I have a phrase book."

"Perhaps you should use it."

"I intend to, but at the moment it's not necessary, is it?" The blasted man's insistence on pointing out my linguistic failures had distracted me from the subject at hand. "What do you mean *I'm the trespasser*?"

"Simply that," he said. "This beach is part of the villa property. And as I have reserved the villa—"

"You what?" Without thinking, I spun around to face him. Fortunately, he had already donned his shirt and trousers, both of which clung to him, in spots where he was still wet, in a most disturbing manner. He was tall and solidly built in the way of a man who enjoyed physical exercise. He appeared to be a few years older than I. His eyes were dark, his features regular, and one might have thought him dashing, even handsome, if one was so inclined. I was not. "That's impossible.

He propped his right foot against a boulder and tied his shoe. "Not at all. I wrote to the villa's owner months ago. I have correspondence confirming that." He finished his right foot and switched to his left. "For the next month, the Villa Mari Incantati is mine."

"As I said, that's impossible." I squared my shoulders. "As the villa has been reserved for me."

"When you wrote to the owner, did she confirm your request?" he asked mildly, working at the laces on his shoe.

"The owner is a dear friend of my aunt, who was supposed to accompany me but was unable to do so at the last minute." Even to my own ears, it didn't sound quite as legitimate as *confirming* correspondence. And given the impromptu nature of this trip to Italy and the fact that Aunt Helena simply visited the villa's owner, an elderly countess who lived in Mayfair, to make the arrangements, it was entirely possible that this stranger's claim to the villa was more valid than mine. "I am confident she arranged everything."

He finished tying his shoe, then straightened. "I assume you have written confirmation as to that."

"Well, I don't, but I'm certain my aunt . . ." Damnation, of course I didn't. And knowing Aunt Helena, I would wager neither did she. She would say she didn't need it, that she and the owner had a verbal agreement. Which was all well and good, but a verbal agreement between two women who weren't here versus a written confirmation in the hands of a man who did not look willing to give up his claim was almost as bad as having nothing at all.

"The aunt who isn't here?"

"Yes, but—"

"Therefore, you have nothing in the way of actual proof as to your claim."

"Not on paper, but—" At once the answer struck me. "The owner was to send the villa staff notice as to our arrival. That should be adequate proof and will clear up this misunderstanding." I narrowed my eyes. "Then you may be on your way."

"Not bloody likely." He smiled and pulled his silk tie around his neck but failed to actually tie it. It gave him a roguish, devil-may-care look. He looked distinctly . . . adventurous. "I arranged to reside here, and here is where I intend to stay." He grabbed his coat and waved toward the path. "Shall we?"

"The sooner we have this resolved, the better," I said in a haughty fashion and started toward the path.

I had no need to be haughty. I was fairly certain he was in the right and I was in trouble. We had arranged to let the villa so quickly that I wouldn't be at all surprised if the staff had never received word. Aunt Helena was not known for either thoroughness or efficiency. I was only comforted by the realization that the majordomo and housekeeper, Silvestro and his wife, Agostina, had been most welcoming upon my arrival, as if they had indeed been expecting me. While I had only been in Italy a day or so, thus far the people seemed remarkably friendly. However, as my welcome had been mostly in Italian, for all I know they could have been saying, *Welcome, madam. Lovely hat. Who are you and why are you here?*

I started up the steep path, the gentleman a few steps behind me. I was very aware of his position behind and, for the most part, below me on the path, and I did hope he wasn't the type of man to stare and think lascivious thoughts. I put the unsettling idea out of my mind. There was nothing I could do about his thoughts, lascivious or otherwise. Besides, our positions couldn't be helped. At least if I tripped and began to slide back toward the beach, he would be there to hopefully break my fall and provide rescue. And wouldn't that be awkward? I had no desire to be obligated to him, and especially not for my life.

There was a short rock wall, no higher than my knees, that guarded the path from the rocky cliff that plunged downward to the sea. The small beach we had come from was one of the few spots I had seen thus far where one could actually access the water. I was not used to a climb like this and tried very hard not to let my exertion show. I couldn't imagine any man would find a woman huffing and puffing her way up a cliff to be even remotely attractive. Not that I cared, but he was rather handsome. I didn't know any woman who wanted to look less than her best in front of a handsome man. It was a matter of pride, really. Nothing more than that.

At least he was not inclined toward conversation, for which I was grateful. I wasn't sure I could talk and climb at the same time. I couldn't help but consider what my next step would be should the staff be unaware of my stay. Resolve washed through me. Regardless of what happened next, I shared one thing with the gentleman. I too had arranged to stay at the Villa Mari Incantati, and the Villa Mari Incantati was where I intended to stay. For Christmas, and two weeks beyond.

At last we reached the point nearly at the top of the cliff where the path widened out and leveled off. There was now only a slight rise to the walled garden and iron gate that led to the loggia—a covered terrace that ran the length of the villa—with a remarkable view of the bay and Mount Vesuvius in the distance. The thought of being so close to the volcano was unsettling, even if it was nice to be able to keep an eye on it. And this was an adventure, after all. What would an adventure be without an element of danger? My Baedeker's Guide to Southern Italy had assured me that there was no real danger, as the volcano had been quiet for the last dozen years or so. Indeed, one could predict the weather by which way the ever-present plume of smoke drifted. Convenient, perhaps, but not overly reassuring.

Aunt Helena had spoken of visiting the ruins of Pompeii, as we would be so close, but now that she wasn't with me, I had no desire to see the remains of what had once been a lively community. The story of how Pompeii had been destroyed and nearly forgotten for centuries had always struck me as terrifying and very, very sad. Beyond that, I was not thrilled at being even closer to the volcano.

We crossed the loggia, even in December a wonderfully inviting spot. Paved with ancient flat stones, winter foliage wrapped around the columns that framed arched openings. The mild nature of the climate ensured all was still green, but only a handful of the hardiest specimens were actually in bloom. I anticipated spending long hours here curled in a chaise lounge reading one of the books I'd brought with me. My escort picked up his pace to reach the glass-paned door before me, opened it and waved me into the villa.

"Thank you," I said coolly and stepped into a large garden room. Three sets of French doors opened onto the loggia. Light flooded the space, thanks to floor-to-ceiling windows on the north wall that provided, as well, a spectacular view of the coastline. Pots and urns filled every unoccupied space and overflowed with a profusion of colorful blooms that were apparently quite willing to thrive in the sunny room when their compatriots out of doors were not.

Almost at once, Silvestro descended upon us with a flurry of enthusiastic Italian. I vowed to never again leave my room without my phrase book.

"Sembra possiamo avere un problema," my nemesis said smoothly.

I wasn't at all pleased that it would be up to him to explain our circumstances, but he was proficient in Italian, and we had already established I was not. I was likely to get us both thrown out. Whether I wanted to or not, I would have to trust that he was an honorable sort. My only solace was the excellent quality of his clothing. Surely a man who wore such clothing could be trusted.

"Un problema?" Silvestro's eyes widened, and his gaze shifted from my interpreter to me and back. Even I could understand *problema*. "Qual è il problema? Cosa posso fare per correggerlo?"

I was now completely lost. As the two exchanged words at breakneck speed, I could have sworn I heard the voice of a long-ago instructor berating me for not taking the study of languages more seriously.

"Ahh." Silvestro glanced at me and nodded. "Un momento." He turned and scurried off down the hallway.

"Well?" I said.

"He says he has correspondence and apparently a book in which he notes matters pertaining to the running of the villa. However . . ."

"However?" I did not like the look on his face.

"Let's wait to see what Silvestro has in his book, shall we? But I daresay you're not going to like it," he added under his breath.

I stared at him, annoyance sharpening my voice. "I have never been fond of men who enjoy being cryptic. Evasive and mysterious are not qualities I find the least bit attractive."

"You think I'm mysterious?" A hint of a smile played about his lips.

"I think you're annoying," I snapped. "Although you have not seen fit to introduce yourself, which I find more rude than mysterious."

His smile grew more smug. "Neither have you."

"I am not accustomed to introducing myself to naked gentlemen I encounter while they are swimming in the sea," I said in a lofty tone.

"I see." His dark eyes, a deep blue, sparkled with amusement. Sparkled! He was enjoying this! "So when are you accustomed to introducing yourself to naked gentlemen?"

I sucked in a sharp breath. This was totally and completely improper and quite, quite shocking. "I beg your pardon!" I narrowed my eyes. "Chiedo scusa!"

He stared for a moment, then laughed. "You do learn quickly."

"Apparently, I will have to." I drew a deep breath and summoned a measure of calm. I did not like being teased. I'd had more than enough of that from male cousins as a child. I did not like feeling helpless, and I absolutely hated not knowing what people were saying. "I do think, given the situation, that we should consider—"

Silvestro came bustling back, a large ledger in one hand and a few loose papers in the other. He placed the ledger on a table. "Signore, signora, vedo qui—"

"Mi scusi," I said quickly, stepped away and gestured to my stranger to join me. "It's ridiculous for me to pretend to understand what the two of you are talking about. If you would be so good as to handle this . . ." I forced a weak smile. "I would be most appreciative."

"Of course," he said in a gallant manner, then studied me for a moment. "Are you sure you can trust me?"

"No." I shrugged. "But I do find your clothes reassuring."

A slow grin spread across his face. His very nice face. "I shall make a note to thank my tailor."

"As well you should," I said in a sharper tone than I had intended, but then, I did tend to be sharp when I suspected something not to my liking was imminent. And suspected, as well, that there was nothing I could do to prevent it.

He raised a brow in an arrogant way, as if he were amused and intrigued at the same time. It was most annoying, and I had the absurd impulse to slap his face. I had never slapped a man's face before and often wondered what vile thing the beast would have to do to deserve such a fate. Now, I was beginning to understand.

"If you will excuse me." He nodded and turned back to speak with Silvestro.

I sighed and returned to stand by the door and gaze at the scene beyond the glass. From this vantage point, the volcano was centered between two of the vine-covered columns that supported the loggia's roof. The sun was beginning to sink below the horizon, and the sky was streaked with pinks and oranges. It was a picture fit for a postal card. No doubt with some sentimental nonsense scrawled on the back.

Silence fell behind me, and I could see the men's faint reflection in the glass. They had apparently finished their discussion. I wasn't at all sure I was ready to hear my fate.

"Well?" I turned to face my stranger and forced a bright note to my voice. "Have you sorted all this out?"

"More or less."

I ignored the reluctant tone in his voice. "When will you be leaving, then?"

The hesitation in his eyes vanished, replaced by a look that might be called a little bit wicked. I had the distinct feeling I had just thrown down a gauntlet. I raised my chin and met his gaze directly. "Well?"

"Oh, I won't be leaving."

My heart sank. I ignored it. It would not do to have this villain think he had the upper hand. Especially if he did.

"What did Silvestro say?" I held my breath.

"He's confirmed that he did indeed have correspondence from the villa's owner as to your—or, rather, your aunt's—arrival."

"Aha!" I fairly shouted with triumph. It was not the sort of exuberance I usually exhibited. I was, for the most part, sedate and cognizant of the rules of proper behavior. One should never gloat over one's successes, after all. But at the moment, I didn't care and wondered if this lapse in propriety was a consequence of adventure. I rather hoped so. It was delightful. "I knew all was in order. I didn't doubt it for a moment." Still, it wasn't well-mannered to rub one's triumph in someone else's face. "I am sorry that your plans have been disrupted, but I understand these sorts of things do happen when one is traveling abroad. However, as this is not the high season, you will surely be able to find other accommodations with very little effort. Perhaps Silvestro can assist you."

His brow furrowed in annoyance. "I have no intention of seeking other accommodations. I said I wasn't leaving, and I'm not."

"You also said my claim to residence at the villa has been verified." I couldn't help myself—I smirked.

"Which does not mean mine has not," he said smoothly. "Silvestro also said my arrival was expected as well."

My stomach sank. "Oh?"

"Apparently, while he did consider it somewhat convoluted, he attributed it to what he calls the bewildering manner of the English."

"Nonsense." I scoffed. "We're not the least bit bewildering."

"As we arrived within a few hours of each other, and you arrived without your aunt, Silvestro naturally assumed we were to meet each other here. A liaison that had been arranged at a location convenient to both of us." He paused. "A Christmas rendezvous, if you will."

"I most certainly will not!" I stared at him. "And I don't think that this is a natural assumption at all."

"He also expressed grave doubts as to whether or not your aunt even exists."

"Of course she exists!"

"Surely you can see his point. Shortly after I arrive, you show up without any sort of chaperone. It's not the least bit implausible to think something had been arranged between us." He shrugged. "Besides, he is Italian."

"I don't care what he is, it's entirely far-fetched to assume simply because a man and a woman reserve the same residence at the same time that there's something scandalous in the works." I ignored the thought that if I had heard of the same sort of situation, I too would have leaped to erroneous conclusions of a sordid nature. "Why, one can just as easily assume that there was a dreadful mistake or some sort of misunderstanding or a confusion in one's calendar."

"As this is not the usual time of year for visitors, Silvestro's assessment of the situation doesn't seem the least bit far-fetched to me. I assume you came from London?"

"Indeed, I did, but—"

"And I am currently residing in Calcutta. If one looks at a map, one might well say that Italy is suspiciously close to a halfway point. Therefore . . ." He paused as if his point was obvious.

"Don't be absurd. London is far closer to Italy than Calcutta is. Why, a man would have to be truly smitten to have come this distance simply for an assignation."

"I would think the distance is insignificant if the right lady is at the end of the journey." His blue eyes twinkled, and heat washed up my face. "Love will entice a man to do all sorts of things he might otherwise not be inclined to attempt."

"Be that as it may, this is not love," I said firmly. "This is an awkward dilemma involving strangers, not . . . *lovers.*" I don't believe I had ever said that particular word in a man's presence before, let alone a man whose name I still did not know, and once again, I could feel my cheeks warm. I ignored it. "Surely you understand we must straighten this out. And I can think of only one way to do so."

"Can you?" His brow rose.

"It's obvious to me." I adopted my firmest voice. "You shall have to find other accommodations."

"As we both have legitimate claims to the villa, why should I be the one to leave? I have come the farthest and expended the greatest effort." He smiled in an overly pleasant manner. "I think you should be the one to go."

"Christmas is but three days away, and I have no intention of wandering Italy aimlessly, looking for a place to stay in some sort of odd reenactment of the story of our savior's birth." I shook my head. "No, as a gentleman, it falls to you to do the proper thing and take your leave."

His smile widened. "And you believe I am a gentleman because of the quality of my clothing?"

"Of course not." Although that did indeed contribute to my assessment of him. "Your accent is cultured and your manner refined. Aside from your penchant to leap naked into the sea—"

He laughed.

"I would say you do indeed appear to be a gentleman." I smiled in as sweet a manner as I could. "Do tell me if I'm mistaken."

"If you judge a gentleman by his willingness to give up his plans in favor of yours, then I'm afraid you are indeed sadly mistaken."

Annoyance surged through me. "Now see here—"

He held up his hand to quiet me. "I have an alternative idea."

I folded my arms over my chest. "Out with it, then."

"As I refuse to turn around and head back to India—"

"And I will not return to England."

"I propose we share the villa," he said. "It's large enough to accommodate both of us. I daresay we can both reside here for the duration of our stay and easily avoid each other."

I stared in disbelief. "That's dreadfully improper."

"It's not as if we would be alone. Silvestro and his wife reside on the grounds, and there are other servants as well. You have brought a maid, have you not?"

"Yes, of course, but—"

"It would be no different than if this was a small hotel. You wouldn't expect me to leave a hotel, would you?"

"Yes," I snapped. "No, I suppose not, but this is not a hotel—it's a private residence. Why, what would people say? This is the height of impropriety, and I have a reputation that I would prefer to keep unsullied."

"What people?" He did have a point. "The servants at the villa speak little to no English. They're not going to be dashing off a letter to England detailing your scandalous Christmas holiday. And, I assure you, I have no intention of telling anyone that I shared a roof on the coast of Italy with a stubborn stranger. You have my word on that. I too have a reputation to maintain."

I waved off his comment. "It's different for men."

He blew a long-suffering breath. "My family is exceptionally stuffy, and my position with the government demands discretion."

I studied him for a moment. He did seem sincere, although I certainly wasn't ready to trust him completely.

"There's no need for anyone to ever know that we resided here together," he added.

I'd already realized he was just as determined to stand his ground as I was. A tiny voice in the back of my head, the very same voice that had urged me to come to Italy on my own, noted that, as no one would ever know, why not share the villa? Weren't new and unusual experiences the very definition of adventure? Besides, there was no other choice.

I heaved a resigned sigh. "Very well."

"Excellent." He grinned. "Allow me to introduce myself. My name is Fletcher Jamison, currently a resident of Calcutta in the employ of Her Majesty's Foreign Service. Silvestro said the letter he received indicated a Lady Waterston would be arriving with her niece. I gather you are not Lady Waterston."

"No, I am Lady . . ." Regardless of Mr. Jamison's promise to keep the details of our stay private, it struck me that not giving my correct name was not a bad idea. "Smithson. I am Lady Smithson." Veronica wouldn't mind my using her name under these circumstances. Indeed, she would quite appreciate it. Not that she would ever know. Good Lord, Veronica would hold it over my head for the rest of my days if she learned of this. She firmly believed that those least willing to bend would eventually snap. She thought I was the least willing to bend of anyone she knew and would have seen my being willing to share a villa—no matter how large—with a man I had just met to be the beginning of a snap. I would have hated for her to have that satisfaction. I extended my hand. "Portia Smithson."

He took my hand and bowed over it. Good. I would have thought poorly of him had he attempted to kiss it, especially under these circumstances. I brushed aside what might have been a stab of disappointment.

"It is a pleasure to make your acquaintance, Lady Smithson." Mr. Jamison released my hand, nodded, then crossed the room to the entry where Silvestro had magically appeared, or possibly had been there all along. They exchanged several phrases in Italian so rapidly that I suspected, even if I had been mildly conversant in the language, I wouldn't have grasped any of it. Silvestro then vanished down the corridor, and Mr. Jamison turned to me.

"There are several suites of rooms overlooking the ocean. My bags were already placed in the suite on the southernmost end of the floor, as it has the best light. I have instructed Silvestro to place yours in the suite at the opposite end. I assume you wish to have as much separation between us as possible."

"That does seem appropriate," I murmured. Not that I feared he would accost me in the middle of the night, or that I might succumb to the temptation of a dashing man within reach. On the contrary, I had never given in to temptation of that kind nor did I intend to. Not that I'd had the opportunity. But it did seem wise to put as much distance as possible between the handsome Mr. Jamison and myself.

"Silvestro says dinner will be served at eight in the dining room or here on the loggia if you prefer."

"I prefer to have it in my rooms, and I would be grateful if you would inform him of that." At once I realized how abrupt I sounded. "My apologies, Mr. Jamison. I do not mean to be impolite, but I have been either on a train or a ship for the better part of a week, and I would like nothing better than a good meal and a bed that is on solid land. Beyond that . . ." I wasn't quite sure how to phrase this. "When my aunt decided not to accompany me, I realized I would be completely alone. I have never been completely alone before. I have a large family and a fair number of friends. I had begun to think of the Villa Mari Incantati as a sort of sanctuary of tranquility and seclusion and solitude. I was—I am—looking forward to that."

"I see." He nodded slowly.

"I do hope I haven't offended you," I added quickly. "But it might be best if we were to keep our distance. You're, well, you're not in my plans."

"Plans change, Lady Smithson. It's one of the few things we can count on in life. However . . ." He smiled coolly. "I too have plans that do not include companionship, no matter how lovely. I will make every effort to avoid intruding on your quest for solitude as I pursue a passion of my own." His gaze slid past me. "And as Silvestro has returned to see you to your rooms, I shall bid you good day." He nodded, smiled and took his leave, exactly as I wanted.

I followed Silvestro down the corridor and up the stairs to my rooms, glancing casually toward the end of the long hallway where Mr. Jamison's rooms were located. It did seem a very long way away, which would serve both our purposes well.

I couldn't help but recall that he had referred to me as lovely. I harbored no false modesty about my appearance. My hair was a deep rich brown, my eyes nearly as dark. My complexion was relatively unblemished, except in the summer when, no matter how hard I tried, I ended up with a smattering of annoying freckles across my nose. My features were even, although my nose was a bit more pert than I would have liked. I was of average height, and at twenty-seven years of age, my figure was still fetching. While no one would call me a great beauty, I was considered attractive. Nonetheless, there was something about a dashing stranger calling me lovely in the most offhand way that was really rather thrilling.

I smiled and glanced again in the direction of his rooms. And wondered exactly what passion Mr. Fletcher Jamison intended to pursue.

3

I have found that after an exceptional night's sleep, I occasionally awaken not only refreshed but with revelations and clarity I neither sought nor anticipated. This was one of those mornings. Typically, this was the result of having eaten something disagreeable the night before or refusing to acknowledge that I had made some sort of dreadful mistake. Last night's dinner was excellent.

I lay in my bed and stared up at the plaster ceiling embellished with paintings of doves and flowers and small, chubby angels. Regardless of Mr. Jamison's legitimate claim to the villa, I should have stood firm and insisted he find other accommodations. As I'd failed to do so, I should, well, take full advantage of his company. A bit of companionship would be most welcome. Especially with someone who spoke English.

I had eaten in my rooms last night at a table set up in front of the French doors that opened onto the balcony that ran along the front of the villa. Margaret declined when I invited her to join me, saying that would be most improper, and even

29

though I had dragged her far away from family and friends at the very best time of year to be with family and friends, she had no intention of allowing her training to lapse. She would much prefer to eat with servants even if she didn't understand a word of Italian, and Lord knew what they might be saying. Which was all well and good, but it was obvious from her tone that she was still annoyed with me for my abrupt decision to abandon England in favor of spending Christmas in Italy.

That my moment of impulse was neither wise nor well thought out was my first revelation. I rarely did anything that was not well thought out. I saw now that it had been the height of foolishness to want to be anywhere at Christmas but with the overly large, often annoying, frequently loud Hadley-Attwaters. Since the moment my aunt and uncle took me in after the death of my parents, to this very day, they had never once made me feel as if I were not a true member of the family. As far as my male cousins were concerned, I was another sister to torment. My female cousins welcomed me, as I evened the balance of power between the boys and girls of the family. Christmas was always filled with festivities and fun and frolic, carols around the fire fed by a giant Yule log, silly plays and pantomimes performed by the younger family members, greenery festooning every nook and cranny of the family's grand house in the country and as enormous a tree as Aunt Helena could find and the boys could manage to squeeze in the door. Even though my Uncle William and oldest cousin Richard were no longer with us, and we had all gone our individual ways, Christmas was still special.

But, while I'd never once said it to any of them, as joyous as Christmas was, there was always the tiniest empty spot in my heart. Aunt Helena might well have suspected, but she never said a word. I would have been most embarrassed and felt like the worst sort of ungrateful creature if she had. David had filled that empty place through the few years of our marriage, although not completely. Perhaps if we had had children of our own . . .

It wasn't merely Aunt Helena's well-meaning yet unrelenting quest to find David's replacement that prompted my flight this year from England and, really, from Christmas itself. But her efforts only served to remind me of what Julia had found with her new husband and what Veronica was in the process of finding with my cousin Sebastian that I had not yet found. I didn't begrudge their happiness, far from it. I was overjoyed for them, and I would never allow them to suspect that I was even the tiniest bit envious. Which was not so much a revelation as an acceptance of my own character failings.

I had not realized, when I had insisted on continuing to Italy after Aunt Helena had decided to return to England, that being independent and alone might also bring on the sort of loneliness and even melancholy I had never experienced. Oh certainly, I was frequently alone in my own house, but it was always with the knowledge that I needn't be alone if I didn't wish to be. There were always family or friends I could call on should I need companionship. What had sounded so perfect when it first entered my mind was now, in reality, disheartening. I had never been one for solitude, which was certainly not a revelation, so why I'd thought I wanted it now made no sense whatsoever. I was in a country whose language I didn't grasp, with a servant who was not happy with me, about to share Christmas with a man I'd just met and had firmly told to keep his distance. I did regret that. He seemed a nice enough sort. It struck me that I should be grateful to Mr. Jamison for refusing to leave. Last night, I experienced a taste of true loneliness. It was not to my liking.

Christmas was the day after tomorrow, and even if I left Italy today, I would never make it home in time. Besides, returning would truly have made me look like an idiot who didn't know her own mind. While that might be accurate, at least in this case, I preferred to maintain the illusion that I was in command of my senses.

Resolve washed through me. I threw off the covers and slipped out of bed. I'd never particularly thought of myself as weak, although I wouldn't say I had more than average courage. But I had weathered widowhood for three years. I managed my own affairs, my household and my finances. If indeed I had embarked on an adventure, my first and perhaps my only adventure, I should make the most of it. It would be foolish not to. After all, I was on my own in a foreign country, residing in a beautiful villa with a volcano in the distance and a handsome stranger down the hall. I did seem to have all the necessary ingredients for adventure.

I pulled on my robe and stepped to the balcony doors. I had left them open last night so that I could fall asleep gazing at the stars overhead and hearing the waves crash against the cliffs. Clouds lingered about the top of the volcano. I would have to check my guidebook to see what that indicated. The morning was bright, if a bit cooler than yesterday. I pulled my robe tighter around me. If I hadn't been so eager to leave England, I would have taken the time to thoroughly research my Christmas destination, and I would have learned that while the weather on the Bay of Naples could be quite lovely at this time of year, rain was to be expected. If I had been aware of that, I might have stayed home. Or insisted on traveling farther south.

Still, today the air was clear and refreshing. The slightest breeze ruffled my unbound hair, and the faint scent of the sea teased my nose. The day beckoned with promise. The most remarkable sense of freedom and liberty stirred within me. At once I realized this trip—this *place*—was not a mistake. This was indeed a sanctuary, no matter how lonely I might be. I inhaled a deep breath and stepped out into the morning.

"Good day, Lady Smithson." Mr. Jamison stood at the balustrade at the far end of the balcony, gazing out at the bay.

I resisted the immediate urge to jump back into my room and hide behind the curtains. Not that between my nightwear and my robe I didn't have on very nearly as many layers as I had when more properly dressed, but I hadn't yet put on my corset. I daresay any number of improprieties could be blamed on a lady failing to don a corset, although I was confident I was made of sterner stuff.

Nonetheless, it was time to embrace my adventure, or at least attempt to survive it. And the first step was to pursue a cordial, platonic sort of friendship with Mr. Fletcher Jamison.

I leaned slightly over the balustrade to better see him and cast him a pleasant smile. "Good morning, Mr. Jamison. I trust you slept well?"

"Quite well, thank you." He nodded in a dismissive manner. It was not an auspicious beginning.

I brushed my hair away from my face, vowing not to worry about my appearance. "It appears we are in for a lovely day."

"Thus far, I would agree with you." An absent note sounded in his voice, as if, having exchanged an appropriate number of words, he saw no need to continue conversing with me. A response I no doubt deserved given my declaration about solitude. Regardless, I had changed my mind, or come to my senses, and I was not going to let his reticence dissuade me.

"Enjoy the day, Lady Smithson." With that, he turned and moved out of sight. Not difficult, given the balcony was as over-furnished as the rest of the villa. Pots filled with greenery, urns planted with small trees and an assortment of wrought-iron furnishings cluttered the balcony and obscured my view of him.

"Although it is far cooler than I had expected," I called after him. I did hate to resort to comments about the weather, but nothing else of substance came to mind. I made my way along the balcony toward him. "But far more pleasant than London at this time of year. Don't you agree?" I stepped around a cluster of pots and pulled up short. "Oh!" Apparently, I had discovered Mr. Jamison's passion.

He cast a quick glance at me from his chair behind an easel, then returned his attention to the canvas in front of him. He had taken off his coat, and his tie hung loose around his neck. One couldn't help but remember how those broad shoulders had looked yesterday, glistening in the late afternoon sun. Not that I had noticed.

"Good Lord!" I moved closer. "You're an artist!"

"No, Lady Smithson," he said coolly, "I am a civil servant."

"In Calcutta perhaps, but here you definitely appear to be an artist." I craned my neck to see what he was painting, but the easel was at an angle that effectively blocked my view, and I suspected Mr. Jamison would not welcome my interest.

His brow arched upward. "You don't approve?"

"I didn't say I didn't approve," I said quickly. But it was my understanding that artists in general tended to ignore the rules of proper behavior. They were, quite frankly, hedonists. Or so I'd heard.

"The tone of your voice did."

"Nonsense." Although I supposed I did disapprove of artists in principle. All that free-spirited impropriety. "Why, you must be an artist if your feelings are this delicate."

He slanted me a quick glance, then returned his attention to his canvas. "My feelings are not the least bit delicate."

I shrugged. "They certainly appear delicate. I suppose you write poetry too."

"No."

I sat down in a nearby chair. "It does seem a pity. To waste all that emotion, I mean."

His jaw tightened. "Lady Smithson—"

"I do think you should call me Portia. It's not entirely proper, but as you pointed out yesterday, no one will ever know. I can't imagine an artist is a great stickler for propriety anyway. Besides, we will be spending Christmas together, which does seem to call for a bit of informality." I favored him with my brightest smile.

He stared at me as if I had suddenly grown two heads. And perhaps I had. I was far more direct with him than I could recall ever being with any man, except perhaps my late husband. I blamed it on Italy. Or the fact that I was using Veronica's name, and she never hesitated to speak her mind regardless of the consequences. And the lack of a corset.

"And the tone of my voice did not imply disapproval, only surprise." I paused. Oh, there might have been a touch of disapproval, but I thought it best not to admit it. "I never would have suspected you were of an artistic nature."

"Why not?" He daubed a bit of blue on his canvas.

"You just didn't strike me as an artistic type, that's all." I tried and failed to keep a defensive note from my voice. I had done nothing wrong. Why did this man make me feel as though I had?

"And you didn't strike me as the type of woman who would appear in public in her night clothes," he said mildly.

"I wouldn't call this public. Nor had I intended to appear anywhere. I simply stepped out on the balcony to savor the morning air, and you greeted me. It would have been rude for me to ignore you."

"And we have already established that you are never rude." His gaze shifted between his canvas and the bay. "If you have now fulfilled the requirements of polite society regarding the exchange of greetings and the avoidance of rudeness, you might want to take your leave." His eyes flicked to mine. "I would hate to intrude on your solitude."

"And I do appreciate your thoughtfulness." Although loneliness might well have been preferable to having anything whatsoever to do with Mr. Fletcher Jamison. He certainly wasn't making this easy. I shoved the thought aside and forced a pleasant smile. "Might I be perfectly honest with you?"

"I have always preferred honesty."

"Have you? I have always thought honesty to be a bit inconvenient." I shrugged, amazed that I had confessed such a thing.

"Oh?"

"Well, yes. Most inconvenient and often unpleasant." I searched for an example. "Say, a gentleman goes on and on about something he considers a great accomplishment." I leaned forward in a confidential manner. "If you are perfectly honest and tell him what you really think, that said accomplishment was not at all great and you did wonder if it could be termed an accomplishment at all, he'll be most offended."

"No doubt," he said cautiously.

"But that's neither here nor there, really, because I do intend to be perfectly honest at the moment."

"Because it's . . . convenient?"

Obviously he did not understand the various shades of honesty as well as I did. I ignored him.

"I discovered last night that solitude is not to my liking." I beamed at him. "So, since we are both alone, for the length of our stay, I propose we should be friends."

"So you are offering the hand of friendship but only in a temporary sense?"

"I'm not sure I would phrase it quite like that, but I suppose it is accurate. We will both go our separate ways when we leave here, after all." I paused. "It just seems to me that it would be foolish of me—of both of us—not to be friends now, as we will be spending Christmas in the same house, and we're both subjects of Her Majesty and . . ."

"And I'm the only one here you can talk to, as I'm the only one here who speaks your language." A slight, wry smile played across his lips.

"You needn't say it like that. As if I were extending the hand of friendship only because you are the only possibility."

"And yet I am the only possibility."

"There is that, but that just makes it all the more perfect, don't you agree?" Again, I smiled brightly.

"Lady Smithson—"

"Portia."

"If you insist, Portia then." He considered me for a moment. "I must confess that yesterday when you suggested we keep our distance, I was a bit taken aback. I have always considered myself to be a friendly, amicable sort, and I had rather looked forward to the prospect of furthering our acquaintance. On a strictly companionable basis, you understand," he said quickly, as if to alleviate any concerns I might have had about his intentions. I wasn't sure if I found his comment reassuring or slightly insulting. "However, the more I thought about your desire for solitude, the more I liked the idea. My life in Calcutta is unceasingly hectic, leaving no time to savor those things that I especially enjoy."

"Painting?"

"Among other pursuits." He nodded. "I came here for a respite from the day-to-day demands of my life. Just as you came for solitude, I suppose I came seeking peace. And while usually I would put interesting conversation with a pleasant female companion on the list of those things I enjoy, our brief discourses have convinced me that, at the moment, I would prefer to keep to myself. So, just as I was not included in your plans, neither are you included in mine." He smiled politely. "Therefore, I shall leave you to enjoy your solitude as I fully intend to savor my peace."

"I see." Indignation rose in my throat. "It's entirely your loss, Mr. Jamison. I am an excellent friend. Loyal, dependable—"

"I had a dog as a boy, Lady Smithson," he said, his gaze returning to his canvas in obvious dismissal of me.

"Poor creature!" I snapped. "Very well, then. I shall spend Christmas alone in my rooms with a romantic novel that will make me swoon and sigh and weep with joy at the end. It will be an excellent Christmas!"

There was more I could say, but at the moment, I felt both triumphant and righteous. *Veni, vidi, vici,* as the Romans would have said, and here in the land that Rome once ruled, I felt very much like a conqueror.

Admittedly, in many ways I had brought this on myself, which made me just as annoyed with myself as I was with him.

"Good day, Mr. Jamison." I nodded, turned and headed back along the balcony toward my door, chin held high. So much for my attempt at cultivating friendship. I had offered him an olive branch, and he had refused it. No matter. I wasn't sure I wanted to be friends with someone who considered me lovely yesterday but only pleasant today. No, I would spend my days here with the books I had brought and long invigorating walks to the village. I would catch up on my correspondence and do whatever else struck my fancy. I was, after all, an independent woman, and I was sure last night's bout of loneliness was nothing more than an aberration. I was simply not used to being alone. There was nothing more to it than that. I certainly didn't need the companionship of some arrogant stranger.

Although—I glanced back down the balcony, Mr. Jamison again hidden from view—I could take his rebuff as a challenge. Or better yet, a game. That would take my mind off being alone, and it would be fun. I smiled. I had always liked games. Particularly at Christmas. Especially when I won.

I had nearly reached my room when I heard the faint but distinct sound of a man's amused chuckle. I was glad he was amused. I would have hated for our meeting to have been completely futile.

I resisted the urge to slam the door behind me. I would not give Mr. Jamison the satisfaction of knowing how irritating I found our exchange. Besides, his behavior only strengthened my determination.

I would forge a friendship with this man, in the spirit of Christmas if for no other reason. The only question was how. And perhaps, once we were friends, I would admit I found him right in one respect.

Plans did indeed change.

4

Exactly how to cultivate Mr. Jamison's friendship occupied my thoughts well into the afternoon. Even attempts to immerse myself in *Belinda*, the novel by Miss Broughton that I had thought would fill my time, failed to engage my attention.

Between my phrasebook and a rarely used skill for pantomime, Agostina and I had managed a form of rudimentary communication. I somehow conveyed to her my desire to have afternoon tea on the loggia, and she somehow understood my meaning. We were both quite delighted at our accomplishment. I considered it a minor Christmas miracle, although she was no doubt used to serving tea when Lady Wickelsworth was in residence. The tiny sandwiches that accompanied the tea were quite nice, but the pastries—most of which incorporated in some manner the lemons that grew so abundantly here—the pastries were glorious. I could quite happily spend the rest of my days on this loggia, eating what Agostina called *zeppole*, or something like that. Regardless, these light-as-air wreaths of pastry piped with a lemon lemon-flavored cream were a heavenly concoction. And a pleasant accompaniment to pondering the dilemma that was Fletcher Jamison.

I was not used to being rebuffed, and I did not like it. Unfortunately for Mr. Jamison, his rejection of my overture only made me more determined. And curious. Why, if he resided in Calcutta, had he come as far as Italy for Christmas? Surely there were any number of places far closer and equally serene where he could find peace. And if he was going to travel this distance, why not go all the way to England for Christmas? He had mentioned his family—why not visit them? Unless, of course, they disapproved of either his vocation or his art. Given Mr. Jamison had termed his family *stuffy*, I suspected the latter.

Or was he perhaps, like myself, looking for a measure of escape? And if so, what was he escaping from? I very much doubted that he had an Aunt Helena thrusting every unmarried female at him like a Christmas offering. What if he was already married and escaping from the bonds of wedded bliss? That was a most disturbing thought. Not that I had any romantic intentions toward him, but I could never be on friendly terms with a man who had abandoned his wife. And perhaps the most intriguing question of all: Was Mr. Jamison more gentleman civil servant or hedonistic artist?

I gazed out at the bay and the volcano in the distance and popped the rest of a third zeppole into my mouth, vowing, as I had with the second, that this would be my last.

"Good afternoon, Lady Smithson." Mr. Jamison's voice sounded slightly behind me and to my right.

"Good afternoon, Mr. Jamison," I said without looking at him. I was trying very hard not to choke on the zeppole.

He paused, no doubt waiting for an invitation to join me. One I was not inclined to extend until I had swallowed my pastry and surreptitiously wiped the sugar from my lips.

"I was wondering if I might have a word with you," he said at last.

"Of course," I choked out the words and waved in the general direction of the chair on the opposite side of the table.

He took his seat, and almost immediately, Agostina appeared with a second cup and a plate for his use. Once his cup had been filled, and he had exerted what appeared to be a considerable amount of charm in Italian, judging by the way the older woman fluttered and giggled around him in the affectionate manner of a mother hen, she took her leave.

"So, Mr. Jamison." I picked up my cup and took a sip. "What word would you like to have?"

"For one thing, I wish to offer my apologies for my behavior this morning." He shook his head. "I am not usually so ill-mannered."

"You are on holiday, Mr. Jamison."

"That is no excuse."

"I didn't think it was."

"Yes, well, as I said, I do apologize."

"And I accept your apology."

He stared at me rather pointedly. "Well?"

"Well, what?"

"Well, don't you wish to apologize for your manner last night?"

"I don't wish to." I sighed. "But I suppose I will if only to be cordial, mind you." I chose my words thoughtfully. "You have my heartfelt apology if you considered me at all rude. I don't always think before I speak."

He gasped in feigned astonishment. "No!"

"Sarcasm, Mr. Jamison—"

"Fletcher."

"Very well, then. Sarcasm, *Fletcher*, is not nearly as charming as it might seem."

"Perhaps not." His tone was somber, but a definite gleam of amusement lingered in his eyes. "If your offer of friendship for the length of our stay has not been withdrawn, I would be honored to accept."

I considered him for a moment. In spite of my determination to be friends, it had been my observation that no man values that which comes too easily. Mr. Jamison—Fletcher—had his opportunity and let it slip through his fingers. "Might I be perfectly honest?"

"Twice in one day?" His eyes widened. The man was a master of sarcasm without saying a word. "I am indeed honored."

I ignored him. "You rebuffed my offer of friendship because I annoyed you last night. I am tempted now to reject yours because of our exchange this morning."

"I see," he said slowly.

"This is a game we could play forever." I met his gaze directly. "I do enjoy playing games, Fletcher." The moment the words were out of my mouth, I knew they were a mistake. I saw the speculation in his eyes. I pretended I hadn't. "Backgammon, croquet and all those lighthearted games one plays at parties. However, I do not wish to play a never-ending game of *Offense and Apology*."

His brow quirked upward.

"Therefore, I propose we start over." I refilled my cup from the teapot festooned with fanciful paintings of lemons and leaves and swirls of blue. "Perhaps each of us could list what we have to offer the other, as friends, that is."

"An application of sorts for friendship?"

"I suppose you could put it that way. Shall I go first?"

He bit back a smile. "Please do."

"Very well." I thought for a moment. "Aside from those sterling qualities I share with hounds"—I cast him a chastising look—"I can converse on any number of interesting subjects and a fair number of dull ones. I am better read than most people suspect. In addition to the games I have already mentioned, I also enjoy a variety of card games. I can play chess, but I'm not very skilled at it." I stared firmly into his dark eyes. "I prefer games that I'm good at, games I can win. And I always play to win."

"Good to know," he said under his breath.

"As I suspect we may spend some of our evenings engaged in healthy competition, I should like to know beforehand if you are one of those men who has difficulties being defeated by a woman. I warn you, I will not allow you to win simply to avoid offending your fragile sensibilities."

"Nor would I expect you to."

"Good." I nodded. While there were any number of ways in which I would allow a man to feel he was superior, one did not grow up in a large family—or at least in my large family—without learning it was to no one's benefit to give anything you did no less than everything you had. A similar sentiment was expressed in Latin on the Hadley-Attwater family crest. "Let's see, beyond that . . ." What did my friends say about me? "Oh yes, I am usually quite cognizant of the rules of proper behavior, which is extremely helpful to those of my friends who have no sense of propriety at all."

"I can see where it would be."

"You have no idea." I shook my head. "I have several friends—well, one in particular who pays no mind to appropriate behavior unless it suits her purposes, very often skirting the edge of scandal itself."

"And you do not approve."

"Absolutely not. There are rules, Fletcher, that dictate how we are expected to behave. Why, if everyone did exactly as they wished, we would have anarchy."

"Not that!"

"I realize you think this is amusing."

"Extremely amusing, given that you have agreed to share the villa with me, which, I believe, you called the height of impropriety."

"That's entirely different." I waved off the comment.

"Is it?" He took a sip of his tea. "It seems to me that impropriety is impropriety."

"That's a decidedly male way to look at it." I glanced at him in a pitying manner.

"It's a decidedly accurate way to look at it."

"Don't be absurd. Our mutual occupancy of the villa is the product of misunderstanding and confusion through no fault of our own. In spite of Silvestro's initial assumption, this was not the planned rendezvous of separated lovers."

Fletcher choked on his tea. Apparently, he wasn't used to women being direct. But I was enjoying saying exactly what came to mind without any thought or concern as to the consequences and with no apology. I wondered if this was how Veronica felt with every unguarded word she uttered. No doubt why she always seemed so smug.

"What we have here is only the appearance of impropriety. And while one should always avoid the appearance of impropriety, in this particular case, we can't." I shrugged. "However, as you pointed out, this is no different than if we were both staying at a small hotel."

"Except it's not a hotel."

"But it certainly could be." I glanced around our delightful surroundings. "And a charming one at that."

His brow furrowed, and he stared at me. "Do you always bend things to fit how you wish to see them?"

"Not at . . ." I considered his question, then smiled. "Why, yes, I suppose I do."

He laughed. "Your candor is both unexpected and refreshing."

"I'm not sure how to respond to that." I put another zeppole on my plate and ignored the thought that I might have to loosen my corset before dinner. "Why is it unexpected?"

"Given your somewhat flexible view of honesty, I wouldn't have anticipated you to be so forthright. Couple that with your comments about proper behavior, well . . ." He shrugged. "You're just not as I imagined you'd be."

"And you're basing that on what? My manner yesterday?" I tore off a small piece of pastry, popped it in my mouth and savored the flavors.

"You were rather indignant."

I swallowed, then lifted a shoulder in a casual shrug. "As I had every right to be."

"For someone in the wrong, I suppose."

"I was no more in the wrong than you were," I said in my loftiest manner. "Now then, it's your turn."

"My turn?" Poor man looked confused. I had no idea why. Our conversation thus far had been quite straightforward.

"To tell me why we should be friends." I settled back in my chair, folded my hands on my lap and considered him in the same manner I would someone applying for a position in my household. "Tell me, Fletcher, why should I be friends with you?"

"I could list my more sterling qualities, but it seems to me there is only one that at this juncture has any merit whatsoever." A slow smile spread across his face. A decidedly smug and superior smile.

"If you think arrogance is a desirable quality, you are sadly mistaken."

He laughed. Again. It was a deceptively contagious laugh. Hearty but not booming, shaded with genuine pleasure and just the tiniest hint of wickedness. Or perhaps that was the look in his eyes. Both were difficult to resist.

"I don't think it's the least bit arrogant to acknowledge that the greatest quality I have to offer you as a friend"—his grin widened—"is that I am the only one here who speaks your language."

I stared for a moment. "I've never had a male friend before." Although I had grown up with four male cousins, which was probably quite similar. "Is this what I can expect?"

"Absolutely."

I laughed at the look in his eye. "Very well, then, Fletcher. I certainly can't argue with that."

"Come now, Portia. You strike me as the type of woman who would argue about anything."

"Do I?" I considered the charge. In truth, I had always tended more toward the avoidance of arguments than leaping into them. "That's very interesting and not at all how most people see me. Not how I see myself, for that matter. At least before I came to Italy."

"Oh?" He reached for his second zeppole, apparently finding them as addictive as I did.

"Without question. I feel like an entirely different person here. I'm not sure why." I shook my head. "Perhaps it's because I have never before traveled alone. I never imagined I would. Nor did I imagine, when my aunt decided to return to England, I would choose to continue on to Italy on my own. It was entirely out of character for me."

"It's quite remarkable, isn't it?" He studied me curiously. "What happens when we step out of the boxes we have always lived our lives in. When we dare to take a chance. To select the road untraveled. To accept, even embrace, the new, the unknown, the—"

"Adventure," I murmured.

"Exactly." He smiled.

I studied him curiously. "You seem the type of man who welcomes adventures."

"Ah, Portia." He shook his head in a resigned manner. "I fear I am as afraid of venturing forth from my box as most people. There are expectations, responsibilities and everything that goes along with them. We can only hope, on occasion, for a momentary respite from those demands from which we can never escape."

"You don't sound like an artist now."

"But I do sound like a dutiful member of Her Majesty's Foreign Service." A note of resignation, or perhaps acceptance, colored his words. I'd never thought being a dutiful member of Her Majesty's Foreign Service to be quite so depressing.

"I gather you don't like your position?"

"My position is excellent, and I am grateful to have it." His tone was firm and left no doubt that this particular topic of conversation was at an end. Which was a shame, as he had certainly piqued my curiosity. I let the subject go for now.

"I have never quite looked at life in that manner."

His eyes narrowed in confusion. "In what manner?"

"Why, the idea of living in a box, of course." I rolled my gaze toward the ceiling. "Goodness, Fletcher, if we are to spend time together, you are going to have to try to follow along."

"Yes, of course. My apologies. I fear I am not used to topics of conversation leaping disjointedly from one to the next like stones skipping on the surface of a pond." He tried and failed to look sincere.

"If I am confusing you, I shall try to speak slower."

"And I shall do my best to keep up." Amusement glimmered in his eyes. I wasn't sure if I liked that he found me amusing or if I was annoyed by it. The former, I thought.

"Tell me, Fletcher." I leaned closer and gazed into his eyes. "Do you expect that I will be a constant source of amusement for you during our stay here?"

"Quite the contrary, Portia." He too leaned closer. "I have no idea what to expect from you. When we first met, I would have said you were one of those terribly upstanding women too constrained by the dictates of propriety to even breathe freely. Today . . ." His gaze searched mine. "Today, I would not dare to categorize you at all."

I couldn't resist an admittedly satisfied grin. "So I am not in a box, then?"

"I have absolutely no idea. Thus far, you are an enigma to me." He settled back in his chair, his thoughtful gaze never leaving mine. "But I would like to find out."

He studied me as though I was an unusual and intriguing creature. I didn't believe a man had ever looked at me in that way before. As if I was of interest beyond my position and fortune and appearance. It was as exhilarating as it was uncomfortable.

What if he found me wanting? Lacking in some way I was not even aware of? Utter nonsense, of course. And furthermore, why would I care? After Christmas, and two weeks beyond, we would each go our separate ways. His opinion of me would make no real difference in my life. Still, for whatever reason, I did want that opinion to be favorable.

"Will you join me for dinner tonight?" he said abruptly.

I started to point out, as I had no intention of eating alone again in my room, his invitation was unnecessary. But it was rather nice.

I smiled. "I would be delighted."

"Excellent." He got to his feet. "Then I shall take my leave for now. I have some work I would like to finish before I lose the light entirely."

"Will you show me your painting?" I asked without thinking.

He paused as if considering the question.

"I would like very much to see it."

"I don't know. I rarely show anyone my work."

"Is it that bad?" I said solemnly.

"It could be." He shook his head. "I am my own worst critic, so it could indeed be quite awful."

"I doubt that. Honestly, what harm would it do to show me?"

"In the guise of perfect honesty, you could tell me you hate it. And what I consider to be an accomplishment is not an accomplishment at all."

"Goodness, Fletcher, you needn't be the least bit concerned about that." A teasing note sounded in my voice. "I shall simply treat you like every other man who asks for an opinion from a woman but only wishes to hear how wonderful he is."

"In that case, then, perhaps." He grinned. "As reluctant as I am to leave right now, I am very much looking forward to this evening. Good day, Portia." With that, he turned and strode into the house, leaving me to stare after him.

And wonder just what kind of box Fletcher Jamison resided in.

5

Dinner on the loggia was nearly the same as last night's: a mere three courses, one of them native fried fish. It was extremely rustic, apparently at Fletcher's request. In the spirit of embracing my adventure, I resisted the urge to comment—although it did seem that civilized meals, with an appropriate number of courses, would transcend the dictates of adventure. However, the fish was excellent.

As was the conversation. Fletcher struck me as extremely intelligent and seemed to expect me to be intelligent as well. The realization took me quite by surprise. That had not been my general experience with men. But I must say I rose to the occasion.

When he commented on the latest uproar in Parliament, when he mentioned the competition for African territory among the nations of Europe and when he spoke of the tenuous relations between Britain and Russia, I was able to more than adequately hold up my end of the discussion. While politics and foreign affairs never especially interested me, I did read more than just the society section of the *Times*. I simply thought it was wise to be well versed on a variety of subjects, although admittedly I rarely used such knowledge. No one expected it of me.

When the talk turned to literature, and he praised Mr. Haggard's *King Solomon's Mines*, I not only confessed to having read the book myself but to having enjoyed it. I'd never told a soul that I had read it, let alone liked it. It wasn't the sort of thing anyone would expect me to read, although it did seem everyone in London had read it or was reading it. I wasn't sure why I revealed this to him, but I had been feeling less and less my usual self since I'd arrived. Less and less restrained, I thought. And there did, as well, seem to be a great deal of freedom inherent in eating out of doors and watching the sun glide gracefully into the sea. It was extremely, oh, liberating was the only word I could think of. Which was interesting, as I had never felt that my liberty was especially curtailed.

"I must confess I am curious, Portia," Fletcher began after we had finished dinner and were sipping the lemon-flavored liqueur produced in the region. Silvestro had come onto the loggia at some point and lit lanterns that now glowed softly behind us, near the villa's open doors. "This part of the Italian coast is popular with the English in the winter for its redeeming medicinal qualities, but at Christmas most visitors return home, and the area is extremely quiet. Why are you here?"

"I told you. My aunt knows Lady Wickelsworth, and she made the arrangements."

"Which does not answer my question."

"No, I suppose it doesn't." I heaved a resigned sigh. "You'll think it's rash and probably foolish."

"Oh, I expect to."

"Then you will not be disappointed." I debated for a moment over exactly how much to tell him. "Have you ever been married?"

"I have yet to be so blessed." A dry note sounded in his voice.

"You don't wish to be married?" I couldn't hide my surprise. Nearly everyone I knew wished to be married. It was in our nature. We did board the ark two by two, after all.

"I'm not really concerned about marriage one way or the other. I'm not opposed to it, nor am I actively seeking it out." He shrugged. "It's been my observation that most people marry for duty or practical reasons or because it's expected of them. I have no particular responsibility to wed, and I see no practical reason to share my life with someone simply because it's expected I would do so."

"And what of love?"

"I don't believe I mentioned love."

"No, you didn't, but it is another reason people wed. Some think it's the best reason." I chose my words carefully. "It sounds to me as if you don't believe in love."

"I neither believe nor disbelieve. I am hopeful of the possibility, but as I have never experienced love, I cannot say that it exists. Nor can I say, however, that it doesn't." He raised his glass to me.

"What rubbish, Fletcher." I scoffed. "You're an artist. I should think love and hate, emotions and perceptions, desires and passions, all of that would be part and parcel of what you try to express with paint and canvas."

He stared at me curiously. "That's remarkably profound. You are full of surprises, Portia."

"I am sorry I cannot be more shallow. Would you prefer I speak of art in terms of pretty pictures and pleasing colors and how well a piece might complement the furnishings in my parlor?" I sipped my drink and tried not to be annoyed. I shouldn't have been, really. I had never thought a woman's intelligence was something to be displayed, but somehow, with him, or perhaps here in this place, I felt differently. As if all the expectations by which I'd lived my life had suddenly vanished.

"You're offended. I am sorry." He grimaced. "Please accept my apology."

"Of course." I waved off his words. "There's really nothing to apologize for. I have never particularly asserted myself when it comes to expressing my opinion on subjects beyond those considered suitable for a lady to discuss."

"Why?"

"Why what?"

"Why do you feel there are certain topics a lady should not discuss?"

"Goodness, Fletcher, don't be so obtuse." I blew an exasperated breath. Really, I thought the man was just baiting me. But even knowing that didn't stop me. "That's the way things are. You know that as well as I. There are rules, if you will, of appropriate behavior."

"Proper behavior."

"Yes. Proper, appropriate, expected, suitable behavior."

"In your box."

"In *everyone's* box." I met his gaze pointedly. "Yours included."

"Probably." He paused. "I must say, I haven't noticed you having any difficulty tonight expressing your opinions on a variety of subjects."

"I am aware of that. It's not at all like me."

"You did say you feel like a different person here." He considered me thoughtfully.

I nodded. "I wonder if it's due to the setting or having to rely entirely on myself or"—even as I said the words, I knew they were a mistake—"the company."

"The company, by all means." He grinned.

"My God, Fletcher, you are arrogant." I huffed, then turned my gaze toward the bay. The reflections of the stars danced on the waters. The faintest scent of something sweet and floral lingered on the light breeze. There was something here, in the air perhaps, or in the sound of the water lapping against the shore, something that had wrapped around my soul. It struck me that I was not the same woman who'd left England, and I wondered who I might be when I returned.

"I would place my money on the setting." I put my glass down, rose to my feet and moved to the edge of the covered loggia to gaze out at the sea. "Look at this view, Fletcher. It's magnificent, but beyond that it's . . . it's magical, that's what it is. There's no other word for it. This is surely what Paradise must look like. Who could fail to be moved by it?" I spread my arms to the sea. "This alone makes one say things one would never say in a London parlor."

"Things about desire and passion." His voice was close to my ear. Good Lord, he was right behind me!

I whirled to face him. He was entirely too close. My stomach fluttered with something akin to panic. "I was referring to your art, as you know full well. I would never discuss"—I nearly choked on the words—"desire and passion with a gentleman, let alone someone I barely know. I do hope you don't think my comment indicated my interest in anything beyond friendship."

"I—"

I narrowed my eyes. "I would thank you to keep your distance, Fletcher. I very much value your companionship but nothing more. I realize our circumstances, my agreeing to share the villa, might have led you to make certain assumptions, but if you intend to seduce me . . ." I squared my shoulders and stared at him. "You should know I have no intention of being seduced. That is not the kind of adventure I am seeking." I sounded a bit pompous perhaps, but it did have to be said.

"I'm afraid you misunderstand." His voice was cool and slightly amused. "I was only bringing you your drink." He held out my glass, his own glass in his other hand.

The hot flame of utter and complete humiliation washed up my face. If I could have melted into a small puddle and disappeared between the stones of the loggia floor at that very moment, I would have greeted my fate gladly. I accepted my glass from him. "Thank you."

I drained the rest of my liqueur, although I was fairly certain it was more potent than I was used to. Good.

"My apologies if I led you to believe the thought of seducing you had so much as crossed my mind."

"No." I forced an awkward laugh. "I would never think such a thing. I don't know why I said that." If ever lightning were to strike me, I would have welcomed it right now. "It simply . . . well . . . you took me unawares, that's all. But I don't . . . no . . . of course not—"

He held out his hand to stop me. "Then we shall say no more about it."

"Ever?" I held my breath. "I would be most grateful for 'ever.'"

"Of course." He smiled. "Probably."

I cast him a weak smile in return. I was not thrilled at being more obligated to him than I already was.

"Good." He nodded. "Because that is no doubt the best way to destroy an excellent friendship. Besides"—he took a sip of his liqueur and gazed out at the sea and the stars—"you're really not the type of woman I prefer."

I didn't know what to say. On one hand, I should have been relieved. Obviously, I was safe from any overtures of a physical nature. On the other, I had just been insulted, even though his preference in women probably ran to models or music hall performers or something else vaguely artistic and slightly sordid. My assumption wasn't at all kind, but then, I wasn't feeling especially kind toward him at the moment.

"Thank God," I said with as much relief as I could muster. It was surprisingly difficult.

"I think so," he said solemnly.

I knew I should keep my mouth shut, but I couldn't resist. "Tell me, Fletcher, what kind of women do you prefer?"

"Well, I like tall, blue-eyed blondes."

"Now it's your turn to be shallow."

He laughed. "I also like a woman I can talk to. Who will not merely listen to placate me, but will truly hear what I have to say. I want a woman who says things that are far more relevant than the newest fashion from Paris or the latest bit of gossip. Beyond that . . ." He thought for a moment. "Someone not quite as concerned with propriety as much as savoring life."

"Can't one do both?"

Even in the dim light, I could see the look of skepticism on his face. "I doubt it."

"Don't be silly, of course you can. Why, I consider myself eminently proper, and my life is quite pleasing."

"Then why are you spending Christmas alone with a stranger in a country where you don't speak the language?" His tone was casual, as if it didn't matter. But it did, and we both knew it.

The question hung in the air between us for a long moment.

"It's quite simple," I said at last. There was no need to go into extreme detail regarding my feelings about Christmas and the happiness my friends had found. "My husband died three years ago, and my aunt feels I have mourned long enough. She thinks it's time I find a new husband."

"I see." He took the glass from my hand, stepped back to the table and refilled it. "The good intentions of our families often have little to do with what we really want."

"She feels she knows what is best for me and is determined to help by having suitable prospects everywhere I turn. In the past year, she has increased her efforts. The closer we came to Christmas, the more I dreaded it." I shuddered. "I knew every party, every gathering, every event my aunt had a hand in would be less about Christmas and more about finding me a suitable match. I had no desire to endure that. So I thought it would be best to flee."

"Like the Israelites from Egypt."

"Faster." I sighed. "Quite honestly, I don't know what came over me. I've never done anything like this. Why, not being home at Christmas is unthinkable, or at least it always has been." He handed me my glass, and I took a thoughtful sip, my gaze fastened on the stars and the sea. "But this year . . ."

"This year, you decided to do what you want rather than what is expected of you."

"I'm not sure it was that well thought out. More of an impulse, really." I shook my head. "I never act impulsively on anything of importance."

"How very prudent and efficient of you."

"Thank you." I'd always been rather pleased that I was prudent and efficient. But tonight it sounded . . . dull.

The silence stretched between us. Easy and companionable. We stood staring out into the night, he slightly behind me. Entirely too close, but I decided to overlook it as the man did seem to generate a fair amount of heat, and it was a cool night.

I wondered what he was thinking. In spite of my best efforts, I couldn't seem to think of anything but how close he was. And how warm. And how I hadn't stood this close to a man in the dark in a very long time. And how terribly romantic it all was, or would be if I were inclined toward that sort of thing. The very thought was ridiculous, as he had no interest in me beyond companionship. Which suited me perfectly, even if it was the tiniest bit annoying.

"What kind of adventure are you seeking, Portia?" If I had not jumped to the wrong and embarrassing conclusion earlier, I might have taken his question in an entirely different manner than he intended. But nothing except curiosity sounded in his voice.

"I'm not *seeking* adventure at all." I glanced over my shoulder at him. "I misspoke when I said that I was. I have been most content with my life."

"Have you?" He paused. "I am nothing more than a casual observer, but it doesn't appear that way to me."

"Well, I have," I said in a sharper tone than I had intended. Admittedly, in recent months, I had come to the unsettling realization that my life was remarkably dull. A truth I was not about to admit. "Extremely content."

"There is nothing wrong with content." The tone of his voice indicated he felt otherwise.

"No," I said firmly. "There isn't."

"Content is safe, secure, undemanding."

Never had safe and secure sounded so very boring. I clenched my teeth. "Indeed, it is."

"Comfortable, complacent . . . expected." He paused. "I suppose one can't ask for more than that."

"No, one can't." I turned on my heel and glared at him. "Tell me, Fletcher, are you content with your life? Is it everything you expected it to be? Is it something to savor, to relish?"

"No," he said coolly and sipped his drink.

"Well, mine is!" I drained the last of my drink. "Now, I believe I shall retire for the night. Good evening." I nodded and headed toward the door before he could utter a word. At the moment, I didn't want to hear anything he might have to say.

I didn't know exactly why I was so angry or, for that matter, who I was angry with, but in a few short minutes, this man— *this stranger*—had defined my life as dull and boring, ordinary and expected. Not precisely in those words, but close enough. Worse, I couldn't refute the charge. Perhaps it was the happiness my friends had found or my aunt's never-ending parade of suitable matches, but more and more, the realization was dawning on me that my life was not as I wished it to be.

I made my way to my rooms, a dozen unanswered questions in my head. I had never thought there was anything wrong with content. It seemed to me that was what people aspired to. I had been happy with David. Admittedly, we had not shared the kind of grand passion one reads of in tales of romance. But we did love one another, and our life together was good. I was—we were—content.

Was Fletcher right? Was content settling for something safe and secure and no more than adequate? Was it accepting the rooftops instead of reaching for the stars? Was he simply making me see what was right in front of me all along?

I sank down onto my bed and stared out the doors onto the balcony and at the night beyond. Perhaps being alone was better than being with someone who made you question everything you thought you knew.

Even if those questions needed to be asked.

6

I paced the width of my room, trying to determine if I had any courage at all. The day had dawned dark and dreary. Rain poured from the heavens, an incessant thrumming on the roof that echoed in my head. Even though a small blaze flickered in the fireplace in my room, gloom invaded the villa, more than matching my mood.

I had awakened later than my usual time, but I had slept fitfully, when I slept at all. I'd had Margaret bring me a late luncheon, relieved to see she was still annoyed with me. I expected Margaret's surly demeanor to continue until we started back toward England and home. If she was to be pleasant now, I would question her health.

Any number of other questions had nagged at me throughout the long night. *What was I to do about Fletcher Jamison?* Which really was a much easier question than *What was I to do about my life?*

I don't know how the man had done it, but with a few brief comments, he had managed to confuse me about who I was and what I wanted. Why, the man could practically see into my soul, which was most unnerving. And had, as well, made me admit, if only to myself, that I had no answers.

I had thus far lived my life truly believing that there were things one was expected to do and things one absolutely could not do. The consequences would have been too dire to fathom. Loss of social acceptance, scandal and ruin, among others. It was always much easier simply to follow the rules.

And has that made you happy? A voice that sounded suspiciously like Fletcher's sounded in my head. *Or merely content?*

I hadn't been *unhappy*, at least not that I'd noticed. Indeed, I would have said my life was quite full. I was sad for a time after David's death, of course, but life continues, and we must continue along with it. Admittedly, I had experienced a certain restlessness of late that I had, for the most part, ignored. The dull state of my existence had already occurred to me. If it hadn't, I probably wouldn't have decided to come to Italy in the first place. Nor would I have continued on my own after Aunt Helena returned to England. And I certainly wouldn't have agreed to share a villa with a total stranger. Why, hadn't I already acknowledged that I was on an adventure?

Perhaps I had changed. The thought pulled me up short. Or perhaps I was changing long before I ever left England. Subtle, yes, but changing all the same. As soon as the idea struck me, I realized it was true. It might simply have taken removing me from my usual surroundings for me to recognize it. I wasn't entirely sure how or where it all might lead, but that was more exciting than it was distressing, which in itself was a revelation.

And did it really matter? Wasn't the unknown part and parcel of adventure? Already, a few minor decisions had made my life far more interesting. I was on the first true adventure of my life, and even though I had decided to embrace it, I really hadn't. At least not yet. Perhaps the sense of freedom I was feeling had nothing to do with the place or the company, but rather that I had no one to answer to but myself. No one to answer my questions but myself. And my only companion was a man I'd just met, a man I would never see again. A man who didn't know my real name.

That, perhaps, was true freedom. The thought was at once intriguing and terrifying. And absolutely irresistible.

I grabbed Miss Broughton's book and headed to the parlor. I was through hiding in my room in a state of uncertainty and indecision. I would settle into one of the comfortable chairs in the parlor and read. Or possibly see what other diversions the villa might offer on a rainy day. If I ran into Fletcher, so much the better.

After all, a woman of adventure did not let the comments of an arrogant stranger influence her plans. A woman of adventure did not let such a man think for so much as a moment that he had the upper hand. And a woman of adventure definitely did not cower in her room like a chastised puppy.

I breezed into the parlor as if I didn't have a care in the world, and indeed, at this moment, I didn't. I noted Fletcher perched on the arm of a chair, arms crossed over his chest, his brow furrowed in thought, gazing out at the rain beyond the roof of the loggia. He stood when I entered the room. I ignored him and moved to the center doors, thrown open to the outside. The air was cool and heavy with moisture but invigorating nonetheless. I drew in a deep, refreshing breath.

"I believe I may owe you yet another apology." Caution sounded in his voice.

"There's no need to apologize," I said blithely and continued to gaze out the doors. I could see no farther than the garden gates, the rest of the world lost behind a curtain of fog and rain. I wondered in what direction the smoke from Vesuvius was wafting now. I did not like being unable to see it should it decide to spew something other than steam from its bowels.

He paused. "You did leave in something of a snit last night."

"Not at all, Mr. Jamison." I glanced at him. "You simply misunderstood."

His brow furrowed. "*Mr. Jamison?*"

"It seems wise." I cast him a pleasant smile. "There are, after all, conventions of proper behavior that one should not dispense with without due consideration. When I suggested we call each other by our given names, I believe I may have been premature. Perhaps we should know each other better before being quite so familiar."

"I . . ." His jaw tightened. "As you wish, *Lady Smithson*." He was obviously irritated. Good. I liked the idea of his being irritated. It seemed fair. "You're certain you're not annoyed with me?"

"Goodness, Mr. Jamison." I met his gaze firmly. "Why on earth would I be annoyed with you?"

He chose his words with care. "I may have said things you didn't care to hear."

"Nonsense." I shrugged. "I admit, I might have been a bit vexed at the time. One always hates to hear one's life analyzed and found wanting, but upon reflection, I realized someone else's assessment of my life is not nearly as important as what I think about it. It's amazing what a good night's sleep can do for one's outlook. Putting things in the proper perspective and all. Don't you agree?"

He stared, apparently struck dumb by my brilliant reasoning. A distinct sense of triumph swept through me.

I glanced around the parlor and decided the chair he had been perched on was best for reading, as it was near the doors and the light was somewhat better. Besides, he was no longer using it. I stepped around him to reach the chair. A distinct scent caught my attention, and I paused. "You smell of oil—linseed, I believe. Are you working?"

"I was."

"But not on the balcony, I assume."

"No, there is a sitting room off my bedroom that is an enclosed balcony. I have set up my easel there to best take advantage of what little natural light is available today."

"And is it going well?"

He shrugged. "Not really."

"I suspect you're eager to get back to it, then." I sat down and opened my book. "I won't keep you."

I knew he was once again staring at me, but I refused to look at him. The man was obviously not used to being dismissed.

"Will I see you at dinner?" His tone was a bit too sharp for my liking.

"Of course. I look forward to it." I turned a page, not that I had read so much as a word. "Fish, I assume."

"I would assume that as well, especially given the day." He paused. "Have a good afternoon, Lady Smithson."

"Best of luck with your work, Mr. Jamison." I turned another page.

He hesitated a moment longer, then started for the door.

"I believe I shall ask Agostina for tea a bit early today. Shall I have her bring you something as well?" I said in an offhand manner, extending, if not an olive branch, then at least a twig.

"That would be most appreciated," he said shortly and took his leave. I now had the rest of the afternoon to myself, which was, in many ways, a great pity.

Still, there was a point to be made, and I was determined to make it. I had indeed left in a snit last night, and I was still irritated by his charges, no matter how discerning they might be. But then, I supposed none of us ever really wanted to hear the truth about ourselves. How we dealt with that truth was another matter entirely, and I was still not certain how to deal with mine.

And while I did think the old adage about killing the messenger was not entirely fair to the messenger, I could for the first time fully understand it. I had no intentions of killing Fletcher. I simply wanted to make him pay, just a little. One should pay for making someone else feel they were lacking in some respect. No matter how insightful or accurate, it still wasn't very pleasant.

The book was amusing, but not nearly as intriguing as Mr. Fletcher Jamison. I had barely read for any time at all when I realized that I was paying as big a price as he. His conversation, even when he said things I didn't wish to hear, was far more interesting than any work of fiction. It had been a very long time since I'd had a candid conversation with a gentleman. Apparently, I missed the man.

I believe that is what is known as karma.

7

Dinner was cordial and even friendly, as if we had both decided to move forward. I was still flushed with what I had considered a victory, and my continued sense of confidence. We ate in the dining room for the first time, earlier than usual, as Agostina and Silvestro were to join their family in the village for Christmas Eve. I had very nearly forgotten it was Christmas Eve, and the thought was more than a little disheartening. I tried to ignore it.

Tonight's meal was not just one type of fish, but seven different fish offerings. The soup currently before me, a tasty broth with an assortment of seafood, was excellent. Fletcher explained this was a traditional Christmas Eve dinner in this region of Italy. Which only served to remind me of my own family's Christmas traditions and the fact that I was very far from those I loved.

"My family," Fletcher began, as if he sensed the direction of my thoughts, "was never one for Christmas. As soon as I was old enough to do so, I was sent to stay with my grandmother and her sister for Christmas."

"Oh." I stared at him. "I am sorry."

"Don't be." He smiled. "It was always . . . exactly how a child thinks Christmas should be. My grandmother and great-aunt wintered in a large house overlooking the sea. They were both firm believers in Christmas, in the magic of the season. My memories of those Christmases are filled with love and laughter and enchantment." He chuckled. "You wouldn't think two elderly ladies would know how to enchant a little boy, but they did." He paused, no doubt gathering his memories. "I know the Christmases we spent together were probably not as perfect as I remember them, but they did seem perfect at the time, and looking back, they still do. My grandmother made certain every Christmas we shared was special. Although, admittedly, they could have been merely adequate, and they still would have been far better than being with my parents."

"Really?" I couldn't imagine such a thing. "Your family wasn't . . . happy?"

"We weren't unhappy. And if we were, no one would ever have admitted it." He thought for a moment. "I don't know how to best describe us. A family of individuals, I think, each going our separate ways, each standing on our own two feet. That sort of thing. My father was usually busy with his business interests, my mother with her social concerns. I spent most of my life away at school."

"Do you have brothers and sisters?"

"No, I'm afraid it's just me. I have a handful of distant relations, but even including them, my family is quite small. I believe it was always a regret of my father's, that he did not have more children, that is. I'm not sure why he would have wanted more. He never seemed especially concerned with the one he had. He died several years ago."

In spite of his offhand manner, as if he were telling someone else's story rather than his own, my heart twisted at thought of the little boy sent away for Christmas.

"My condolences."

"Thank you. My mother, on the other hand, never wanted more than one child. I suspect she was eternally grateful when I turned out to be a boy." He pinned me with a wry look. "She had done her duty and felt she needn't do anything more, if you will."

"I have no siblings either. My parents died when I was quite young, and I grew up in the home of my aunt and uncle and seven cousins."

"Seven?"

"My family is substantial. And boisterous." I paused, remembering Christmas Eves with everyone gathered around the table. "Christmas Eve was always wondrous, filled with merriment and anticipation and magic." A wistful note colored my words. "That day, we would find the largest tree possible for the house—we were usually in the country at Christmastime. Decorating the tree and the house itself would take all day, and we would begin the burning of an enormous Yule log. After dinner, someone would read Mr. Dickens's *A Christmas Carol*, although, inevitably, one or more of us, depending on age, would fall asleep before the reading had ended." I smiled with the memory. "I don't believe I ever heard the end of the story."

He gasped with feigned disbelief. "You never heard *God bless us everyone*?"

"I'm afraid not. Well, not as a child, that is."

"I am shocked, Lady Smithson," he said in a stern voice, "at such an affront to Christmas."

"I suspect I have been forgiven." I picked up my wine and took a sip. "As Father Christmas was quite good about bringing me what I truly wanted every year."

"No empty stocking on Christmas morning?"

"Never," I said staunchly.

He raised a skeptical brow.

"Never," I said again, resisting the urge to laugh at his skeptical look. "Goodness, Mr. Jamison, you needn't look at me like that. I think we have already established that I have never been one to flout the rules of proper behavior and expectations."

"Although one does have only your word for it." He shook his head in a manner that would have been most irritating had I not been well aware that he was teasing.

"I assure you—"

"Shall we do that after dinner?" he said abruptly. "Read *A Christmas Carol*, that is."

"Oh, I think not." I cast him a grateful smile. "But thank you for suggesting it."

"You seem a bit"—he searched for the right word—"melancholy tonight. I thought perhaps you were missing your family."

"I am." I sighed. "However . . ." I forced a bright smile. "Here is where I chose to spend Christmas this year, and I refuse to regret that choice."

"Because it's an adventure?"

"Exactly." I nodded. "An adventure that is my Christmas gift to myself. Besides, it's not as if I was a child taut with excitement at the thought of Father Christmas's impending arrival. I daresay he wouldn't know where to find me this year anyway."

"It has always been my understanding that Father Christmas is not confined by borders." His tone was solemn, but his eyes twinkled. "He will find you, you know."

I laughed, my mood at once lighter. No, this was not the Christmas Eve I had always experienced. Which did not mean it couldn't be every bit as nice. Different but nice. After all, here I was in a cozy villa in Italy, with a fire burning brightly, an excellent meal in front of me and a charming man trying very hard to lift my spirits. It was very nice indeed. "I should hope so. I would hate for my Christmas wish not to come true."

"And what is your Christmas wish, Lady Smithson?"

"My dear Mr. Jamison." I shook my head in a mournful manner. "If I told you, then it certainly would not come true. I daresay that's one rule it would be foolish to break."

"And we can't have that." He grinned. "If you will excuse me." He stood and left the room.

I turned my attention back to my soup and my thoughts. But he had made me smile. Fletcher really was a very nice man. Not many men of my acquaintance would go to the effort of trying to make me feel better about being away from my family, especially after I had been so sharp with him. Guilt washed through me at the thought. Perhaps I had not been entirely reasonable.

Fletcher returned in a few minutes with two sheets of stationery and a pencil. He took his seat and addressed his soup with renewed enthusiasm.

I waited for a long moment, then surrendered. "Dare I venture a guess as to the purpose of the paper?"

"Come now, Lady Smithson." He cast me a pitying look. "Surely you know that for Father Christmas to grant a Christmas wish, you must write it down, then burn it in the fire." He leaned toward me and lowered his voice in a confidential manner. "The smoke, you know, carries the message to him."

"Does it?" I asked as if I had never heard that before.

"It does indeed." He settled back in his chair. "I thought after dinner we would write our wishes and send them off."

I frowned. "Isn't it too late? For Father Christmas to be able to grant our wishes?"

Fletcher paused, his spoon halfway to his mouth. "Surely I'm not hearing what I think I'm hearing. Do you doubt the abilities of Father Christmas?"

"No." I choked back a laugh. "Of course not. Never."

He fixed me with a stern look. "I should hope not. We would hate to awaken tomorrow with nothing in our stockings."

"We would indeed." I laughed, then shook my head. "I must thank you, Mr. Jamison. This is a far more delightful Christmas Eve than I had anticipated when I awoke this morning. I had expected, well, I'm not sure what I expected. But I did not expect to enjoy myself."

"Do you know what the best thing is about not worrying about expectations?"

I narrowed my eyes and studied him across the table. "Are we still speaking of Christmas, or have we returned to last night's discussion?"

"I don't know. Will you leave in a snit?" He finished his soup and put his spoon down.

"Possibly." I bit back a grin. "But I shall try to restrain myself. So tell me. What is the best thing about not worrying about expectations?"

He raised his wine glass to me. "You don't have to try to live up to them."

"But you do, don't you?" I said without thinking.

"Me?"

Apparently, I'd caught him by surprise. I looked up from trying to scoop the last bit of soup onto my spoon.

"Why do you say that?"

"Because it seems clear to me, Mr. Jamison." I finished the final spoonful just in time for Silvestro to appear and replace my bowl with a plate overflowing with fish, most fried, each and every one displayed in an all too lifelike pose. I smiled my appreciation, and Silvestro beamed back at me. I might not understand the language, but I could still communicate. Well, somewhat.

"You were saying," Fletcher said the moment the servant withdrew, "before the fish arrived. About my living up to expectations. What did you mean?"

"It's obvious." I cut a piece of some sort of cod. "You're a civil servant in Calcutta, when you would prefer to be an artist. It appears to me you are living up to someone's expectations, or possibly society's, but certainly not your own. Someone else's box, if you will." I tasted the fish. Light, tender and perfectly seasoned. I couldn't help a tiny, highly improper moan of satisfaction. Which only made me realize Fletcher hadn't said a word. I glanced at him. "Am I wrong?"

"I . . ." He stared for a long moment, then blew a long breath. "You continue to surprise me, Lady Smithson."

"Do I?" I smirked. "How delightful."

He laughed. "Now then, shall we continue last night's discussion of British-Russian relations?"

It was obvious from the resolute set of his jaw that he was not going to answer my question. Which was far more telling than if he had tried to deny my charge.

"Oh, let's," I said brightly, although I would have preferred to discuss practically anything else. I had nearly exhausted my limited knowledge of the current tenuous relationship between the two empires last night.

Fortunately, the conversation soon shifted to other topics. We spoke about things we liked and things we didn't, finding we were in agreement about far more than either of us would have expected. And we shared more of our own Christmas memories. He told me a little about life in Calcutta, and I spoke a bit about my family and my friends. Oh, I didn't use any names, of course. As easy as our conversation was, it seemed wise not to be too free with the details of my life, and I sensed he was a bit guarded as well. Before I knew it, Silvestro had served fruit and cheese, and he and his wife had taken their leave, telling Fletcher they would return later in the evening. Aside from Margaret, who had informed me before dinner she planned to retire early to write letters home in an effort to ease her distress at being away for Christmas, we were alone.

I suppose I should have been leery of being alone in the villa with a man I barely knew, but somehow I wasn't at all concerned. I had no doubt Fletcher was indeed a gentleman who could be trusted. Even so, it was rather exciting.

"As it is Christmas Eve, would you care to join me for a glass of Strega?" he said as we strolled into the parlor.

I'd had a great deal of wine with dinner but was remarkably unaffected. I credited the fish. "That would be lovely, I think. What exactly is it?"

"A regional liqueur." He moved to a table where Silvestro had conveniently left a crystal decanter partially filled with a yellow-colored liquid and two glasses. "It's a *digestif*, intended for drinking after dinner." He poured a glass and handed it to me.

"And extremely potent, I imagine." I held my glass up to a lamp and studied it dubiously.

"That's why one glass is usually enough."

"Enough for what?" I said under my breath.

"For whatever you wish." He filled his own glass, then raised it to me. "To spending an unexpected Christmas Eve with . . . a new friend?"

I raised my glass to his. "To new friends and the unexpected."

He took a long sip of his drink, and I followed suit. The taste was . . .unusual. Sweet and herbal with hints of mint and juniper. It was as strong as I suspected and warmed me down to my toes. I had no doubt it was excellent for digestion.

"How very . . .unique." I choked out the words, blinking to keep my eyes from watering.

"It's made in Benevento, not far from here." He took another sip. "According to one legend, it was first made by beautiful female fairies, who used the potion to cast love spells on unsuspecting humans."

"I imagine this would do it." I smiled weakly.

"The word *strega* means *witch* in Italian."

"This is a love potion, then?" I considered my half-empty glass. "It does look enchanted."

"Yet another legend has it that any couple who drinks it together is united forever."

My gaze jumped to his. I wasn't sure I was willing to make a magical commitment to a man I hardly knew. Still . . . Perhaps not a commitment, but . . . There was something about him that was undeniably appealing, something I liked. He was amusing and terribly nice and really quite handsome. My gaze slipped to his lips, and I couldn't help but wonder how his lips would feel against mine. With very little effort, I could lean forward—

"Of course—"

My gaze snapped back to his.

"It's my understanding that the liqueur has been made for only about twenty years or so. I suspect the legends are more potions to increase sales rather than anything to do with love."

"I would certainly buy it," I murmured and took another sip. He laughed.

"But it really doesn't seem fair, does it?" I asked. Using a potion to make someone love you. How would you know if that person truly loved you or not?"

"Oh, I imagine you would know." His gaze remained locked with mine. His dark eyes endless and compelling and . . . dangerous. Terribly, wonderfully dangerous. "If someone truly loved you."

I sipped thoughtfully and considered him. "So says the man who doesn't know if he believes in love." I knew I was in hazardous waters, but I couldn't seem to help myself. "But then, you also said you have never been in love."

"No. Not yet."

"Perhaps that's what you should wish for. For Christmas, that is," I added quickly.

"Perhaps." He sipped his drink, looking just the tiniest bit puzzled and completely wonderful.

A voice in the back of my head—I believed it was the real Lady Smithson's—urged me to abandon prudence, take a chance, throw caution to the winds and fling myself into his arms. I had never had that urge before.

Another voice—the mother I never really knew—insisted I summon my resolve and remain true to my principles. A proper lady, a perfect lady, would never give in to the kind of sordid temptation offered by a handsome stranger. And I was, or at least I had always been, a proper, perfect lady.

I drew a deep breath. "It's late. I should probably retire."

"And I had the distinct feeling it was only the beginning." He stared at me for an endless moment, and something inside of me shivered. He cleared his throat. "Of the evening, that is."

I moved toward the door. "I shall see you tomorrow, then."

"Wait." He stepped toward me, and again, my heart fluttered.

"Yes?" I held my breath. Was this it? Would he kiss me?

"Now that we have laid to rest the ghosts of Christmas Past, we must look ahead."

I shook my head in confusion, ignoring a distinct stab of disappointment. "Forgive me, but I don't know—"

"Our Christmas wishes. We haven't made them yet." He set his glass down. "I'll get the paper." He left the parlor, and I sank into a chair.

I had the oddest sense of loss, the strangest feeling that I had just missed something of importance. Had he intended to kiss me? Surely not. Aside from gazing into my eyes as if he could see into my very soul, he had made no particular overtures, nothing, really, to make me think he was so inclined.

Or had I been about to kiss him? It was an absurd thought, but there had been a moment . . . I drew a calming breath and took another sip of the liqueur. This could surely be blamed on the Strega and the stories of the legends surrounding it. I raised the glass and stared at the golden liquid.

I was not the sort of woman who freely kissed men. Indeed, aside from David, I could count on one hand the number of times I'd been kissed. And, excluding David, I could not recall a single instance when a kiss had been my idea. Yet, had Fletcher not spoken when he had, I might well have leaned closer and pressed my lips to his. It was a shocking realization. Even more surprising was my immediate regret that I had missed the opportunity.

Fletcher returned in less than a minute. "I know this is not the Christmas Eve you are used to, but perhaps whatever you wish for will make up for it."

"No, it is not my usual Christmas Eve." I smiled up at him. "But it is one I shall remember always."

"We can't ask for more than that." He presented the stationery and pencil to me with a flourish.

"Good, because I have no idea what to wish for."

"Come now, Lady Smithson." He settled in the chair closest to mine. "Surely there is something you want."

"One would think." I stared at the blank page in my hand.

"Some desire of your heart perhaps?"

"My heart's desire? Goodness, that's a great deal of importance to place on one mere wish," I said under my breath, still staring at the empty paper.

"Well, it's not a mere wish, is it?"

I looked up at him.

"It's a Christmas wish." He shook his head. "I have it on very good authority that a Christmas wish is given additional weight."

"Oh?" I arched a skeptical brow. "And whose authority would that be?"

"My grandmother's." He smiled a vaguely sad sort of smile. "She always insisted on a Christmas wish."

"She's no longer with you, is she?" I asked, although I was fairly certain of the answer.

"On the contrary." He picked up his glass and swirled the Strega in an offhand manner. "She is always with me, especially at Christmas."

"You're lucky to have that," I said. "I was so young when my parents died, I barely remember them at all. And while my aunt and uncle and cousins never made me feel that I was anything other than a cherished member of the family, there always seems to be something lacking at Christmas."

"Indeed, there is." He nodded. "But enough of looking backwards." He adopted a stern tone. "You have a wish to think of."

"I'm still thinking." I narrowed my eyes. "Aren't you going to write one?"

"I already did." He pulled a folded sheet out from his waistcoat pocket. "Unlike you, I have no problem deciding what to wish for."

"And did you wish for your heart's desire?" I teased.

"Yes." His gaze met mine, and a slow smile spread across his face. "I believe I did."

"At least you know your heart's desire." I sighed.

"And you don't?"

"No, I'm afraid not. I would think—" Abruptly, I knew exactly what to wish for. I cast him a triumphant grin. "Never mind. I know what I want." I scribbled my wish on the paper, then folded it in half and again.

"Excellent. I was confident even the terribly proper and newly adventurous Lady Smithson would come up with the perfect Christmas wish."

"I'm not sure how perfect it is. I suppose we shall see."

He laughed and held out his arm. "Allow me to escort you to the fire."

I glanced at the fireplace, no more than five or so feet away.

"It's not the distance, you know," he said in a solemn tone, "but the importance of the occasion."

"I cannot argue with that." I rose to my feet, took his arm and ignored the tiny tingle of awareness that shot through me at the solid feel of his muscles beneath my touch.

He chuckled. "And I thought you could argue with anything."

"Come now, it's Christmas Eve," I said primly. "Even I would hesitate to argue on Christmas Eve." I grinned. "Unless I was right, and you were very, very wrong."

He laughed and escorted me the few steps to the fireplace. I released his arm and waved my folded wish at him. "Shall we do this one at a time or together?"

He nodded thoughtfully. "Together, I think."

"Very well."

We stepped closer to the fire and tossed our wishes into the flames. The fire caressed the edges of the papers as if deciding whether they were worthy of consuming. Then at once both notes caught and burst into flames. In a few seconds, there was nothing left but ash still holding the shape of the wishes. A moment later, they crumbled into nothingness.

For long minutes, we stared into the flames. I couldn't help but wonder what he had wished for and if it had anything to do with me. It was absurd of course. He barely knew me. Still, it seemed we had shared something truly special on this Christmas Eve.

"Thank you," I said softly, then glanced at him. He was studying me as if trying to decide something important.

"No," he said at last. "I should be the one thanking you. You have made this Christmas Eve one I too shall remember always."

Again, his gaze, dark and intense, caught mine, and longing rushed through me. I really knew nothing about this man, and yet it seemed that I knew everything. Still . . .

"Well . . ." I said awkwardly, and the moment vanished.

"Well, indeed." He chuckled in a self-conscious manner.

"I think I shall retire for the night. I know it's still early," I added quickly, "but I did not sleep well last night, and I find I am rather weary."

"Then you should certainly retire." His blue eyes twinkled with amusement, as if he knew I wasn't seeking sleep as much as escape.

He took my hand and raised it to his lips in a slow and measured fashion. Without warning, my heart hammered in my chest, and my mouth was abruptly dry. His gaze locked on mine. "I hope we can continue to be friends."

I swallowed hard and tried to say something clever. "Of course." Not clever, then. I cleared my throat. "I would like that."

"Excellent." His lips lingered over my hand. I held my breath. "I am looking forward to spending Christmas Day together."

"Perhaps the rain will stop." Good Lord, did I have nothing better to say than to comment on the weather? Apparently not. "I should have wished for that."

"I'm glad you didn't. There is nothing better than being trapped indoors on Christmas Day. But I do hope all your Christmas wishes come true, Lady Smithson."

I should have pulled my hand from his, but I had no desire to do so. At that moment, I would have gladly let him hold my hand forever. I cast him a weak smile. "Portia."

He smiled, straightened and released my hand. "I shall bid you a good evening, then, Portia."

"Good evening, Fletcher." My gaze lingered on his for a moment longer, then I turned and started for my rooms.

I fairly floated up the stairs, which was probably due to the wine with dinner and, of course, the Strega. Although I certainly didn't notice the effects of either. A feeling of anticipation and even wonder engulfed me, which, upon reflection, were not unusual on Christmas Eve. But I suspected it had more to do with the man I'd shared the evening with than anything else.

And I too couldn't wait for Christmas Day.

8

For the second morning in a row, I slept far later than I had planned, because for the second night in a row, I scarcely slept at all.

I had toyed with the idea of attending Christmas services at a church in town, even though it was Roman Catholic and I was not. I had always privately believed that God was God, and it was only in how we chose to worship him that we were divided. However, with my limited understanding of Latin and even less of Italian, I no doubt would have spent the service in a fog of dutiful ignorance.

The questions that had filled my head through the long restless hours of last night now had less to do with concerns about my life and everything to do with the man with whom I'd shared Christmas Eve.

Why hadn't I kissed him when I had the chance? That was one question I already had the answer to. I was simply not that type of woman. Still, hadn't I already come to the realization that I was no longer the woman I had always thought I was? That I had changed, that I was not the same? Besides, a single kiss did not mean I would end up in his bed. I was certainly not inclined toward that sort of thing. Why, it had been three years since I had shared a man's bed.

And isn't that long enough? Veronica's voice rang in my head.

As with all the other questions plaguing me in recent days, I had no answer for that. At least, not while awake. But my rare moments of slumber last night had been filled with disturbing and admittedly erotic dreams of Fletcher. Apparently, I had paid far more attention to the unclothed parts of him I had seen when he emerged from the water on my first day here than I had realized. My dreams had taken much of what had happened last night—his gazing into my eyes and kissing my hand and the feel of his arm beneath my touch—and everything that hadn't, and, well, in my dreams they did. In my sleep, he took me into his arms and kissed me thoroughly, until I could scarcely catch my breath. And when I thought I could bear no more, we were both unclothed and writhing on the bed in the sort of unbridled ecstasy I had only ever imagined. But then, it was a dream, after all. It wasn't real. It was a fantasy wrought from curiosity and dark, smoldering eyes and unfamiliar foods.

When I woke, the bedclothes were twisted and in disarray as if he had actually been in my bed and we had truly shared a night of utter, mindless passion. It was no wonder that I was so tired this morning. Although, in truth, our assignation was nothing more than a scandalous nightmare brought on by something I ate. Or the Strega. It hadn't really happened. Nor would it.

Why not? Veronica's voice asked. *You don't plan to see the man again, and it's not as if anyone would know. You've already decided you have no intention of even confiding in me, one of your dearest friends, who will always keep your secrets about your clandestine Christmas rendezvous.*

Christmas rendezvous, indeed. That was exactly the sort of thing Veronica would say if she were really here, and exactly why I did not plan to tell her. I ignored her voice in my head in the very same way I would have ignored her if she had been here in person.

I had barely stumbled out of bed when Margaret informed me, with that disapproving look she had mastered, it was nearly time for Christmas dinner, a large midday feast, as was the tradition here. I had no idea how she managed to get that information, as she spoke no more Italian than I, but I was certainly not about to ask. She also told me, with a subtle hint of satisfaction, as I had slept so late, I had missed any possibility of breakfast. But she did earn my eternal gratitude by bringing me a large serving of a sort of fruitcake and a cup of strong, thick coffee—exactly what I needed. This must have been why I kept her in my employ. It certainly wasn't for her sunny disposition.

I was at once eager and reluctant to see Fletcher today. Would the bond we'd forged last night remain? Or would we be strangers again? I nearly forgot my concerns when I came down the main stairway and the most delightful aromas assailed me. Of exotic spices and garlic and tomatoes. These were not smells I associated with Christmas, but they were delicious and comforting nonetheless. With the rain still falling outdoors, the villa seemed warm and cozy and like home.

I didn't encounter anyone on my way to the parlor and wondered if Fletcher was in his rooms. Painting perhaps. I would still like to see his work. Now that we were on better terms, maybe I could convince him to show it to me.

I stepped into the parlor. Or perhaps I wouldn't need to ask. In the middle of the room stood a muslin-covered easel. What on earth had he done? I stepped toward it.

"Good, you're here." Fletcher's voice rang behind me, and he brushed past me into the parlor. "Merry Christmas, Portia." He paused as if he wasn't sure if he should throw his arms around me or kiss my cheek or simply nod. Instead, he grabbed my hand and shook it heartily. "A very merry Christmas, indeed."

"God bless us everyone," I murmured and stared at him. Impolite I know, but I couldn't seem to help myself

His eyes were rimmed in red and slightly wild looking. His clothes were rumpled, as if he had slept in them. His hair was disheveled, his necktie hung loose. He was grinning like a madman, and he still held my hand clasped in his.

I carefully pulled my hand free. "What on earth has happened to you?"

He grinned. "I have been assisting Father Christmas."

"All night?"

"Not all night." He ran his hand through his hair. It resisted his efforts and now stuck up in a manner too strange to be amusing. It was rather endearing. At once I could see him as a little boy on Christmas morning. "But most of it."

I chose my words with care. "What exactly did assisting Father Christmas entail?"

"I wanted to have everything ready before you came down." He cast me a curious look. "I expected you long before now. I thought you were entirely too disciplined and proper to sleep late every day."

"Did you?" I smiled in what I hoped was a mysterious manner.

"How unexpected," he said under his breath.

Unexpected? How . . . delightful.

He looked around the room, grabbed a chair and positioned it in front of the easel. He swept his hand toward the chair. "If you please."

I opened my mouth to protest, then sat instead.

"I knew from what you said last night and, more importantly, what you didn't, that you are missing Christmas with your family much more than you let on."

"Yes, I suppose. But—"

"This is not the first time I've stayed at the villa, and I've long considered it a special sort of place."

"I agree, but—"

"I know this sounds extremely sentimental, and I am not a sentimental sort usually, but at Christmastime, well . . ." He grimaced. "I could be a ten-year-old boy."

"Aren't we all children at Christmas?"

"Exactly." He beamed. "I would hate you to leave here remembering this only as the Christmas you were not with your family, so I thought you needed a touch of home. First . . ." He disappeared behind the easel, then returned with two twists of newsprint. He handed me one. "Here is your Christmas cracker."

"Is it?" I studied the alleged cracker dubiously.

"I admit it's not going to snap, and you will have to untwist it instead of pull it apart, but yes, it is what will pass this year for a Christmas cracker."

"And a fine cracker it is too." I smiled with delight. Minor as it might seem, no one had ever done something like this for me before. I untwisted the paper to find another piece of newsprint, this one intricately folded. "And this is?"

"A hat, of course." He cast me a chastising look, as if I should have known, and indeed, I should have. Why, what else could it be? He untwisted his own cracker and pulled free the folded newsprint, shaking it out and placing it on his head. It resembled an admiral's hat and was quite nicely done. "What do you think? Will it do?"

"I think it's perfect." I unfolded my own hat and put it on my head.

"Very fashionable." He grinned. "But there's more. Are you ready?"

"Of course. It's Christmas morning." I nodded and tried not to bounce in my chair as I might have when I was a small child. But then, this unexpected Christmas surprise made me feel very much like a child, eager to see what Father Christmas, or, rather, his assistant, had brought. "I am more than ready."

"Very well." He started to pull the muslin off the easel then paused. "Don't expect too much. I was in something of a hurry."

"Goodness, Fletcher." I huffed. "You're going to drive me mad if you don't show me at once what you have hidden."

He grinned. "All right." With a grand flourish, he pulled the sheet away.

My breath caught. I had of course expected some sort of painting, but I hadn't expected this.

"I don't know what to say." I shook my head.

"I fear it's not my best. I don't work as frequently in watercolors as I once did," he said apologetically, "but as I wanted this to dry before you saw it, I decided—"

"It's wonderful." I couldn't tear my gaze from the painting. Here was the Christmas I remembered. Fletcher had painted a large tree decorated with glass ornaments and candles and sweets and stars and here and there a paper decoration that a child might have made. Behind the tree, wood-paneled walls were no more than a suggestion, and through a doorway, there was the faintest hint of figures in celebration. It was all as I had described it to him last night, bits and pieces of the past. The painting had that delightful translucent quality watercolor often had, and there was a mystical, charmed appearance to it. A vision, a memory of Christmas Past.

"I thought of trying to find an actual tree, but it was too late to do so, and I—"

"This is perfect, Fletcher." I shifted my gaze from the work to the man. "Absolutely perfect."

Caution shone in his eyes. "You like it, then?"

"I adore it." I turned my attention back to the painting. "It's not as if you have captured Christmas exactly, but more my remembrances of it. The essence of my memories, if you will."

He grinned. "You do like it, then."

"It is perhaps the most wonderful Christmas surprise I have ever had." I glanced at him. "May I take it with me? When I leave, that is."

"Of course. I painted it for you."

"Thank you." My gaze returned again to Fletcher's dream of Christmas. "I don't believe I have ever had a gift quite this special."

"That, my dear Portia, is a grave oversight."

"But I have nothing for you."

He smiled. "Your company on this Christmas Day is the greatest gift of all."

"The greatest gift of all?" I raised a skeptical brow. "Now you're being silly."

"As well I should," he said staunchly and leaned forward in a confidential manner. "It is Christmas, you know. If one can't be silly on Christmas . . ."

I laughed. "You're absolutely right."

"And I have all sorts of silliness planned."

"I do hope so." I grinned, feeling very much as if I were a child again. A child on Christmas Day. There was no better feeling in the world, although admittedly I had nearly forgotten that.

"I thought we would play games: charades and twenty questions and backgammon and—" He eyed me suspiciously. "You did say you play backgammon, didn't you?"

"I did." I nodded. "And I am quite good at it."

"Excellent, as I would hate to beat you too easily."

"That will not be a problem, Fletcher. Although . . ." I frowned thoughtfully. "Perhaps, as I have no present for you, I should allow you to win. As my Christmas gift to you."

"And a thoughtful gift it is too." He grabbed my hand and pulled me to my feet. "As much as I am grateful for the offer, I fear I shall have to decline." He grinned in a decidedly wicked manner. "I have no need of assistance."

"Oh?" There was a slight breathless note in my voice. I was not sure why. The man still held my hand, and I saw no need to pull away.

"No." His gaze searched mine. "I have no doubt I can claim victory without any help."

"Can you?" It struck me we were no longer talking about backgammon.

"I have always enjoyed winning when it was more of a challenge." His gaze shifted to my lips, then back to my eyes. "I don't think one appreciates victories that come too easily."

"Then you prefer to fight for what you want?"

"I don't know that I prefer it, but I will. After all, when you find something that's worth having . . ." He stared at me for a long moment, and once again, I felt that irresistible pull toward him, as if I were falling forward helplessly. "It is worth any battle necessary."

"What if you lose?"

"One never starts a fight one doesn't think he can win."

"But there's always the chance of failure."

"Ah, but it is that very risk, that possibility of defeat, that makes victory all the sweeter."

"Is it?" I leaned closer, the slightest note of yearning in my voice.

"Always." He stared at me for an endless moment, then abruptly shook his head as if clearing it and released my hand. "Agostina planned to serve dinner as soon as you came down. We should go—"

"Yes, we should." I released a breath I hadn't realized I held. "The villa smells wonderful."

"And the taste is even better. Agostina always outdoes herself at Christmas. Shall we?" He offered his arm, and I hooked my arm through his. He took a step, but I held back.

"Fletcher." I smiled into his dark eyes. "Thank you again for the painting. I shall treasure it always."

"It was entirely my pleasure." He smiled and escorted me into the dining room.

In the back of my mind, I wondered how he knew what Agostina always cooked for Christmas dinner.

While I had long considered a meal of fewer than six courses to be less than civilized, in the few days I'd been at the villa thus far, I had begun to grow accustomed to the less complicated array that Agostina served. Christmas was another matter altogether.

There was dish after dish of delicious culinary offerings. A rich broth and pasta soup was followed by courses of pillows of pasta stuffed with cheese, savory sauces of tomatoes and onions and peppers, platters of roasted lamb and wild boar, along with plates and bowls of potatoes, aubergines, artichokes, olives, dried figs and local cheeses. All accompanied by crusty breads and endless glasses of a rich, red wine and followed by an array of sweets, including, of course, zeppole.

When we weren't sighing with pleasure at the feast Agostina had prepared, we were laughing at whatever story one of us was telling at the moment. We exchanged tales about incompetent government employees and the exploits of some of my less than proper friends and relations. His stories were shaded by details about life in India, mine seasoned with tidbits of gossip I'd heard from my family or my friends. I had never condoned gossip myself, but one could not help but overhear.

With every word, I knew him a little better, and he knew me. While I do think he was being as cautious about the identifying details of his life as I was being with mine, I couldn't help but feel a little guilty. After all, no matter how much I shared with the man, I still had not told him I was not Lady Smithson. And the longer I kept up the lie, the worse it would be when the truth was revealed. Still, I kept reminding myself, once we left the villa, I would never see him again. It was not quite as comforting a thought as it had been a few days ago.

After dinner we settled into backgammon, and I encouraged him to believe I had let him win the first game. Although, from the smirk on his face, I don't think he did indeed believe it. The evening was odd in its comfort, as if we had spent time together before. Christmas perhaps, or simply ordinary days. Days made special by the company. As if this—the two of us together—was right.

"I must say, Fletcher," I began, "and do not let this go to your head."

He gasped. "Never. I did not let my winning the first game go to my head."

"Actually, I believe you did." I returned my gaze to the board. "Apparently, I was too sated from dinner to give the game the attention it deserved. Do not expect that to continue." I considered my next move. "As I was saying, between the food and the company, that was possibly the most delightful Christmas dinner I have ever had."

"And have you had any other Christmas dinners alone with a man you barely know?" He rolled the dice.

My gaze jumped to his, but he was studying the board. "Don't be absurd."

"I only have your word as to the sort of woman you are. And you did agree rather quickly to sharing the villa with me." A teasing note sounded in his voice.

I kept my gaze fixed on the board and my tone matter of fact. "If you are trying to annoy me, Fletcher, I must tell you it's not working."

"Odd. I thought it was." He moved one of his men.

"If it was, you would know." In spite of my best efforts, there was a sharp note in my voice, and I rolled the dice a bit more enthusiastically than I should have.

"You do know I am teasing." He paused. "Which probably makes no difference, does it?"

"None whatsoever."

For a long moment, he didn't say a word. "I seem to find myself apologizing to you over and over again."

"Perhaps that's something you should work on." I moved my markers. "What do you feel the need to apologize for now?"

"Teasing you, of course."

"I grew up with four male cousins, Fletcher. I daresay I am immune to teasing."

"Not that I've noticed," he said under his breath, rolling the dice. "There is nothing wrong with content, you know," he added abruptly.

"That's not the impression I got of your opinion the other night."

"I can be a bit unyielding in my opinions."

"As can we all." I took a deep breath and looked at him. "Fletcher."

He moved one of his men, then glanced at me. "Yes?"

"I was indeed content with my husband, with my life. In hindsight, it might not have been the grandest of passions, but I did love him and he loved me. I could have been quite happy being content for the rest of my days."

He nodded and moved a second piece.

"However, now I think I want more than content."

"I can understand that."

I would also like"—I braced myself—"to see more of your work."

His eyes widened. "Of all the things you can choose, that's what you want?"

"I didn't realize I was making a grand declaration encompassing the rest of my life." I tossed the dice. "Yes, right now, that is indeed what I want."

"I rarely show anyone my work."

"I am not anyone."

He thought for a moment. "I will make you a bargain."

"Oh, I do love bargains."

"You can see my work if you agree to pose for me."

"Naked?" The word came of its own accord, and heat at once flushed my face.

His brow shot upward. "Would you consider that?"

Why not? I returned my gaze to the board and moved my men. My comment was as much a surprise to me as it was to him. "Yes, I believe I would."

"Well." He sat back in his chair and studied me. "Imagine that."

"You're shocked, aren't you?"

"I might well be, yes."

"Correct me if I'm wrong, but it's entirely possible that you and I will never see each other again once we leave here." I glanced up at him.

He nodded. "I hadn't thought of that, but I suppose you're right."

"I know that has led me to be, oh, I don't know, somewhat less restrained in my speech and behavior than I usually am." I met his gaze directly. "I am on holiday, Fletcher, unrestrained from expectations by family or friends or myself. It's remarkably intoxicating."

He stared, the look in his eyes admiring. That too was intoxicating. "You continue to surprise me, Portia Smithson."

"Goodness, Fletcher." I sighed and shook my head. "I continue to surprise myself."

9

The rain continued in the days following Christmas, but Fletcher and I paid little attention to the weather. We were far too busy enjoying each other's company. All in all, it was quite like the days of my youth when all my cousins would be home from school, and we would do nothing more than play games and talk and enjoy simply being together.

Oh, we weren't together every minute. He spent a great deal of time painting, although he had yet to show me his work. Nor had I posed for him—with clothes or without. Neither of us had brought up the subject. I think we both feared I had changed my mind and feared even more that I hadn't.

We continued our backgammon rivalry, and on any given day, one of us would be no more than a game or two ahead of the other. He was very good, but so was I.

On the day after Christmas, Boxing Day in England, we found ourselves abandoned for most of the day. I knew there was no such holiday in Italy, although Margaret did expect to have the day to herself, and I was not about to tell her otherwise. Fletcher informed me that Silvestro and Agostina would have the day free as well, a tradition their English employer had started years ago. He assured them we could fend for ourselves for the day, reminding the couple that there was more than enough food left from Christmas to feed a small army.

Two days after Christmas, we toyed with the idea of playing backgammon for more than the satisfaction of winning, although I was not sure there was anything in this world more satisfying than beating an arrogant man, but decided against wagering money. I knew from his clothes and the way he spoke that he was well-educated and possibly from a well-to-do family, but he was also a government employee, and I hated the idea of his losing more than he could afford out of some misplaced sense of pride. We decided instead to play for information. One question per victory.

Sometimes the questions were silly. *What is your favorite animal?* (His was the Bengal tiger, because it truly was a magnificent beast. Mine was the dodo bird, because it was gone now, thanks to mankind, and I believed remembering the creature was the least we could do.) *If you could be anyone in history who would you be?* (He said Leonardo da Vinci, for obvious reasons. I said Cleopatra, also for obvious reasons.)

Sometimes, the questions and answers were more revealing than anticipated.

"My turn for a question." I fairly chortled with delight. It was the third day after Christmas, and I was doing extremely well.

Fletcher sighed. "You have won three games in a row."

"I know." I grinned. "I am trying not to be too smug."

"And failing," he muttered.

"Now, now, Mr. Jamison." I wagged my finger at him in a chastising manner. "There will be none of that. You lost, and now you must pay. Try not to be afraid."

His brow rose. "I am not afraid."

"Nor should you be." I scoffed. "None of the questions have been especially difficult. Where would you most like to visit? What color do you prefer? Really, Fletcher?" I cast him a condescending look. "Blue? Not summer-sky blue or flawless sapphire blue, but just blue. One expects more from an artist than just blue." I shook my head. "Besides, it's not at all the right color for you, you know."

"I shall keep that in mind," he said dryly. "And you should be able to come up with better questions."

"Very well, then." I said the first thing that popped into my head. "What is your greatest fear?"

"Not living up to expectations," he said without hesitation, then paused as if he hadn't meant to admit that. But the answer lingered in the air like a forbidding cloud. "I don't know why I said that."

"I do," I said lightly, hoping to lessen the abrupt intensity of the moment. "It's a universal fear. We all share it. Fear of not living up to the expectations of parents or families, mothers-in-law or society."

"Mothers-in-law?"

I ignored him. "You said it yourself. There are expectations and responsibilities faced by each and every one of us. We can only hope for a, oh, a holiday from those expectations now and again."

"You are entirely too pretty to be this clever." He smiled in a reluctant manner. "And you are far smarter than anyone would suspect."

"Most women are, Fletcher." I handed him the dice. "As I have won the last three games, you may roll first."

"How very gracious of you."

"I know."

He spilled the dice onto the board. "And what are you afraid of, Portia?"

"Volcanoes."

"Volcanoes?" Fletcher bit his lip, but he clearly thought this was funny. "Volcanoes like Vesuvius?"

"Not like Vesuvius," I said coolly. "Vesuvius specifically."

"Why?"

"I have no idea. Admittedly, it's not entirely rational, but I do not like living in the shadow of a volcano." I shrugged. "Perhaps I lived in Pompeii in a previous life."

"Reincarnation?" Again, he looked as if he were about to burst into laughter. I, however, was not amused.

"I read a great deal, Fletcher. No one seems to realize that," I added under my breath. "I do understand the concept. Now." I held up my hand to keep him from speaking and no doubt saying something sarcastic. It was hard for him. I could see it in his eyes. "I know the volcano has not spewed anything of significance for thirteen years, eight months and two days—"

"You know that, do you?"

"It seemed a wise piece of information to have. However, something unpleasant could happen at any time."

"By unpleasant you mean fiery rocks raining down from the sky? Molten lava? That sort of thing?" The man could barely keep a straight face.

I didn't understand why. It was not as if I was fearful of something like a spider that I could crush under my foot. Although I was not fond of spiders.

"Exactly." I nodded. "I do understand the threat of anni-hilation may be the price one pays for Paradise, and I realize my concern might be considered silly. Therefore . . ." I straight-ened my shoulders in a show of bravery. "I am not about to let my concerns send me screaming off into the night. I'm not terrified, simply aware."

"We could take an excursion to the top of Vesuvius to view the crater," he said thoughtfully, as if he were actually considering such a thing. "It might alleviate your fears."

"Are you insane?" I stared at him with all the indignation I could muster. "I needn't meet the devil face-to-face to know he exists. The last thing I want to do is stick my head in a volcano!"

"I simply thought it might help." He adopted an inno-cent expression I did not believe for a moment.

"And I am grateful for that." What was the man thinking? I drew a calming breath. "I must say, I feel very foolish at the moment, so let's continue the game as if you had asked a ques-tion no more significant than my favorite book. Oh." I pinned him with a stern look. "And should you ever win again—"

"And I will."

"—you have forfeited your next question, as you have already asked it out of turn and been given far more extensive an answer than I wished to give."

"Fair enough." He nodded.

"And it's my turn." I rolled the dice. "Do not think I shall be easier on you simply because you've been losing."

He chuckled. "I would never think that."

It struck me that we had both revealed something we would have preferred to keep to ourselves. Mine was silly, really. A fear I hadn't even realized I had until I was here, with the volcano ever present in the distance. His was something he had lived with all his life. My fear could be abated simply by returning home. His was far more complicated.

Four days after Christmas, the rain finally stopped, and the sun broke through the clouds. Fletcher and I took the opportunity afforded by the break in the weather to walk the twenty minutes or so into town. The roads were muddy, but I hadn't seen anything of Sorrento yet, the charming ancient town perched on the rocky cliffs. I must say, my Baedeker's had not done it justice. The view over the bay from the public gardens was magnificent, and we shared a few moments of companionable silence. Although my thoughts were far from the picturesque vista and firmly on the man by my side.

With every day spent in Fletcher's company, I liked him more and more. I liked how he laughed and the way a lock of his hair fell over his forehead when he concentrated. I liked the look of passion in his eyes when he was working and the wicked twinkle I'd see unexpectedly on occasion when he looked at me. I didn't know what that meant, or indeed what I wanted it to mean. But with every hour, every minute, I liked him more and more.

I was snapping, there was no other excuse for it. Exactly as Veronica had predicted. There was no doubt that between Veronica, Julia and myself I was the one most concerned with proper behavior and the appearance of propriety. The one least willing to bend. The one most likely to snap. And Lord help me, I wanted to snap. With every inadvertent brush of his hand against mine, every unguarded glance, every shared moment, I wanted it—wanted him—more and more.

And more and more I wondered what he wanted. Why, the man hadn't even tried to kiss me. Sometimes, I would catch him looking at me, and it was clear he wanted to. What on earth was holding him back? Was he that much of a gentleman? Shouldn't there be at least a touch of hedonistic artist behind that honorable facade? I was beginning to suspect his true purpose was simply to drive me mad. In that, he might well be succeeding.

I had awakened this morning with renewed resolve. At some point late in the night, as I tossed and turned and again dreamt of being in Fletcher's arms, it had dawned on me that if he was what I wanted, he was what I should have. I was a woman of adventure, after all. Even if having him wasn't the sort of thing I did. But then, I'd never really had the chance either, had I? Nor had I had the desire.

Now it seemed I had both.

"I have been thinking about what you said yesterday," Fletcher began, his gaze focused on the vista before us.

"If I recall, I said a great many things yesterday. Most of which needn't be repeated," I added. "Ever."

"You mean that irrational nonsense about the volcano?" He waved off my concern. "I've forgotten it entirely."

"Hmph."

"But you also said we might never see each other again after we leave the villa."

"When we first decided to be friends," I said slowly, "we did say we would go our separate ways when our stay here was ended."

"I suppose we did." He nodded. "Nonetheless, I have been giving it further consideration."

"Oh?" I held my breath.

"I think it's very practical."

Disappointment stabbed me and with it annoyance. Absurd, of course, as I didn't know what I'd hoped he might say. But I did know it wasn't praise for the *practicality* of never seeing each other again. "Practical?"

"Without question," he said firmly, and that too annoyed me. "It simply makes sense. For one thing, you live in England, and I reside in India."

"But England is your home."

"Yes, of course, but I have no idea when I'll be back there permanently. It might be years."

"So it's only *practical* to accept that we will probably never see each other again?" With every word, I was becoming more and more irate. It scarcely mattered that I was the one who had first said it. That I had realized, and indeed accepted, the very same thing some time ago. But now, well, now things were different. At least for me. "That our, our *friendship* is indeed finite? Destined to end?"

"It seems to me"—caution sounded in his voice—"you have been practical from the beginning."

"Oh?"

"Come now, Portia. I would be a fool not to have noticed. Every time we talk, you are careful not to reveal too much of your life." He paused. "Admittedly, I have done the same thing."

"Because it's *practical*." I fairly spit the word.

"It is. Or, rather, it was." His brows drew together. "It made perfect sense. After all, we were strangers."

"And now?"

"And now . . . we aren't," he said weakly.

"Perhaps we should have stayed strangers," I said sharply, turned and started back the way we had come.

"Where are you going?" he said behind me.

"It appears to be clouding over again. I would hate to be caught in the rain. It's only *practical* to return to the villa."

"Portia," he called after me. "Just because the chances are good that we will never see each other again doesn't mean that's what I want."

I turned on my heel and faced him. He nearly stumbled into me. "What do you want, Fletcher?"

His eyes widened, and a look akin to terror passed over his face. The look of a man tripped up by his own words, or that of an animal caught in a trap. A rat perhaps. "Well, I don't know."

"I didn't think so." I huffed in disdain, turned and continued on.

His strides were far longer than mine, and in two steps he was by my side. "What do you want?"

"Oh no, you are not playing that game with me." I sniffed.

"What game?"

"The game where you will not tell me what you are thinking until I tell you what I am thinking first!"

"I'm not playing any game."

"Mr. Jamison." I stopped and glared at him. "You're right. We will never see each other again, and it's only *practical, sensible* and *reasonable* to understand that and accept it. There. Are you happy?"

"Not especially."

"Good!" I started off again. I knew I was being entirely unreasonable, but I couldn't seem to help myself.

"I daresay you're not being either practical, sensible or reasonable at the moment," he yelled after me.

"Nor do I wish to be!" I threw back over my shoulder. "I have been entirely too practical, sensible and reasonable for much of my life. I am tired of it!"

He was fast enough to catch up with me, but instead, he chose to follow a short distance behind. Wise of him. "You're angry at me, I can tell."

"How perceptive of you!"

"I'm not sure what I've done."

"An intelligent man like you can surely figure it out!"

We walked on in stony silence on my part, utter confusion on his. But he was wise enough to keep his mouth shut. If I was indeed being reasonable, although I had no desire to be anything other than angry at the moment, I would admit that he couldn't be expected to know the directions my thoughts had taken in regards to him. In regards to us. I wasn't being the least bit fair to him.

I didn't care.

I was very aware of him no more than a few feet behind me all the way back to the villa. I would have thought my ire would have eased with every step, and yet it only seemed to increase. It struck me that I was not merely irate but hurt. I thought we were sharing something beyond simple friendship. Not love, of course. I would never again mistake affectionate companionship for deep, abiding, forever love. I had made that mistake once. And it had been quite nice, and I had been content.

I would not settle for content again.

I was completely irrational, and I realized it. This wasn't at all like me. Not Portia, Lady Redwell, who was so cognizant of proper behavior that I was considered more than a little stuffy. Who was so unwilling to cause difficulties or, God forbid, scandal, that I had always done exactly what was appropriate and acceptable, right down to marrying the sort of man it was expected I would marry. Which perhaps wasn't fair to David. He was a good man, and I never doubted that he loved me. But I also suspected that he would have been every bit as content with someone else, as probably would I. It was not a good revelation to have about one's husband or one's marriage, and I hadn't recognized the truth of it until long after

David was gone and I realized, while I did miss him, my life had not ended with his.

When we reached the villa, I drew a deep breath and turned to face Fletcher. He stopped in mid-step and eyed me cautiously. As one might look at a volcano set to erupt.

"I owe you an apology, Fletcher." I clasped my hands in front of me.

"Do you?" he said carefully.

"You were absolutely right. It is *practical* to accept the limited nature of our friendship. We might very well never see each other again after we leave the villa. We're no more than ships that pass in the night, really."

He took a step closer. "Portia, I—"

"Goodness, Fletcher, there really isn't more to say. At least I have no more to say on the subject." I narrowed my eyes, and challenge sounded in my voice. "Do you?"

He stared at me for a long moment. "No," he said at last. "No, I don't suppose I do."

"Excellent." I cast him my brightest smile. "Now then, if you will excuse me, I fear I feel a headache coming on, and I think I should rest a bit before dinner."

"Yes, of course." He nodded. "I do hope you will still be able to join me for dinner."

"As do I." I nodded, turned and entered the villa, pausing for no longer than it took to hand Silvestro my hat and mantelet, then continued to my rooms.

As much as I will acknowledge I was not being the least bit reasonable, it made no difference. I was angry. At him and perhaps at myself, although I couldn't quite say why. If I was being perfectly honest, I would have to admit that I really didn't know what I wanted from the man, what I expected from him. It was obvious, as well, that he had no idea what he wanted from me. If anything.

All I knew for certain, alone in my room on an overcast day in Paradise, was that I might well have just had the tiniest taste of what a broken heart might feel like.

I resolved not to taste it again.

10

I sent my regrets for dinner and retired early. Not that it did any good. I certainly did not sleep well, and when I did, Fletcher was there, a constant presence, confusing and at once aloof and irresistible. And certainly, in my dreams, he did not hesitate to kiss me. It was most annoying. I rose the next morning in a foul mood. Even Margaret dared not cross me. She was wiser than she looked.

I decided it was best to avoid Fletcher for the time being. At least until I decided what I really wanted of him. I took my meals in my room and, as the skies were clear, wandered down the treacherous path to the beach. I perched on a boulder trying to read the exploits of *Belinda*. But the heroine was tiring and her hero spineless, and the story of true love gone awry was more annoying than entertaining. It did not engage my attention, and therefore I spent much of the day composing in my head a strongly worded letter to *The Weekly Review of Art and Literature* disputing its account of the novel as encompassing *brazen wit and stormy passion*. I found the wit dull and the passion even duller.

Still, my displeasure at *Belinda* did take my mind off my displeasure with Fletcher. I assumed he spent the day painting, but he made no effort to cross my path, and I did not seek him out. By the time I retired for the night, I had reached the inescapable conclusion that he had made no promises to me—either said or unsaid. Nor had he done anything whatsoever, except be thoughtful and generous, to make me think there was more to our friendship than appeared. The fact that he did not know that I had decided to pursue him for strictly immoral purposes could not be blamed on him.

It was for the best, really. I wasn't the type of woman to throw myself into a man's bed. I'd never been that type of woman, and I would wager I would not be that type of woman in the future. Just because I had borrowed Veronica's name, and she was outspoken about her own preference for being a mistress instead of a wife, did not mean I could follow in her path.

Tomorrow, I would be cordial to Fletcher, and we would resume our friendship and enjoy the rest of our time together. No matter what unsettling thoughts or disturbing dreams I might have about him tonight.

I bolted upright in my bed. My heart thudded in my chest, blood roared in my ears, panic stole my breath. My stomach twisted and lurched. The rumble that had awakened me sounded again, and I leaped out of bed.

Dear Lord, this was it! All my fears realized! We would be engulfed in ash and flames at any minute! Even now it was probably too late! I tore out of my room and raced down the corridor to Fletcher's door. I pounded with my fist for what seemed like an eternity but was probably less than a minute.

He flung the door open, wild-eyed and completely disheveled, exactly like a man just dragged out of his bed.

"What! What is it? Are you all right?"

"It's happening, Fletcher! Just as I feared!" I was ranting and making no sense, but I couldn't stop. Nor did it matter. "I knew this would happen! I just knew it!"

He stared at me. "Huh?"

"Fletcher! Wake up!" I grabbed his shoulders and shook him.

"Bloody hell, you haven't even kissed me, and we're going to die! We're doomed, Fletcher, doomed!"

"Doomed?" he said slowly.

"For God's sake! Vesuvius is erupting! Can't you hear it?" Why didn't the man understand? "We have to flee! Away from the coast!" On one of the first nights here I had determined that was the best route to escape Vesuvius. I believed in being prepared. "Now, Fletcher—now! We have to wake up Silvestro and Agostina, and we can't leave Margaret! We have to hurry!"

It was obvious that the man wasn't sure if he was awake or just dreaming.

"Fletcher, wake up!" There was only one thing to do. I drew back my hand and let it fly. He caught my hand right before I made contact with his cheek.

"I am awake," he said in a far more lucid voice than I would have expected.

"Thank God! But we must—"

"Vesuvius is not erupting." He glanced up and down the hall, grabbed my hand and yanked me into his room, then shut the door behind me. "Good God, woman!"

"Don't be stupid, Fletcher, of course, it is! What are you doing?" I tried to wrench away, but his grip tightened. "We have to leave here at once!"

"Come with me."

"Fletcher!"

"Portia!" He pulled me across the room to the French doors that opened onto the balcony and threw open the door. He grabbed my shoulders and spun me around to face the bay. "Look out there. What do you see?"

"No! I can't look!" I turned my head back against his chest, squeezing my eyes tightly closed. I had no desire to see doom spewing from the volcano. "I don't want to look! I don't want to see death approaching!"

"Death is not approaching!" His voice rang with assurance. Poor deluded creature. "Open your eyes, Portia."

"No!"

"We're not going anywhere until you do." A threat sounded in his voice.

"Fine!" I braced myself and opened my eyes. "But only to save your life!"

"What do you see?"

"I don't see anything," I snapped. "It's dark and raining." At that moment, lightning flashed and thunder cracked the night. I jumped, and the oddest sound came out of my mouth, a sort of squeaking, squealing noise.

"I assume that's what you heard." Amusement sounded in his voice.

The truth struck me like yet another bolt from above, and my breath caught. "Vesuvius is not exploding, then?"

"I can assure you it isn't."

"And we're not going to die?"

"Not tonight."

Relief rushed through me and with it awareness. At once I was acutely conscious of his body against mine. His grip on my shoulders eased, but his hands remained. It struck me how safe I felt with him, even against the threat of approaching annihilation. At that moment, I remembered everything I had said and realized as well there was nothing more humiliating in the world than having a man you were attracted to know of that attraction. Especially when he had not indicated any attraction on his part. Now that I knew we weren't facing imminent death, I truly wanted to die.

I should have pulled out of his embrace, but then I would have had to face him, and I would rather face Vesuvius.

"I have not been sleeping well of late," I said at last. "I have had the most disturbing dreams."

"Of volcanoes?"

I nodded. "And of you."

"Oh?"

"It's not important." I uttered an odd sort of laugh and moved away from him to stare out at the night. "Obviously, I confused thunder with volcanic eruption." Again, that awkward, self-conscious laugh sounded. "I was sound asleep. As I said, I haven't been sleeping at all well, but tonight I think I was simply exhausted. I was sleeping quite soundly until the volcano erupted."

"It was thunder."

"Yes, well, I know that now." I hadn't thought at all about my state of undress or his, I in my nightgown, he in men's silken pajamas. One didn't worry about proper clothing when the world was coming to an end. Nor had I considered the fact that we were in his room, alone together in the middle of the night. Until now. Yet another thing to be embarrassed about. "I do apologize for waking you." I inched toward the door. "I should be going."

"I would like to hear about those dreams."

I finally looked at him. He was clearly amused. And he had every right to be. I had just made an enormous ass of myself. I drew a deep breath and met his gaze. "Honestly, Fletcher, if I were to tell you, it would make you even more arrogant than you are now. Why, it would go straight to your head, and you would be unbearable."

He chuckled. "That's a distinct possibility."

"I really should go. This isn't at all, well, appropriate."

"Completely inappropriate, I would say." He shook his head. "Not the least bit proper."

"Dear me, no." That strange little laugh burst from me again. Good Lord, why did I keep doing that? I sounded like a madwoman. "I do want to thank you for being so, well, strong and gallant in my moment of—"

"Insanity?"

"I was going to say utter terror, but I suppose insanity is just as accurate." I smiled weakly. "So you do have my gratitude. I'll be going now." I moved toward the door, but he stepped into my path.

"Not quite yet."

"No?" I adopted an innocent expression.

He studied me closely. "About that other matter."

"Other matter?" I had hoped that had slipped by him in the midst of my panic-stricken tirade.

"Yes." His eyes narrowed. "You mentioned that I have not kissed you."

"Did I?"

His dark gaze caught mine. "I distinctly heard you say I hadn't kissed you."

I wanted to deny it. To utter that odd laugh again and claim he had not heard me correctly. Surely I would not say something so outrageous. So improper. But denial did seem rather pointless. Apparently, when one had faced death, even if only in one's own mind, one could muster a certain amount of courage.

"Very well, then." I blew a long breath. "My initial inclination at this moment is to deny that I said that, but I have decided not to." I raised my chin and met his gaze firmly. "Admittedly, while it has been a long time since I have engaged in anything more than casual flirtation, I was fairly certain you harbored some interest in me. An interest, I will confess, I shared. However, you have been nothing but a perfect gentleman, and it is now obvious to me that I was clearly mistaken and–"

"Good God, Portia." He stepped close to me and framed my face with his hands. I held my breath. "I have wanted to kiss you from the moment you spoke bad Italian on the beach."

"But—"

"Shut up, Portia." And with that, he pressed his lips to mine in a kiss ridiculously slow and gentle. Nothing more than a hint or a promise, and yet heat spread from the touch of his lips to mine, washing through me, curling my toes. His breath lightly caressed my lips, teasing and drawing me closer.

His hands slipped from my face, and I wrapped my arms around his neck. His hands slid around my waist, and he pulled me close. The thought flitted through my mind that the appropriate thing, the *right* thing, would be to pull away. But I had no desire to do so, as nothing had ever seemed so right.

At last he drew his lips from mine and stared down at me. "There hasn't been a day that has passed that I haven't wanted to do that."

"Then why haven't you?" The words came of their own accord, but I did not wish to take them back.

He shook his head, his gaze boring into mine. "I would never do anything that you did not want me to do."

"Goodness, Fletcher." I drew his lips back to mine and murmured against them, "you are going to have to learn to read me better than that. We have wasted a great deal of time." Again, I pressed my lips to his, and passion exploded between us.

Within moments, we had discarded our clothes in a frenzy of desire too long denied.

The heat of his naked flesh against mine stole my breath. Without conscious effort, we tumbled onto his bed. I explored his hard body with my fingers, my mouth. I was mad with hunger, wanting him, needing him. A madness he shared.

His mouth was everywhere at once. The line of my jaw, the hollow of my throat. He worshiped at my breasts until I moaned and my back arched. His hands caressed me, stroked me, gentle yet demanding. And I demanded in return.

I rained kisses on his neck, tasted the salt of his skin, reveled in the male scent of him. My hands explored the planes and valleys of his chest, his stomach, his hips. I ran my fingers over his erection and reveled in carnal satisfaction when he sucked in a hard breath. When his hand slipped between my legs, I thought I would swoon from the sheer ecstasy of it. Every touch of mine, every caress of his only heightened the yearning need that threatened to consume me. Consume us.

At last he joined with me, my legs wrapping around his. And we moved together in a rhythm, natural and right and forever. Tension wound tighter and tighter within me until at last my body convulsed around him in an explosion of sheer sensation and utter ecstasy. Dimly, I felt him shudder against me, and he moaned.

For a long time, neither of us moved. I had no desire to do so and wasn't sure I had the strength. I had experienced release before, but infrequently, and never as consuming as this. I had thought I would surely die and die gladly.

This was not the time to compare intimacy with David with what I was discovering with Fletcher, and yet I couldn't help myself. Relations with David had been most pleasant, but never had I felt uncontrolled, wild with desire. That had not been David's fault, nor had it been mine. After all, in love-making as in everything else, we had been content.

At last we lay together, our hearts still beating as one, his arms around me. I could not recall ever feeling quite so decadent, quite so wonderful. There was nowhere in the world I would rather be than wrapped in his arms. And no other arms I would rather have around me. Tomorrow I would no doubt give this feeling a great deal of thought and due consideration. A voice in my head would point out that the all-encompassing passion of tonight was obviously attributable to the immorality of it, forbidden fruit, as it were. That Fletcher and I had no future together, our worlds were too far apart. That we would indeed probably never see each other again. But right now I wanted to do nothing more than savor it.

"Portia," Fletcher said at last.

I curled tighter against him. "You have the sound of a man who has been thinking."

He chuckled. "I'm afraid I have."

"No good can come of that, you know."

"Perhaps not." He paused for a long moment, and I held my breath. "But it has occurred to me—"

"No." I rolled onto my side and placed my finger against his lips. "I don't want to hear it."

He caught my hand and kissed my palm. I shivered with renewed desire, leaned forward and replaced my finger with my lips. "Unless you are going to say it has occurred to you that we should take full advantage of being naked together in your bed to continue to explore each other in all sorts of ways we haven't yet thought of . . ." I nibbled on his bottom lip and trailed my hand lightly down his stomach to his growing erection. "Then I really don't want to hear it."

"Portia." He groaned my name against my lips, and he grew harder in my hand. The oddest sense of power washed through me and with it need, renewed and unrelenting.

I wanted him again. Wanted to feel him inside me. Wanted him to take me, fill me. I had never been this wanton, this wicked. I surrendered to decadent passion and pure bliss.

I slid my leg across his and shifted to lay on top of him, then sat up. My legs straddled him, and I could feel his erection nestle between the cheeks of my derrière. In the dim light, I sensed more than saw him smile. I leaned forward and let my breasts brush against his chest. His harsh intake of breath sent a shiver of satisfaction and something far more delightful through me.

"Unless you are going to say that it had occurred to you that we could continue what we started here well into morning, I'm not interested."

"Well, it was not what I was thinking . . ." His hands wrapped around my waist. "But that had occurred to me . . ." With a swift movement, he shifted, and I lay beneath him.

"Good," I murmured and again claimed his lips with mine. And once more joined my body with his.

We scarcely slept at all, save in short, deep stretches. Barely time to recover before reaching for each other again. By morning, we were at once exhausted and yet not entirely satisfied. We were, I believe, insatiable. The very thought made me want to giggle. Whoever would have imagined? Portia, Lady Redwell? Insatiable in a virtual stranger's bed?

Still, I sighed, there were things that needed to be said. Decisions that needed to be made. I slipped out of bed and found my nightgown. I threw it over my head, then stood in the open balcony doorway, wrapped my arms around myself and gazed out at the rain.

"You have clothes on, Portia," Fletcher's sleep-weary voice sounded from the bed. "I thought we had agreed not to do that today."

I laughed. "I don't recall any such agreement."

"I can see where it might have slipped your mind. You were otherwise engaged at the time." He chuckled. "Come back to bed."

I resisted the urge to do exactly that. "I have been giving a great deal of thought to what you said the other day."

He groaned.

"What?" I glanced at him over my shoulder.

"The last time one of us made that statement, it did not go well."

I smiled. "Unless you intend to be irate, irrational and indignant, I suspect it will be fine."

"I'll make no promises." He threw back the covers, then got to his feet and searched for his clothes.

I should have looked away. It would have been the proper thing to do, really. But then, I was not aware of the rules of propriety governing the aftermath of a night of wild, impetuous passion, and I quite enjoyed watching the way he moved. Watching the shadows play over the hard, lean lines of him. He pulled on his pajama trousers and moved close, standing behind me and enfolding me in his arms.

"Very well, then," he said softly against my ear. "Go on."

"I think you're right." The rain had eased since last night, but I could see no farther than the end of the garden. "It is only practical to accept that we may never see each other again when this holiday is over."

He was quiet for a long, silent moment, and his arms tightened slightly around me. "Is that what you want?"

"What I want, Fletcher . . ." I drew a deep breath. I had no idea what might happen in the future and, in truth, no idea what I wanted in that future. For good or ill, I knew only what I wanted today. "What I want is to ignore what might happen tomorrow. What I want is to enjoy what we have found together here and now." I twisted in his arms to face him and slid my arms around his neck. "What I want is to savor every moment with you. I know I for one am having an unexpectedly wonderful time."

His arms wrapped around my waist. He pulled me close, and his heart beat against mine. "Probably because you had no expectations."

"Exactly." I smiled up at him. I could have said so much more but thought it wiser to refrain.

I was unsure of my feelings, my emotions. And unsure as to what it all meant. I had spent a great deal of my life thinking that what I truly wanted was what was expected of me. In recent months, possibly longer, I'd had a growing awareness that that was no longer enough.

There was more than enough time to consider what significance there might be to my making love with Fletcher. Now that there was no volcanic eruption to contend with, we had time. At the moment, I refused to consider how little time there was.

I had reserved the villa for Christmas, and two weeks beyond. My reservation was nearly at an end.

11

Never had time moved so swiftly. Never had the days flown by so fast. But then, I imagine they always did when one was conscious of every minute, every hour. When one was lost in passion and intimacy and joy, and trying to savor every feeling and commit every moment to memory. I never imagined scandal and decadence would be quite so wonderful.

"Would we like each other had we met in London?" he asked me late one morning, before we had risen for the day.

"I don't know." I thought for a minute, not that the idea hadn't already occurred to me. "I suppose that would depend on whether or not we were trapped together in a large house with no one who spoke English."

He laughed. "That was exactly what I was thinking."

I was at once relieved and uneasy about his admission. It was comforting to know that our thoughts were somewhat aligned in this and yet disconcerting as well. Was our relationship no more than a product of being away from all we knew?

Of that unique kind of freedom that came from distance away from friends and family and, yes, expectations? I didn't know. One more question that I didn't particularly wish to answer. Not at the moment.

But I was happy, blissful. Eternity in hell was not too high a price to pay, the cost of sin and all. We drifted through the days in a passion-filled haze. It was the epitome of scandalous behavior. We enjoyed the days it rained and we were forced to stay indoors. We reveled in those days when the sun broke through the clouds and we walked to the town square and along the cliffs. We talked endlessly about matters of importance and about nothing of significance at all. We did not see eye to eye on any number of topics, ranging from art and literature to science and invention. We argued nearly as much as we laughed, and we laughed a great deal. Even when fully clothed. And I discovered he was indeed more hedonistic artist than civil servant.

I would read while he painted, and he finally allowed me to see his work. Privately, I thought my Christmas tree the best of it, but I admit I know nothing of art. I didn't dislike his paintings, but I found them a bit too modern for my tastes. I tended to like objects in a painting to be more recognizable and realistic. Not that I admitted this to Fletcher, although he never asked my opinion. I believed that showed a man who either had supreme confidence in what he did or simply didn't care what anyone else thought. In Fletcher's case, I thought it was a bit of both.

I attempted to pose for him, but it wasn't as productive for his work as it might have been had we both not been so easily distracted. It was, however, delightful.

Margaret was suitably appalled by my shocking behavior, of course. But we had been together too long, and I didn't question her loyalty. I had always expected that she would keep my secrets, although, admittedly, I had never given her any- thing to gossip about. I had long suspected the social standing of servants among their peers improved when they supplied the juiciest bits of gossip. Perhaps that was why she had been more pleasant since Fletcher and I had begun what even the most discreet among us would not fail to call an affair. I tried to care what she thought, and I was certain I would care when I returned to London, but at the moment, I didn't.

Admittedly, I experienced a certain amount of guilt, as if I were being unfaithful to David. It was absurd. David was extremely practical, and while he might have looked askance at the impropriety of my liaison with Fletcher, he would not have condemned my moving forward with my life. I daresay, had I been the one to have died, David might well have remar- ried by now.

The man, the villa, the setting, even the volcano, it was all intoxicating. Seductive. Like a dream one never wanted to awaken from. But as much as I tried not to think about it, the clock ticking toward farewell was always there. We were always conscious of it. It was always hanging unsaid in the air. But for Christmas, and two weeks beyond, I did not consider the consequences of my actions. Nor did I care.

It was magic. There was no other word for it, certainly no other reason. And with every passing day, the emotions we shared grew more intense, every moment more bittersweet.

We did not speak of the future. We made no promises. Love was never mentioned, and while I felt a great deal for him, I was not sure it was love. It was certainly passion, and it was wonderful. And the most remarkable Christmastime.

In no more than the blink of an eye, it was over, and we said good-bye at the villa. It was very nearly the same kind of day it had been when I first arrived. I wondered if he would swim after I left. He was to leave tomorrow.

We stood together in front of the carriage hired to take me to Castellammare. From there, Margaret and I would take the short train ride to Naples. And tomorrow morning, we would be on board a ship heading toward Southampton.

"Very well, then." I gestured at the carriage. Margaret was already waiting inside. "I should be off."

"Yes, of course." He offered me a hand.

I stepped onto the first step.

"Although I have been thinking." His gaze met mine, my hand still in his.

I stopped and held my breath. "Yes?"

"Perhaps . . . I don't know." He shook his head. "Perhaps, if I have the opportunity, that is, I shall return next year for Christmas."

My heart sped up. "Do you think so?"

"It's certainly a possibility. Although I'm sure you will wish to stay with your family for Christmas." He released my hand.

"No doubt." I forced a smile and stepped up into the carriage. I settled into my seat then, without thinking, twisted and leaned out the window. "But it is a lovely place to be at Christmas," I said quickly. "I might well return myself, although a great deal can change from one Christmas to the next."

He nodded. "Without question."

"You could be sent somewhere even more remote than India."

"And your aunt could find you the perfect match."

"Indeed," I agreed. "Any number of things could happen."

He shrugged. "Well, I did say perhaps."

"I would certainly make no promises," I said.

"Nor would I."

My gaze meshed with his, and oh Lord, my heart ached in my chest. "But it is a possibility."

"A definite possibility."

I wanted nothing more than to fling myself out of the carriage and into his arms. I'm not sure why I didn't, except for a lifetime of following expectations and behaving properly.

"Until next Christmas, then. Possibly." He smiled up at me. "Safe travels, Lady Smithson."

"Take care, Mr. Jamison," I said, fighting the oddest catch in my throat, struggling to keep my smile firmly in place.

Fletcher nodded at the driver, and we started off. Margaret didn't say a word. We were barely out of sight of the villa when she silently handed me a handkerchief. I noted it was a souvenir printed with scenes of Sorrento, and my eyes blurred.

Every day of my travels, in a carriage, on board a train or a ship, I told myself that Fletcher and I were not to be. We were from different worlds. He had been an adventure, after all. Beyond that, we hadn't been completely honest with each other. We had admitted that. I had remained guarded with him, and I think he with me. If he had asked me to stay, and part of me had ached for him to do so, I would have said no. But he didn't ask. And I didn't offer.

I certainly had no intention of returning to Villa Mari Incantati next Christmas. Nor, I suspect, did he. It was the sort of thing one said when one was reluctant to say farewell knowing that it might well be forever. Why, I could be married by this time next year. His circumstances could change. Any number of things could be different next year. Next Christmas.

This Christmas was no more than a moment. To remember and cherish and keep close to me always. But my life had nothing to do with this place and this man. And I was ready to return to my life as I knew it. A life that had always been pleasant and, yes, content. Even Fletcher had admitted there was nothing wrong with content.

Nothing at all.

And the closer I came to home, the easier it was to ignore the nagging thought in the back of my mind and totally disregard the distinct, melancholy feeling that I was indeed climbing back into a box.

Part Two

England 1886

12

My life resumed its normal state almost immediately after my return, as if I had never left. My aunt continued to herd one man after another in my direction. My unmarried cousins lent whatever assistance Aunt Helena might need in her efforts so as not to distract her and thereby turn her matchmaking attention toward them. Any concerns I might have had regarding the possibility of a child vanished within days of leaving Italy. There was little to indicate I had ever been away. Everything in my life was exactly as it had always been. Nothing had changed.

Except me.

After the exuberant color of southern Italy, London was shades of black and gray, which suited me. Veronica wed my cousin Sebastian a scant week after my return. It was a joyous event, and I couldn't have been happier for my dear friend. Of course, Sebastian's marriage left only myself and my cousins Miranda and Hugh as yet unwed. Miranda had been a widow for only two years, and it did seem she was not quite ready to move on with her life, although she was always the quietest of the family and one never quite knew what she was about. As Hugh was a man, Aunt Helena didn't seem to think his need to wed quite as urgent as mine, and she renewed her efforts toward finding me a match, although it did seem her only requirement in a suitable prospect was little more than he be unmarried. And breathing.

I had fallen back into my old ways of doing what was expected of me. Life was much easier that way. I had hung Fletcher's Christmas painting in my bedroom, which seemed like an excellent idea, as I would not have to explain it to anyone, and I put Fletcher Jamison completely out of my mind. Or, rather, I tried. Admittedly, he would reappear in the most unexpected ways, the most inconvenient moments. The first time I danced with a man after my return, I realized Fletcher and I had never danced together. It was most distracting, and while I was usually quite an accomplished dancer, I feared my partner was grateful when the dance ended. Fletcher frequently made an appearance in my dreams as well. Along with Vesuvius.

I had been home for nearly a month when, at my aunt's urging, I accepted an invitation to a ball given by Lord and Lady Dunwell. While I had not enjoyed solitude at all in Italy, now that I was home, I relished my privacy. And yet, I was exceedingly restless, and a ball did sound enjoyable. I should have known better.

I was scarcely in the door when Aunt Helena introduced me to a gentleman I had briefly met on another occasion, and then she conveniently abandoned me to greet an acquaintance, although I suspect she simply wanted to leave me alone with the man. No sooner had I managed to evade his attentions than Aunt Helena appeared with another prospect in tow.

And again, she disappeared. Fortunately, I spotted my eldest cousin, Adrian, and his wife, Evelyn, and made my escape, promising another dance later in the evening. A promise I had no intention of keeping.

"Good evening, Adrian. Evelyn, how wonderful to see you." I kissed Evelyn's cheek and spoke low into her ear. "Save me."

Evelyn's eyes widened. "From what?"

A waiter handed us each a glass of champagne, and I downed mine with an unbecoming sense of desperation. "Aunt Helena, of course." I turned to Adrian. "Your mother is in rare form tonight, cousin. Every time I turn around, she is introducing me to yet another candidate for my hand. All of whom seem to think the way to my heart is by stepping on my feet and clutching me entirely too tightly in the guise of dancing." I lowered my voice. "One more dance and I daresay I shall be crippled for life. As my favorite cousin, I beg of you to rescue me."

"Your favorite, you say?" Adrian raised a skeptical brow. "I thought Sebastian was your favorite."

I huffed. "Sebastian is my favorite youngest male cousin. You are my favorite oldest male cousin."

He bit back a smile. "And Hugh?"

"Hugh is my favorite . . ." I scrambled for the right word. "Barrister cousin. Yes, that's it." I needed Adrian's assistance, and if he would help me, he would indeed be my favorite. I tried and failed to keep a note of panic from my voice. "Now will you help me?"

"What do you want me to do?" he asked cautiously. Goodness, one would have thought I needed him to help me rob the Bank of England, not merely escape his mother and too-eager suitors.

"Would you be so good as to drive me home?" I peered around him, trying to find any of the less than noteworthy matches my aunt had tried to foist me on tonight. "Now, if you please. Before Aunt Helena returns with yet another victim in tow." I shuddered. "I have had quite enough."

"I am sorry, Portia." Evelyn cast me a look of sympathy. "But we have scarcely been here any time at all. Leaving now would be considered most impolite."

"Nonsense." She was right, of course, but I didn't care. "You don't even like Lady Dunwell. Not that I blame you." Lady Dunwell's amorous escapades were very nearly legendary. But then, so were her husband's. In that way, at least, they were a perfect match.

"If you could manage to survive for, oh, say, another hour or so." Adrian glanced at his wife.

Evelyn nodded. "That would be sufficient, I think. Another hour wouldn't make it appear as though we were eager to leave."

"Not that we are," Adrian muttered, then smiled apologetically at me. "And then we would be delighted to see you home."

I groaned. "In another hour or so, your mother will have me married with a dozen children."

Adrian choked back a laugh.

I narrowed my eyes. "It's not the least bit amusing."

"Of course not, dear." Evelyn patted my arm.

Adrian cleared his throat. "My apologies." He studied me curiously. "I thought you wanted to marry again."

"Indeed, I do," I said with a sigh. "But I wish to marry someone who is not thrust at me. As if he were a canary, and I was a . . . a . . . a hungry cat!" Indignation swept through me. "I am perfectly capable of finding a husband on my own."

"Not thus far," Adrian said under his breath. In another setting, I would have been hard-pressed not to have smacked him for that.

Instead, I ignored him. "However, this is an exceptionally large and pretentious house. Perhaps I can find a peaceful place to, well, hide until you are ready to depart."

Evelyn nodded. "And the least I can do is help you find a suitable spot."

I had always liked Evelyn, but no more so than at this moment. "A parlor perhaps?" I thought for a moment. I had been in this house once before, but that was some time ago. "Surely they have a music room? I know there's a conservatory. Or a library?"

"No," Evelyn said quickly, although it did seem a library would be perfect. "You never know who might show up in a library. But a parlor is an excellent idea."

"It's rather cowardly, though, don't you think?" Adrian said mildly. "Hiding from Mother, that is."

"Yes. And I don't care." I glared at him. "Thus far this evening I have been presented to one gentleman who was not looking so much for a wife as a mother for his herd of children and another who, well, let us simply say he was not to my liking."

"Judging on appearances, Portia?" Adrian shook his head in a chastising manner. "I never imagined you were that shallow."

"Stop teasing her, dear." Evelyn frowned.

"I simply want someone who stands taller than my chin," I said in a sharper tone than I had intended, but I was wearying of playing fox and hounds with my aunt's potential matches. Being the fox grows tiresome quickly, and I no longer seemed to have the patience I once had. "I do not think I am asking for the moon."

"Perhaps not." Amusement gleamed in Adrian's eyes. I was so glad one of us was enjoying this.

"As for my shallow nature, I am more than willing to debate that with you at another time." I cast Evelyn a pleading look. "Now, I think we should—"

"Too late, I fear." Adrian gazed over my head.

I groaned. Once again, I was trapped. Aunt Helena was approaching with yet another gentleman. This one was at least taller than I and not unattractive. Still, I would reserve my opinion until he opened his mouth.

"Adrian!" Aunt Helena beamed at her son. "And Evelyn. So lovely to see you both. I had no idea you would be here tonight."

"Nor did we, Mother." Adrian kissed her cheek.

"Nonetheless, I am most gratified to see you here." My aunt lowered her voice. "It's a most influential gathering."

"Helena." Evelyn cast a pointed glance at the gentleman waiting to be introduced.

"Oh dear, where are my manners?" Helena sighed. "The bane of growing older, I suppose." She turned to her latest offering. "May I present my son and daughter-in-law, Lord and Lady Waterston. And this"—a flourish sounded in my aunt's voice, and I resisted the absurd urge to drop a regal curtsey—"is my niece, Lady Redwell. Portia, this is Mr. Sayers."

"Ah yes." Mr. Sayers took my hand and raised it to his lips, his gaze never leaving mine. He was entirely too practiced and well-rehearsed, an assessment that was not at all fair of me. Why, he could be my perfect match. But I doubted it. Amusement quirked his lips. "The widow."

There was little more humiliating than being presented as a desperate widow. I pulled my hand free and summoned a weak smile. "I see my aunt has been talking to you."

"Oh my, yes." A satisfied note sounded in Aunt Helena's voice. "It seems I went to school with Mr. Sayers's mother. Unfortunately, I can't seem to remember her, but then, it was a very long time ago. Once again, you have my apologies, Mr. Sayers."

"None are necessary, Lady Waterston," he said smoothly. Too smoothly, I thought. There was something about him that was entirely too polished. "As you said, it was a very long time ago."

"Still, it is impolite and most annoying." Aunt Helena sighed. "My memory is not what it used to be. Yet another distressing result of the passing years."

"Better than the alternative," Adrian murmured.

My aunt cast her son a disparaging look.

"Lady Redwell." Mr. Sayers addressed me, and my heart sank. "I would be most grateful if you would do me the honor of joining me in a dance."

"What an excellent idea." A smug twinkle sparked in Aunt Helena's eyes. No doubt she already had me wed to the man. "You have scarcely danced all evening."

Adrian coughed.

The idea of fleeing into the night flashed through my mind, but my aunt would probably race after me with a special marriage license in one hand and a bouquet of bridal flowers in the other.

I summoned as genuine a smile as I could manage. It was only one dance, after all. "I would be delighted."

Mr. Sayers nodded to the others and escorted me onto the dance floor. He was an excellent dancer and fortunately not one of those talkative gentlemen who felt compelled to expound on one topic or another while leading me through the steps of a dance. I was grateful to him for that, although, in spite of his gallant nature, it did strike me he was no more interested in me than I was in him. Yet another way in which he gained my gratitude. The dance ended, and he accompanied me off the floor. Before the moment became too awkward, I used the same excuse my aunt had employed earlier and claimed to see someone I simply had to speak with. Relief flashed on his face so quickly I might have been mistaken, but I doubted it.

I had no desire to stay in the ballroom. My appearance here tonight was a mistake. I preferred to be by myself right now, although I suspected that would pass. It had simply not passed yet.

I made my escape through the first door I encountered. I was fairly certain I remembered where the conservatory was, and I headed in that direction. Hopefully, it would be blissfully empty, and I could hide for the next hour.

The Dunwell conservatory was as large and pretentious as one would expect from Beryl Dunwell, but I had always had a fondness for conservatories. The moment I crossed the threshold and closed the glass-paned door, letting the scent of earth and exotic blossoms surround me, I was no longer in cold, damp London but somewhere warm and bucolic. Italy perhaps.

I sighed and moved deeper into the conservatory. Lush greenery surrounded me, along with memories of the villa. How long would it be before an unexpected sight, a chance scent, a sound or a flavor would no longer snap me back to thoughts of Fletcher? How long would it be before I wanted it to? Probably far sooner than I wished. Whether I wanted to admit it or not, while I did try to ignore all thoughts of him, he was never gone for long. It was to be expected, of course. I'd left Italy not quite a month ago. It was too soon to expect that I would not think about him at all. And entirely too soon to consider returning to the villa for Christmas. A great deal could happen between February and December. To me and to him. Chances were he would have forgotten all about me by Christmas. And even as I tried to tell myself I would have forgotten all about him as well, somewhere deep inside, I didn't quite believe it. Somewhere in the vicinity of my heart, I feared.

I wandered aimlessly for a moment or two, pausing here and there to examine an orchid or blossoms of jasmine or heliotrope. My London house did not have a conservatory, and I vowed to look into having one built.

The vague hint of something harsh and heavy and completely foreign to a conservatory tickled my nose. It was the smell of something burning, something vile, the smoke coming from deeper in the conservatory, toward the far outside wall. There was no mistaking that smell. I made my way around a large, circular planter overflowing with palms and ferns, stepped around a small potted tree and spotted my quarry. My assumption was correct.

A tall gentleman, deep in thought, stood smoking a cigar in the open doorway that led into the Dunwell gardens.

"See here," I said sharply, "you are not supposed to smoke in a conservatory! No matter whose it is!"

I must have startled him. He sucked in a sharp breath and began to choke, then to cough.

"Oh dear." I stepped closer. "Are you all right?"

He glared at me and continued to cough.

"Do you need help?" I stared at him. Of course he needed help. I quickly circled him, then pounded on his back. I could have sworn plumes of blue smoke spewed out of the man's nose, although I was probably mistaken.

At last, he caught his breath.

"All right now?" I asked brightly.

"Yes." He gasped. "You may stop pounding."

I snatched my hand away. "Don't you know better than to smoke your cigars in a place like this?"

"I wasn't. There was a door. I was in the open doorway. More outside than in, really."

I crossed my arms over my chest. "You were letting the cold air in."

"I was keeping the smoke out." He waved his arms to disperse the lingering smoke.

"I detest cigars," I said staunchly.

"At the moment"—he cast a rueful look at the cigar still in his hand—"so do I." He flipped it out the open door, and I refrained from saying anything.

I nodded at the door. "You really should close that. It's dreadfully cold outside."

"I had every intention of closing it." He pulled the door shut. "And I am well aware of the cold."

"Then you should also be aware that most of the plants—"

"Is this your conservatory?" His brow furrowed.

"It really doesn't matter." I sniffed. "You should not have been smoking cigars in here."

"No, of course it's not yours," he said, as if I hadn't spoken. "This is Lord Dunwell's house, and I have met Lady Dunwell. You are definitely not her."

"Thank goodness," I said under my breath, then cast him a pointed look. "Now that you are finished, I assume you will return to the ball?"

"Yes, I suppose." Although he made no attempt to leave.

"Well?" I fluttered my fingers toward the house. "Go on, then."

He studied me curiously, and I had the most insane desire to tug at my bodice and smooth my skirt to make sure my dress was still in place. I judged him to be a few years older than I and dashing enough with sandy-colored hair and sky-blue eyes. He had, as well, a confident air about him, but then someone secretly smoking a cigar in a conservatory would probably have to. "Why don't you leave, and I'll stay?"

"I need a moment of . . . solitude." Yes, that was good. "I was feeling somewhat faint. The crowd, you understand." I flipped open my fan and fanned my face. "It's a female sort of thing." That should scare him off. Men always seemed terrified of that kind of detail.

He stepped closer, concern in his blue eyes. "May I be of assistance?"

"No!" I shook my head. "But thank you. Now please go, before someone finds us in here together. Alone. Voices do carry, you know, and someone is likely to stumble in here at any minute. I am not interested in scandal, and this is precisely how gossip starts."

"I'm aware of that too." He continued to stare at me as if I were an insect pinned to a display board. "My God." He grinned. "You're hiding from someone, aren't you?"

"Don't be absurd," I said quickly, but apparently not quickly enough.

He chuckled, and the corners of his eyes crinkled. "I was escaping as well."

"Oh?" I tried to feign interest, but all I really wanted was for him to leave.

"There is a persistent older woman who is stalking me like a game hunter on safari."

On second thought, this was intriguing. "Go on."

"She is determined to introduce me to her niece."

"I see." And wasn't that interesting? "Are you considered a catch, then, Mr. . . .?"

"Lindsey. Lord Lindsey, actually." He smiled. "Thomas."

"Now then, my lord." This was really quite delightful. "You did not answer my question. Are you considered a catch?"

"Well, yes, I suppose." He shrugged. "It's not the sort of thing you're aware of every moment, if you are a decent sort."

"And are you a decent sort?"

"I must say, I came in here to escape and enjoy a quiet, pleasant cigar, not be interrogated. But yes." He nodded firmly. "I do consider myself a decent sort."

"How wonderfully humble of you."

He grinned. "I can be humble as well."

"No doubt." I paused. "So which of us is going to be a gentleman and bravely go forth, leaving the other blissfully alone?"

"I am usually thought of as a gentleman."

"Excellent." I waved toward the door. "Good evening."

"But I don't know your name."

"No, you don't."

He cast me a look of regret. "You could be letting quite a catch escape, you know."

"I am willing to take that risk."

"Say, I have an idea." He leaned toward me and lowered his voice. "If we remain quiet, no one will hear us, and we can share this sanctuary. It is a very large place. Why, if I were to go around that plant and behind that palm, you wouldn't even know I was here."

"Oh, I would know."

"Are you really going to make me go?" A pleading note sounded in his voice.

"Yes." I smiled. "I think it's for the best."

"Very well." He heaved an overly dramatic sigh. "But you do understand you could be throwing away the catch of the year?"

"I suspect if you were the catch of the year, I would have heard of you by now," I said in as gentle a tone as possible.

"That's what happens when one is as humble as I am." He shook his head in a mournful manner. "This is your opportunity to snap me up before some other lady sees what a wonderful catch I am."

"I beg your pardon." I bit back a laugh. "Why on earth would you think I would be the least bit interested?"

"You're obviously not married."

"Obviously?"

"Married women generally do not take refuge in the middle of a ball, unless, of course, they are engaged in some sort of illicit activity, and you do not strike me as that sort."

I stared at him. I had no idea what to think, although I did note a twinge of relief. "Was that a compliment, or have I been insulted?"

"I did not mean it as an insult. I find a certain awareness of appropriate behavior to be quite admirable in a lady."

"Oh." I did not know how to respond.

"Furthermore, I would imagine you are a widow. You are entirely too lovely to have reached the age of majority without someone having married you."

"I do appreciate the sentiment, but—" Some rational, solid, proper voice inside me—my mother's perhaps—told me not to say another word. I almost obeyed it. "Thank you."

"Three years, I would imagine," he said slowly.

Caution washed through me. "Yes?"

He stared at me for a long, considering moment. "You're the niece, aren't you?"

"If I was, I'm not sure I would admit it now."

"I suspected your aunt had exaggerated." He smiled. "She didn't."

Again, he caught me off guard. I had no idea what to say. I do not like being flustered. I was not one of those women who looked helpless and charming when flustered. I tended to look annoyed and blotchy. It was not attractive.

"Again, thank you."

He nodded and turned to leave, then turned back. "You do realize, if I were to escort you back to the ballroom and we were then to share a dance or perhaps several, your aunt would be ecstatic."

"You have no idea." I shook my head. "But I would not put you in that position. Besides, the countless other females looking for a good catch would be crushed at the possibility that you are off the market."

"They shall have to bravely carry on."

"I warn you, my aunt will have us married by the end of the month."

"It's a risk I am willing to take." He grinned. "You see, I have an iron-clad escape already in the works."

"You would have to," I said wryly.

"I am leaving the country tomorrow, and unfortunately, I expect to be gone for several months."

"Fleeing the country, while it does seem extreme, might well be your only salvation."

"Unfortunately, I have little choice." He paused. "May I call on you when I return?"

"I don't know." I fluttered my fan. "Any number of things could happen in several months. Why, I could no longer be amenable to having you call on me."

His brow rose. "Are you amenable to it now?"

I laughed and surrendered. "I suppose I am not disposed against it."

"Good." He took my hand and raised it to his lips in a manner every bit as smooth as Mr. Sayers's, but with Lord Lindsey, it seemed natural and effortless. And quite, quite charming. "Then I shall hope nothing happens to change your mind."

I withdrew my hand. "You are very nearly as determined as my aunt, aren't you?"

"Oh, I can be very determined." He grinned again. It was an exceptionally nice smile, and I returned it. "Especially when I find something that might well be worth pursuing."

I laughed. "Well, then, my lord, I would be delighted to dance with you."

"I knew you would." He offered his arm. I hesitated, then drew a deep breath and rested my hand on his arm. There was no flash of heat. No moment of awareness. My toes did not curl, my insides did not flutter. Not that it mattered, but it was interesting to note.

By the end of the evening, I was very much aware that there might possibly be a new gentleman in my life. I wasn't sure how I felt about that.

But I wasn't opposed to finding out.

13

In March, I began to study Italian, only because of my new-found realization of the benefits of knowing how to communicate in another country. I certainly had no intention of returning to Italy in the foreseeable future, but it was possible I would return one day, and it would be nice to know the language. Besides, a well-bred lady should be conversant in a variety of languages. I also began planning a conservatory for my London house. And I found myself attending more and more gallery exhibitions of promising new artists.

By June, I had mastered sufficient Italian to call for a carriage and comment on the weather, but little else. I was not known for my patience, but I refused to give up. I would conquer Italian. Or it would conquer me, but one of us would not survive. I also finalized the design for my conservatory and started plans for a folly in the garden at my country house. My cousin Miranda was assisting me, although it did seem that I was assisting her, as she was far better at this sort of thing. Her late husband had been an architect. Between my new projects and my usual charities and social obligations, I was extraordinarily busy.

Still, I was well aware that I was not the same woman I had been before my sojourn in Italy. I certainly didn't feel the same, although no one else seemed to note any change in me. Or so I thought.

Julia and Veronica and I did not see each other as often as we once did. It was to be expected, of course. They were occupied with their families—Julia had had a daughter in the spring—and I was otherwise engaged. Our weekly rendezvous at the ladies' tea room at Fenwick and Sons, Booksellers had fallen to no more than once a month, and some months not even that. But with summer upon us and each of us planning to retire to the country for the warmer months, Veronica insisted we meet. I hadn't realized how much I had missed this company of women.

"Portia," Julia began after we had exchanged greetings and the latest gossip, "Veronica and I have been talking."

"Have you?" I smiled at my friends, but there was something in her tone that did not bode well. "And what, of any number of topics, have you been talking about?"

"You," Veronica said bluntly.

"Really? I had no idea I was that interesting." I refilled my cup. "In fact, I thought I was rather dull."

Veronica and Julia traded glances, obviously deciding which one was to go first. Apparently, Julia won. Or lost.

"We have noticed, in recent months . . ." Julia said, decidedly uneasy. I'd never seen either of my friends uneasy before. "Well, you seem . . . I don't know, not your usual self."

"Not your usual self at all," Veronica added.

"An improvement, no doubt." I smiled and added sugar to my tea. "So how precisely do I not seem my usual self?"

"We have noticed that you are very often preoccupied."
Julia's tone was cautious. "And rather quiet—withdrawn, we
would say. You're not nearly as, oh, buoyant as you used to be,
and you are entirely too thoughtful."

"You"—Veronica pinned me with a firm look—"are
never thoughtful."

"Never?" I gasped in feigned shock. "Surely on occasion?"

"No," Veronica said staunchly. "Never."

"It's one of the things we love about you," Julia said
quickly. "We've noticed as well a certain restlessness."

"I thought I was withdrawn and preoccupied."

"You are. It's most confusing." Veronica studied me
closely. "Which is very nearly the only thing about you that
hasn't changed."

"Utter nonsense." I scoffed. "I can't imagine how you've
drawn these conclusions. You two have scarcely seen me this
year."

"And that is entirely our fault," Julia said.

"No, it's not." Veronica's brows drew together. "Portia is
the one who keeps canceling our gatherings."

"I have been busy."

"Too busy for your friends?"

"No." I shook my head. "Of course not."

"And you've been secretive." Veronica narrowed her eyes.
"For as long as we have known you, you have never been able
to keep a secret."

"And I am not keeping a secret now," I said lightly and
sipped my tea.

"You're different than you were before you went to Italy."
Concern showed in Julia's eyes. "We are worried about you."

Veronica leaned forward. "We are your dearest friends in
the world. If there is something amiss in your life, we want to

know." She reached out and covered my hand with hers. "We want to help."

My gaze shifted from Veronica to Julia. They both gazed at me with looks of apprehension and worry.

"What on earth are you two up to?" At once the answer struck me. "You think I'm ill, don't you?" I sucked in a sharp breath. "You think I'm dying!"

"No, of course not." Julia waved off the charge.

"Are you?" Veronica said at exactly the same time.

"Don't be absurd." I stared at my friends and realized they were as much sisters as friends. And realized as well I had no idea why I hadn't told them about Fletcher. Oh certainly, there were all sorts of valid reasons. I didn't want Veronica to hold my indiscretion over my head, and I would have hated for Julia to think less of me, although I was fairly certain she wouldn't.

"Portia," Julia said carefully, "we understand why you might not want to talk about it, but it's obvious, at least to us, that you are hiding something."

Veronica nodded. "It's not at all uncommon for people who are ill to go to Italy for medicinal purposes. For the waters and fresh air and that sort of thing. And to see specialists."

Certainly there were legitimate reasons for my reticence to confide in them, but ultimately, this was *my* secret. I'd never had a secret of my own, and I hadn't been ready to share it, as if the telling of it somehow would diminish its significance. Besides, I did think the less I thought about last Christmas, the more likely I was to forget all about it. And him. Admittedly, I had been wrong.

Now, perhaps it was time.

"Portia, we are your dearest friends," Veronica said, "and if you are ill, we—"

"I'm not dying," I said quickly. "Well, not any more than we are all inevitably dying someday." I adopted a casual manner, took a particularly decadent small cake from the platter and braced myself. "I met a gentleman."

Stunned silence hung over the table. For a moment, I thought I'd killed them.

"You what?" Veronica's eyes could not have gotten any bigger.

"You're certain you're not dying?" Julia studied me.

"Positive."

"And where exactly did you meet this gentleman?" Suspicion rang in Veronica's voice.

"In Italy."

"Where in Italy?"

"Goodness, Veronica, if you wish to think I'm making up a story simply to distract you from concern about my impending death, I can assure you I'm not. I have never felt better. But if you choose not to believe me . . ." I shrugged and took a bite of cake.

"It's not that we don't believe you." Julia shook her head as if to clear it. "It's just so, so unexpected."

"And where in Italy did you meet this gentleman?" Veronica could be like a dog with a bone. "Specifically, if you please."

"At the villa. There was a bit of a mix-up as to who had engaged the villa for Christmas. You know how those things happen when you're traveling." I considered another bite of cake. "So we shared."

"You shared a villa with a man you'd just met," Julia said slowly.

"A stranger?" Veronica's voice rose.

"Well, you know what they say. Those least willing to bend . . ." I adopted my most innocent look and took a sip of tea.

Veronica opened her mouth to say something, but nothing came out save an odd, sputtering sound. Julia's mouth dropped open as well. I'd never seen anyone so taken aback as my two dearest friends. It was most satisfying.

"I see," Julia said at last.

"I must say, I was prepared for your unfortunate demise, but this revelation of yours has taken me completely by surprise." Indignation sounded in Veronica's voice. "We have been extremely worried—"

"We never would have imagined this." Julia snorted.

"I am sorry, but—"

"The least you can do now is make amends. A few particulars will suffice." A decidedly wicked smile curved Veronica's lips. "We want to hear all about it. Every delicious detail."

"We are assuming it was delicious," Julia added.

Veronica waved away the comment. "It would be pointless otherwise. Was it pointless?"

"My choices are pointless or delicious?"

Veronica nodded.

"Well, then, it was most definitely"—I smiled a wicked smile of my own—"not pointless."

"I knew it!" Veronica's eyes sparked with triumph. "I knew one day all that propriety of yours would snap you like a twig."

"A delicious twig." Julia grinned.

"No one knows any of this." My gaze shifted from one friend to the other. "You must promise to keep this completely confidential." I didn't need to ask. Of all the people in the world, I knew these two would keep my secrets.

Julia nodded. "You have our word."

"*We* have always been good at keeping secrets," Veronica said pointedly.

"Very well, then." I drew a deep breath and told them everything. Well, not every detail, but more than enough. It required two more pots of tea and another round of biscuits.

It was a relief, really, to finally talk about my adventure. It is said that confession is good for the soul, and I wasn't certain that my soul was soothed by the revelation of my scandalous Christmas, but I did feel remarkably like a weight had lifted. When I finished, neither of them seemed to know exactly how to respond.

"And you know nothing more about him than his name?" Julia asked.

"I know he is a civil servant with a position in India. I surmised that he is well educated, but I really know nothing more than that."

Veronica stared in disbelief. "Good Lord, Portia, didn't you ask?"

"No." I took a sip of tea. "It didn't seem necessary. It was painfully obvious to both of us that we were from different backgrounds, therefore the likelihood of any sort of future was slim."

"Are you going to return this year for Christmas?" Julia asked.

"I doubt it," I said coolly. "My stay at the villa was definitely an adventure, but over and done with. It was a moment out of time, as it were. I'm not sure how else to describe it."

"Magic," Julia murmured.

"That's as good a word as any." And hadn't I already thought the same thing myself? "As for returning for Christmas . . ." I shrugged. "I'm not sure it's wise."

"Oh, my dear, you abandoned wise some time ago." Veronica leaned forward and met my gaze directly. "You absolutely must go."

"I have no idea what might happen between now and Christmas."

"Regardless," Veronica continued, "the story is not over yet. Perhaps this was just some sort of coincidence, ships that pass and all that, but what if this was fate?"

Julia stared at Veronica. "I have never heard you put any credence in fate before."

"Nor will you hear me do so in the future. But the one person I never truly imagined would plummet from her lofty perch of propriety has never fallen before. It puts everything in an entirely different perspective. For two people from different ends of the earth to have no choice but to spend Christmas together, at a villa called *Mari Incantati*, it does seem that some greater power has had a hand in it." Veronica turned to me. "You do know what that means, don't you? In Italian?"

"My lessons in Italian have not progressed quite that far."

"It means *Enchanted Seas.*" Veronica considered me thoughtfully. "Portia, whether he is right for you or not, this man has obviously occupied your thoughts for the last six months. Regardless of the fact that he's not titled or wealthy, or part of our social world, it's obvious this was something quite special. The *wise* thing to do is return to Italy to find out what it all means."

"He did not promise to be there."

"What if she goes"—Julia glanced at Veronica—"and he does not?"

"Well, that's the end of it, then, isn't it?" Veronica nodded firmly. "She'll know they are not supposed to be together and know as well he is not the man she thinks he is. And is certainly not worth mooning over."

"I have not been mooning," I said mildly.

Veronica cast me a skeptical look.

"I haven't." Although, now that it was mentioned, perhaps I had. Still, there was nothing I could do until Christmas.

"I know I for one"—Julia chose her words with care, her gaze meeting mine—"would be quite disappointed in you if you decided not to go."

I stared in surprise. "I expected that from Veronica, but not from you."

"Thank you." Veronica smirked.

"Given all you have said, and perhaps all you haven't, I agree with her." Julia paused, obviously to choose her words. "I am usually the first to urge caution, but you cannot continue with your heart in some sort of limbo."

I rolled my gaze toward the ceiling. "My heart is not in limbo. What an absurd idea."

Julia and Veronica exchanged knowing glances. Were they right? Was my heart truly involved? Did my friends recognize something I hadn't? Or wouldn't?

"Admittedly, there is a certain amount of risk." Julia thought for a moment. "It's entirely possible he won't come, or that he will, but it won't be—"

"Delicious." Veronica nodded.

"I wasn't going to say delicious, but I suppose the meaning is the same. And, Portia, you said this was an adventure. Isn't risk part and parcel of adventure?"

"Risk goes hand in hand with love as well," Veronica added.

"It seems to me," Julia said, "the risk would be well worth it."

"Besides, now that you have snapped"—Veronica grinned—"it would be a pity if you were to completely return to your unbending ways."

"And we wouldn't want that." I studied my friends and realized my mistake. From now until Christmas, Veronica would be unrelenting in her efforts to convince me to return to Italy. And Julia would be right by her side. Still, perhaps encouragement was what I needed, although I would prefer it in less enthusiastic doses.

"Very well, then, I shall make you a bargain. If the two of you refrain from bringing up this question until, oh, say, December, I will then listen to your arguments and give them due consideration." I shook my head. "I have no desire to be the subject of an unending campaign of persuasion."

"Agreed." Julia nodded.

"The middle of November is the best I can promise," Veronica warned. "Goodness, Portia, if I were to see you heading blindly over a cliff, I would never stand by silently and let you fall. Although I suppose, in this case, you are more refusing to peek over the edge of the cliff for fear of falling. It's my duty, as your friend, to nudge you a bit."

"This man might not be your fate or the love of your life," Julia said, "but what if he is?"

Veronica nodded. "Don't you owe it to yourself to find out?"

"I said I will think about it." I adopted a firm note and promptly changed the subject, my friends reluctantly following my lead.

I had already thought about it a great deal. Indeed, the question of next Christmas was always in the back of my mind. But I saw no need to make any sort of decision now. I had time. Now that I was home, it was obvious to me that in spite of one Christmas, and two weeks beyond, one adventure does not an adventuress make. I might have changed enough to have thrown caution aside and fallen into an adventure with a man who remained very much a stranger, but I hadn't changed enough to commit the rest of my life to a man society—as well as my family—would see as an inappropriate match. I would not be one of those women who blithely threw away a lifetime of expectations. I did not have that kind of courage. And I'd never been the sort of woman who embraced adventures.

Even ones colored by passion and touched by magic.

14

"It's not to my liking," a vaguely familiar male voice said from behind me.

I stood considering the still life by an artist I had never heard of and probably would not hear of in the future. The exhibit at the Rossier Gallery of new and allegedly promising artists had opened a few days ago to the cautious approval of critics.

"I would much rather an apple look like an apple rather than a smear of red paint," the man continued. "I find random blobs of paint unappealing."

"Do you?" I continued to study the work but glanced at him out of the corner of my eye to confirm his identity. "Then you are not fond of the impressionist school?"

"I much prefer the old masters," Lord Lindsey said firmly. "I suppose you like this sort of thing."

"I admit, I didn't until recently. I too have always preferred an apple to look like an apple. However, now I find the more I see of it, especially this exaggeration of impressionism, if you will, the more I am starting to appreciate the nuances and emotions caught by the artists." I moved to the next work, and he followed me.

"I fear I am dreadfully mired in the past and tradition, especially when it comes to questions of art," he said. "There is nothing I appreciate more than a well-done hunt painting, or a portrait that is a reasonable likeness of the subject."

"I daresay most of us would prefer that portrait not be quite as reasonable but rather better than we actually look."

"You do have a point."

"I have any number of points." I adopted a casual tone. "It is September, my lord. I thought you intended to call on me. Unless, of course, you have at last fallen prey to the machinations of one of my aunt's cohorts and have finally been caught."

He chuckled. "No, I am as yet uncaught."

"Then your failure to call on me can only be attributed to a change of heart."

"Or, the fact that my travels out of the country took far longer than I anticipated. I did not complete my business in a satisfactory manner until recently, and I did not return to London until last week."

"I see. All is well, then?"

"It is."

At last I turned to him and smiled pleasantly. "Well, then, you should have called on me last week." I nodded and turned to leave.

"Tomorrow," he said quickly.

I turned back to him. "Tomorrow?"

"I shall call on you tomorrow, if you are amenable to that," he added.

"I suppose you won't know until tomorrow." I flashed him a brilliant smile.

"Unless I can determine it now." He offered his arm. "May I accompany you on your stroll around the gallery?"

"To view art you don't especially like?"

"I am willing to make sacrifices." He sighed in an overly dramatic manner and dropped his arm. "One would think a catch such as myself would not have to make such sacrifices."

"We all have to make sacrifices, Lord Lindsey."

"Thomas," he said. "I know it has been some time, but you did agree to call me Thomas."

"Did I?" Certainly I remembered, but a man who expressed interest in you then failed to so much as drop you a note in more than half a year did not deserve to know that you recalled him at all. Nor was it necessary to tell him the months had flown by and I'd barely given his absence a second thought. That would have been rude.

"You did, indeed. The very last dance we had, I asked you to call me by my given name. You said that wouldn't be at all appropriate, given that we had just met and scarcely knew one another."

I nodded. "It does seem awfully forward."

"But, I assured you, I intended for us to know each other much, much better."

"Intentions, my lord . . ." I shook my head in a chastising manner. "The road to hell, you know."

He winced. "I promise to do better in the future." Again, he offered his arm. "I do hope you can overlook my failings."

"I shall try." I took his arm. "But I will make no guarantees." We moved on to the next painting. "Not even a note, Thomas? In nearly seven months?"

"I am the worst sort of inconsiderate fiend," he said contritely. "But I do believe I can be trained, and I am willing to learn."

"Exactly what every woman wants to hear."

He chuckled. "According to my mother, that is indeed exactly what every woman wants." The amused note remained in his voice, but there was a new edge of candor. "I implore you, Portia, to take pity on me. I have no sisters, and I have never been married, so the nuances of female expectations tend to escape me. I will make mistakes as we go on, and I do hope we will go on."

"I see no reason why we can't be friends."

"I will accept friendship." He paused. "For now."

I glanced at him, and at once I realized he was subtly declaring his intentions. He was a very nice man, and I did like him, but I wasn't sure I wanted him to set his sights on me.

And why not, my mother's voice whispered in the back of my head. *Fletcher made no promises to you nor you to him. You don't really know anything about him. He's not at all the kind of man you should marry, not that he seemed interested in marriage. You owe Fletcher nothing, let alone fidelity and loyalty.*

Still, even if I owed nothing to Fletcher, I did owe honesty to Thomas. "Might I be perfectly honest?"

"Please do."

"I'm not certain I wish to be more than friends."

"But we will be friends?" he asked hopefully.

"I see no reason why not."

"Then that's all I'm asking." A note of satisfaction sounded in his voice. "For now."

"For now?" I raised a brow. "And just how long is *for now?*"

"As long as necessary, Portia. I am in no great hurry, and the last thing I wish is to hurry you into something you are not ready for." He paused. "I realize, regardless of how much time has passed, it cannot be easy to move on after losing a spouse."

I started. David was the last thing on my mind. "That's very thoughtful of you."

"I have always believed that all things come to those who wait." We moved to the next painting. "I warn you, I am a patient man."

"As well as determined?"

He grinned. "It is a combination I intend for you to find irresistible."

"That's flattering, Thomas, but . . ."

"But we scarcely know each other. I understand that, Portia." He stopped and met my gaze firmly. Sincerity shone in his blue eyes. "I am not asking for more than you are willing to give. At the moment, your friendship is enough and, given my failure to pursue a relationship with you after our first meeting, far more than I deserve. But understand that I do intend, or at least I hope, that friendship between us is only the beginning."

"The beginning," I said cautiously.

"Yes." He nodded. "At least for me. I am hopeful that it will be for you as well. But while I am fairly certain I know what I want, it is obvious that you do not. As much as it grieves me deeply to admit it, I suspect you have not spent the last seven months thinking of me, whereas I have thought of nothing but you."

I stared at him for a shocked moment, then scoffed. "I don't believe that for an instant."

"Not even for a fraction of an instant?"

I laughed. "No."

"Ah well." He sighed. "I shall have to work on that." He tucked my hand back in the crook of his arm, and we proceeded to the next painting, a blur of colors depicting a field of flowers. "Whether you choose to believe me or not, I assure you I am quite sincere."

"Then we can add sincerity to your other sterling qualities of determination and patience." I bit back a grin.

"Don't forget thoughtful. You called me thoughtful just a few minutes ago."

"And how considerate of you to point that out."

"I thought so." He leaned closer in a confidential manner. "I did confess I am considered a catch."

I laughed.

"And you must admit I am amusing." He grinned. "Come now, Portia, I daresay you and I have a great deal of common ground. I think we will get on quite well together. As friends."

I paused, and then plunged ahead. "For now."

His eyes lit with satisfaction, and he nodded. "For now."

Thomas did indeed call on me the next day and the day after that. And on very nearly every day, whether he appeared in person or not, there were flowers. Flowers of every variety and hue, until my house had a distinct floral smell to it. I had never been the object of a man's attention before, at least not in such a grand and extravagant manner, and I must admit I was flattered and I liked it. He was certainly making an impression.

Aunt Helena was definitely impressed and more than a little smug. She pointed out to me that she had identified him as an excellent prospective husband even if she had not actually introduced us. She did not hesitate to mention, on more than one occasion, what a perfect match we were. Why, we very rarely even disagreed. Thomas was exactly the kind of man I was always expected to marry, just as David had been. In spite of her regret that she had not played a bigger role, she was decidedly self-satisfied in what she—and everyone else assumed—would be the end result of our friendship.

Except me.

Not that I didn't like Thomas. I did. Quite a bit, actually. But then, everyone seemed to. He was kind and generous and clever. He got on well with Adrian and Hugh and Sebastian. He charmed my female cousins, Miranda and Bianca and Diana. Even Julia and Veronica seemed taken with him. Or at least they never said anything against him.

Thomas was as good as his word. He allowed our relationship to grow as it would, without demands or pressure. It was quite . . . easy, I thought. And very nice. But even though we had made no promises to each other, to all the world we had the appearance of a couple firmly headed toward the altar.

Before I knew it, December was upon us. Neither Veronica nor Julia had brought up Italy, and the question of my returning to the villa. I had hoped they had forgotten about it. Too much to hope for, I know, as I certainly hadn't. But there was Thomas now, and while I wasn't in love with him, I did feel a certain affection for him. And loyalty.

Still, with every day closer to Christmas, I was aware of an increasing restlessness. I ignored it, telling myself it was simply the anticipation inherent in the season. Nothing more significant than that. Why, who didn't feel a bit restless in the weeks approaching Christmas?

Ten days before Christmas, Thomas escorted me home from a dinner with my family. To my surprise, Julia and Veronica greeted us in my parlor.

"My, this is certainly unexpected." I looked from one friend to the other. Identical expressions of feigned innocence shone on their faces. "Why are you here?"

"To wish you Christmas cheer, of course," Veronica said brightly.

"Lord Lindsey." Julia offered him a genuine smile. "How lovely to see you again."

"Isn't it?" Veronica's smile was just a bit tighter than Julia's. "We had no idea you would be here. And so late in the evening."

"It's not yet ten o'clock." I narrowed my gaze and studied my friends. "Aunt Helena wished to retire early tonight."

"Portia and I were about to indulge in a brandy," Thomas said smoothly, crossing the room to the table where my butler had placed a decanter of brandy and glasses. Thomas and I often shared a brandy when he accompanied me home from one event or another. "Would you care to join us?"

"I think not." Julia cast me an apologetic look.

"Excellent idea, my lord." Veronica smiled. She and Julia were up to something.

My gaze shifted from one woman to the other. "What are you doing here?"

They traded glances. Guilty glances, at least on Julia's part.

"There is a matter we need to discuss." Veronica accepted a glass from Thomas. "I agreed not to bring this up until mid-November and—"

"But I thought it best to wait past that," Julia added. "And Veronica agreed"—her gazed slipped to Thomas and back to me—"given you've been . . . busy."

"But it's ten days until Christmas, Portia." Veronica's gaze met mine. "We think you need to make a decision."

"We would hate to see opportunities missed out of inertia or procrastination or avoidance." Julia squared her shoulders. "We fear that's what you're doing."

"I see." They were right, of course, not that I intended to admit it. I turned to Thomas. "Would you give us a moment alone, please?"

He took a sip of his brandy, then shook his head. "I don't think that would be wise."

I cast him a sharp look. There was a distinct note of possession in his voice, as if he had the right to dictate what I could and could not do. As if he were far more than a friend. At once I realized this was not the first time I'd heard that slight edge of ownership in his voice. I had ignored it. It really hadn't seemed important. Until now.

I chose my words carefully. "I do think it would be better if I spoke to my friends alone."

He studied me for a long moment. "As you wish. Ladies." He nodded, turned and strode from the parlor.

Once the doors had closed behind him, I turned to my friends. "Don't you think this discussion can wait until tomorrow?"

"It has already waited too long." Veronica huffed.

"We are not here on a lark. We gave this a great deal of thought and discussion. The time has come for action." Julia glanced at Veronica and continued. "We wouldn't have said a word if you and Lord Lindsey had come to some sort of understanding. But from what we've seen, and what you've said—"

"And all that you haven't said." Veronica sipped her brandy. "You may not realize it yourself, but we know exactly what you've been doing."

"Oh?" I crossed my arms over my chest and tapped my foot in annoyance. "Perhaps you would care to explain it to me, as I have no idea what you're talking about."

"You have put off making a decision about returning to Italy until it's too late for you to do so." Julia's blunt words hung in the air.

They weren't entirely right. I had realized exactly what I was doing.

"So we have made the decision for you." Veronica smiled with satisfaction.

"What do you mean?" I said slowly, almost afraid of the answer.

"We have booked passage on a ship bound for the Mediterranean that stops in Naples. Barring any unforeseen delays, you will arrive at the villa no later than the day before Christmas." Julia paused. "It sails at midnight."

I stared in disbelief. "Midnight tonight?"

"Well, if one wants to be accurate, that would be tomorrow morning, but yes, in a little over two hours."

"I can't possibly be ready in a little over two hours." I protested. "I haven't packed or made any arrangements—"

"We arranged for your bags to be packed," Veronica said. "Sebastian will inform the rest of your family that you won't be joining them for Christmas. And Julia and I will take care of any other details as necessary."

"This is absurd." I glared at my friends. "I have no intention of going to Italy tonight."

"Have you decided not to go at all, then?"

"I haven't made any decision yet," I hedged.

"Precisely why we've made it for you." Veronica considered me for a moment. "Unless, of course, you have decided to marry Lord Lindsey. He seems a decent enough sort."

"He is a decent sort. He's a very nice man, and I like him very much," I said. "However, I haven't decided to marry him, as he has not asked."

"He will." Veronica snorted. "Everyone knows it. The only question is when."

"I would think the question is whether or not I will accept."

"Why wouldn't you?" Julia asked. "You are well matched. He is all that your aunt and your family want for you. All you've ever wanted, really. In many ways, he's very much like your late husband. The two of you have a great deal in common and seem to get on quite well."

"Indeed, we do," I said staunchly. "Why, we scarcely ever disagree."

"What more could you want?" Veronica shrugged. "I daresay you will probably be quite content together."

I stared at her. "Why did you say that?"

"Because I think you will be content," Veronica said slowly. "Isn't that what you want?"

"Tell me, Veronica, Julia, are the two of you content?"

"It's not the same for us." Caution edged Julia's voice. "We are both deeply—"

"Madly and passionately," Veronica interrupted.

"—in love with our husbands. We have each found something I don't think we ever expected to find."

Veronica smiled. "Magic."

"I could be in love with Thomas," I said, my voice a bit sharper than I had intended. "If I tried."

"One doesn't try to be in love, Portia," Veronica said in a gentle tone. "In fact, one might well try very hard not to be. Love is confusing and bewildering and awkward."

"I loved David, and it wasn't the least bit confusing." Without thinking, I raised my chin. "It was comfortable and quite lovely, and we were . . ."

Content.

The word hit me like a slap across the face. I had acknowledged it long ago, of course, but David was the past, and Thomas was, or could be, the future. And it would be a nice future, safe and secure. And I would be . . . content.

Even Fletcher had admitted there was nothing wrong with content. But I looked at my friends and realized, as selfish as it might be, that I wanted what they had found. I wanted deep and mad and passionate.

I wanted magic.

"Very well." I nodded.

"Very well what?" Julia stared at me.

"Very well." I drew a deep breath. "Apparently, I am going to Italy tonight. Or, rather, tomorrow."

"Excellent." Veronica grinned in what might have been triumph, or possibly relief. "Your maid has traveling clothes ready for you to change into, and she has your things packed."

"My maid?" I shook my head. "You mean Margaret?"

Julia nodded. "She's been extremely helpful and seems quite eager to accompany you."

"My Margaret?" I couldn't quite believe that.

"Unless there is another Margaret. Now . . ." A brisk note sounded in Veronica's voice. "There is no time to waste if you are going to make the sailing."

"No, but . . ." I winced.

A light dawned in Julia's eyes. "Oh yes, well, we'll leave you to it, then." She caught Veronica's eye and nodded toward the door.

"I'd nearly forgotten about him." Veronica grimaced. "We'll wait in the foyer." She cast me a look of encouragement, then she and Julia took their leave.

Victoria Alexander

I had time to do little more than brace myself before Thomas entered.

"Dare I ask what that was all about?" He eyed me cautiously.

"Well . . ." There didn't seem to be any easy way to say this. "I've decided to go to Italy."

He stared as if I was speaking a language he didn't understand. Italian perhaps. "You've what?"

"I'm going to Italy, Thomas. For Christmas."

"Why?" His brow furrowed in confusion.

"I spent last Christmas in Italy, and it was quite delightful, so I have decided to return." I drew a deep breath. "Tonight."

"Tonight?" Disbelief rang in his voice.

"Midnight, really, so that would actually be tomorrow."

"I don't understand." He shook his head.

Nor did I expect him to. But I wasn't entirely certain I understood it myself, even if it did seem . . . right. "As I said, last Christmas—"

"But last Christmas we were not, you and I were not—"

I arched a brow. "Friends?"

"More than that, I thought." A harsh note colored his words.

Guilt stabbed me. "If I have led you to believe—"

"No," he said sharply and ran a hand through his hair. "No, you have done nothing beyond offer your friendship. It has been obvious to me from the beginning that you have been quite careful about that. I thought it was simply the reluctance of a widow to move forward." He paused. "Very well, then. As your friend . . ." He met my gaze firmly. "If you are going to Italy for Christmas, I shall go with you."

"That's a very generous offer, but . . ." I shook my head. "I'm afraid I am going to have to decline."

167

"I see." He studied me for a long moment. "There's a man involved, isn't there?"

"That's really none of your concern, Thomas," I said in as gentle a tone as possible.

"Of course it's my concern." His brow furrowed, and he huffed a short breath. "I want to marry you, Portia. I know I haven't said it—I didn't think you were ready—but I do think my intentions were clear."

I wasn't sure what to say. Perhaps his intentions were clear, and I had simply ignored them. It struck me that it would be so easy to accept what he offered. To be content. But he deserved more than that, and so did I. "I am sorry."

He considered me thoughtfully, then nodded, his jaw tightening. "I am a patient man, Portia, but I warn you, this decision of yours is irrevocable. If you go to Italy, I will not be here when you come back. Our *friendship* will be at an end."

My breath caught. "I will . . . regret that, Thomas."

"Bloody hell, Portia." He stepped close, grabbed my shoulders and yanked me into his arms, pressing his lips to mine. Shock froze me in place, and he released me.

"My apologies. I don't know . . ." He stared at me for an endless moment, then heaved a frustrated sigh. "I wish you all the best, Portia." He nodded and strode from the room.

I stared after him. The last thing I wanted to do was hurt him, yet I should have realized from the beginning it was inevitable that I would.

Thomas offered me everything in the world I had once had. It was simply no longer enough.

There was every possibility Fletcher would not be at the villa, but my friends were right. If I didn't go, I would always wonder. And wonder as well if I could indeed be the kind of woman who abandoned all she knew for love.

I would never know if I had the courage for that, if I didn't have the courage for this.

For this Christmas.

Part Three

Christmas 1886

15

My heart beat faster the closer I came to the villa, thudding in my chest like a child's rubber ball against a walk. On board the ship, I'd had hours to consider the ramifications of what looked more and more like a reckless, ill-advised and, no doubt, disastrous whim. In my head, Veronica's voice bolstered my courage, pointing out my heretofore unacknowledged desire for adventure and the fact that, for a full year, I had not been able to get Fletcher Jamison out of my thoughts. Her arguments were countered by the voice of my dead mother, reminding me that a proper lady—a perfect lady—did not have illicit liaisons in Italy or any other country. And, God forbid, especially not at Christmas. I scarcely remembered my mother at all, as she and my father had died during a sea voyage when I was barely a year old, but for my entire life, she had always been the voice of propriety. Or perhaps she was my conscience. Regardless, I was an adult, a widow, and capable of making my own decisions regarding my behavior. For good or ill. Even if they were wrong.

The biggest question, of course, was whether or not Fletcher would be there. But there were other considerations as well. I had made no advance arrangements, although Veronica had assured me she would telegraph Silvestro as to my impending arrival. Julia had offered to pay a call on Lady Wickelsworth to determine if the villa had been let to any unknown parties. I would have hated to arrive unexpectedly on a new tenant's doorstep at Christmas. Julia promised to have a telegram waiting for me when I disembarked in Naples, should the villa be occupied by anyone other than Fletcher. In which case, I might well turn around and go home.

Julia didn't say it aloud, but we both realized an inquiry to Lady Wickelsworth would also reveal if Fletcher intended to return. I would certainly want to know if there were new residents of the Villa Mari Incantati, but I wasn't sure I wanted to know if the villa was unoccupied. If he had not come back. After all, by that point, it would be too late.

I reached the villa late in the afternoon on the day before Christmas. As I approached, I could have sworn the clouds parted and a shaft of sunlight illuminated the villa, the *Villa of the Enchanted Seas*. It did indeed look enchanted. There might well have been a rendition of Handel's *Hallelujah Chorus* somewhere in the distance as well. It was completely absurd, no more than a product of imagination run amok coupled with an unnerving mix of trepidation and eagerness. What on earth was wrong with me? I shook my head to clear it. At once the villa was again as it had always been and unchanged from last year. Across the bay, Vesuvius loomed, as menacing a presence as ever. The celestial choir vanished.

What if . . . I swept the question from my mind. I would know the answers to all my *what ifs* soon enough. I drew a deep breath and braced myself for whatever might happen next.

Silvestro greeted us at the door.

"Good afternoon," I said in my halting Italian, grateful I had continued my studies, even while denying any intention to return to Italy for Christmas.

Silvestro's eyes lit with delight. "Signora! You speak Italian!" he said in his language, with the same sort of joy one usually reserved for the birth of a child. Unfortunately, obviously swept away by delight, he then launched into a stream of Italian so fast and complex I could do little more than stare at him open-mouthed.

I smiled and nodded—I did so hate to disillusion him as to my fluency. He was so elated. Silvestro directed Margaret to her room and carried my bags to the same rooms I had stayed in last year, chatting all the way. Finally, I could stand it no longer.

"Signore Jamison?" I asked, trying to appear unconcerned but failing to hide the hopeful note in my voice.

"Ah." He nodded in a knowing manner that might have been insulting under other circumstances. But here and now, whatever the man was thinking about my presence, he was right. After all, while last year had been unexpected, this year was planned. This was indeed a rendezvous between lovers. The very idea made me blush, but it was no more than the truth. It would be hypocritical of me to pretend otherwise. Oddly enough, I, who was always so cognizant of appearances, didn't particularly care what he thought. Apparently, it was the mark of illicit behavior to disregard concern about the appearance of impropriety. Silvestro continued on, confident in my ability to understand him. Obviously, my greeting had been far more polished than I had suspected.

"Signore Jamison?" I tried again, and again, Silvestro's explanation was beyond my comprehension.

At last I held up a hand to stop him. "I don't understand. Non capisco." I shrugged helplessly.

He stared at me for a moment, then realization dawned in his expression.

"Si, Signore Jamison, ahhh." He nodded and proceeded to gesture and pantomime in an enthusiastic manner. He waved toward the balcony doors, leading me to believe Fletcher was indeed here and in the same spot where I had first discovered him painting last year. At least, that's how I interpreted Silvestro's attempt at communication. I knew full well I could be completely wrong, and Fletcher might not be here at all, but I preferred to cling to hope, even if I was as apprehensive as I was excited.

Silvestro flung open the French doors, and I indicated he did not need to accompany me farther, which he did seem to understand. He swept an enthusiastic bow as I stepped passed him, then discreetly vanished into the house. The late afternoon sun welcomed me and bolstered my courage. I drew a deep breath and started toward Fletcher's end of the balcony.

I peered around a potted palm, and my heart caught at the sight of him.

Fletcher stood before an easel, deep in concentration. He was angled slightly away from me, allowing me to study him for a moment, unobserved. He slapped paint onto the canvas in what appeared to be a haphazard, yet joyous, manner. There was an air about him, in the way he moved and worked, of determination and confidence. In manner alone, it was obvious that this was not the same man I'd spent Christmas with last year. His appearance had altered as well. He was somewhat, oh, *scruffier* than he had been. His hair was slightly longer and disheveled, as if he continuously ran his hand through it. He looked as if he hadn't shaved in at least a day. He wore no coat or necktie, and his shirt was open at the throat, at once inappropriate and most attractive. He seemed, as well, taller in height and broader of shoulder than I remembered. Not as if he had grown, but rather expanded. As if there was greater substance to him now. There was no question that the man before me on the balcony was more hedonistic artist than government employee. Not at all proper and decidedly dangerous.

A description of Lord Byron flashed through my mind: *mad, bad and dangerous to know.* I shivered at the thought, and something inside me fluttered with anticipation. Dear Lord, I wanted this man. What kind of woman had I become? And why didn't I care?

I braced myself and took a step toward him. "Good day, Fletcher."

His gaze turned to mine, and his eyes narrowed, as if he couldn't quite believe what he was seeing. "Portia?"

I cast him a weak smile and nodded.

"Portia!" His dark eyes lit with welcome and desire and what might have been joy. At least, I interpreted it as such. He strode toward me.

"Merry Christmas," I said in an inane attempt to say something that wasn't entirely idiotic.

He laughed and swept me into his arms. "It is now."

His lips claimed mine, and I lost myself in a maelstrom of emotion and desire and need.

He could take me right here on the balcony in front of Silvestro and Agostina and whoever else might be in the house. In front of the gods of Vesuvius itself, and I wouldn't care. I had missed him more than I had dared to admit, even to myself.

"Oh God, Portia." He raised his head from mine and gazed deeply into my eyes. "I didn't know if you would come. I had hoped, of course, but—"

"I feared you wouldn't come either." I swallowed hard against the emotion welling inside me. "We made no promises, after all, and—"

"Didn't we?" Again, his gaze searched mine, and I realized that perhaps we had made promises. Unspoken, but promises nonetheless. With every word, every look, every kiss.

My heart swelled, and at once I realized, or perhaps accepted, that this man truly had claimed my heart. Regardless of what might happen tomorrow, or next week, or next Christmas, he owned my soul.

I stared at him. "Margaret is unpacking my bag."

He smiled slowly. There was no doubt in my mind that he knew exactly what I was thinking. Just as I knew his thoughts. "Agostina and Silvestro are busy with the preparation of tonight's dinner. It is Christmas Eve, you know."

I nodded. "Seven dishes of fish."

"You remember."

"I remember." I held my breath. "I remember everything."

"As do I." Again, his gaze locked with mine, and the need, the longing, in his eyes echoed my own.

I wanted to be coy, to pretend I did not want to be naked in his bed, my body entwined with his. I wanted to be correctly aloof, appropriately reserved, but it seemed pointless. It had been nearly a year since I'd had his arms around me. Since I'd known the heat of his flesh next to mine. Since I'd felt the joining of my body with his.

I blithely tossed aside a lifetime of doing what was proper, along with the last vestiges of hesitation, wrapped my arms around his neck and pulled his mouth back to mine.

"Fletcher," I murmured against his lips.

"Portia," he breathed my name and crushed his lips to mine. Any sense of decorum or restraint, mine or his, fled in the face of overwhelming, unrelenting need. Urgency, as I've never known before, held me in its grip.

We stumbled into his room, his hands never leaving my body, my lips never parted from his. It struck me how absurd I would think this blinding need—this disregard for anything but the unrelenting desire to press my naked flesh to his—was should it be described to me. I would laugh at the very idea of passion so demanding it swept away rational thought. Caught willingly by lust and yearning, nothing had ever been so right.

We tore at each other's clothes until they lay in heaps and drifts around the room, until at last our bodies pressed together, flesh against flesh, fire against fire. We fell onto the bed and explored each other in a frenzy of need and desire. I had not forgotten how the planes and valleys of his body felt beneath my touch. My dreams had not allowed me to forget. But this was real, and this was right. Our bodies entwined in desperate fervor. We writhed on the bed, twisting the bed-clothes into hopeless knots, in exploration and discovery of each other once again. He tasted of man and desire and passion. And, God help me, of forever.

I moaned in his ear, and he murmured something that sounded French. *French?* It was momentarily disconcerting, as I didn't recall him speaking French when last I was in his bed. While my French was substantially better than my Italian, the haze of arousal that muddled clear thinking, even while enhancing all other sensations, made his words impossible to comprehend. Yet there was something about the way he said whatever it was he said that melted my very bones. It was—he was—intoxicating.

When his body claimed mine, I wondered that I didn't perish at the joy of it. The familiar tension, the exquisite feeling of being wound like a spring, ever tighter, built deep within me. I felt his body tighten, stiffen. He thrust hard, and the tremors of his release shivered through me. He slid his hand between us and had no more than touched me when my own release tore through me with uncontrolled urgency. My back arched, and I screamed softly and marveled at the exquisiteness of it all. How could something so wonderful be considered sin?

Afterward, we lay together for endless moments, legs entangled, wrapped in each other's arms, our breathing slowly returning to a semblance of normality. We floated in that lovely aftermath of sensation, and Lord help me, I had missed it. I'm not sure I have ever felt so cherished.

"It has been a very long time since last Christmas," he murmured against me, "but worth waiting for."

"Um . . ." I smiled, too drained to do more.

It was with great reluctance that we eventually parted and shifted to a less entwined position. There was a bit of embarrassment as well, at least on my part. I had never before behaved so wantonly. Even last year, caught in the throes of newfound passion, of that nearly forgotten time of getting to know one another, intimately if not well, I had not been this unrestrained. But then, our lovemaking seemed different this year. It was certainly more explosive, which struck me as due to more than merely pent-up desire. It was deeper somehow, more intense, I thought, although last year I wouldn't have imagined that possible. I wondered if it could be blamed on the forbidden nature of our union, which made no sense, as it was every bit as forbidden last year. Or perhaps it was the result of our year-long separation and the anticipation of being together once again. As much as I had tried to deny it, to myself as well as to my friends, I had wanted to return to the villa even before Julia and Veronica had forced my hand. I simply hadn't had the courage to do so without prodding.

Yet, I had wasted no time in leaping into his bed. Perhaps wanton was becoming a habit, because, as much as I had felt a twinge of dismay as to my enthusiasm, I had no true regrets. It did seem well worth it. Once more, I reached out for him . . .

"Agostina will be calling us for dinner any minute now," Fletcher murmured against the back of my neck.

"I would think so." I resisted the temptation to collapse against him, into his arms. He was allegedly helping me with my dress, but as he punctuated every few words with a kiss or caress, he made little progress. Not that I cared.

He heaved a resigned sigh. "You should finish dressing."

"Perhaps, if you were to pay more attention to the fastenings on my dress, I could indeed finish." I attempted a chastising tone but failed. His questionable efforts to assist me were far too delightful to hurry along. Still . . . I released a sigh of my own. "I assume they're joining their family in the village tonight?"

"Well, it is Christmas Eve."

"Yes, it is. And I would hate to delay them." I paused. "Do you realize you spoke French to me while we were . . ."

"Engaged?" A grin sounded in his voice.

I ignored it. "I'm not very fluent in anything other than English, but I do recognize French when I hear it. You've never spoken French to me before in the midst of . . . of an *engagement*, and I am curious as to why you did so now."

"I was trying to impress you."

"I was extremely impressed." I cast him a wicked look over my shoulder. "But not by the French."

He chuckled. "And yet, you did seem to like it."

Heat washed up my face. I had always secretly found a continental accent to be rather exciting. "That, my dear Mr. Jamison, is not the point."

"And I thought it was entirely the point."

"I simply wondered why." I bit back a grin. "I didn't say I wish you to stop."

He paused as if surprised by the direct nature of my words. I hadn't thought I could surprise him after last year. It was gratifying to learn I still could.

He laughed. "While I was unaware that I had lapsed into French, I will remember its effect on you."

"See that you do," I said in an overly prim manner that belied the shiver of anticipation skating up my spine. "What did you mean by lapsed?"

"Simply that I have spoken French more often than English this past year. Done." He turned me around to face him and smirked with satisfaction. "I could be a lady's maid if it comes to that."

"By all means, Fletcher." I rolled my gaze at the ceiling. "I know the qualities I always look for in a new maid are government service, preferably in India, and the tendency to kiss the back of my neck while helping me dress."

He laughed again and pulled me into his arms. "Then I should do very well." He paused. "I shall explain everything after dinner."

I drew my brows together. I wasn't sure I liked the sound of that. "Everything? I don't understand."

"You will." He leaned down and kissed the tip of my nose. "After dinner."

"Perhaps you don't recall, but I am not an especially patient sort. I would prefer to hear everything, whatever *everything* may be, now, if you please."

"It can wait," he said firmly. "I don't want Agostina and Silvestro to be late for their family, so I suggest you go to your rooms—"

"Where Margaret is no doubt scandalized by my absence." I grimaced. I had left her to her own devices the very moment we had arrived at the villa. She was once again unhappy that I had decided to return to Italy for Christmas and hadn't hesitated to let me know her feelings, in that subtle way she had perfected, with every mile we traveled away from England.

"Where the ever-faithful Margaret—"

"The judgmental and condemning Margaret."

"Will be wondering what has become of you and, more than likely, be waiting to help you change for dinner."

"Probably." I sighed and reached up to brush my lips across his. "I have missed you, Mr. Jamison."

"And I have missed you, Lady Smithson."

I resisted the immediate urge to wince and instead cast him a weak smile. I had nearly forgotten about that tiny little deception. I should tell him the truth, explain why I had not given him my real name, but certainly not now. After he explained *everything*, then perhaps I would as well. Yes, that did seem like a plan.

A scolding voice in the back of my head noted that men did not usually take well to deception. Utter nonsense, really. Women took deception no better than men. But what was done was done. There was no way to undo what did seem to me to be a relatively insignificant falsehood. Besides, he'd been no more forthcoming with the details of his life last year than had I. Why, I had no idea if his name was really Fletcher

Jamison at all. If you looked at it from the proper, albeit somewhat twisted, angle, I was simply being cautious. Although even I would be hard-pressed to accept that as an excuse. And at the moment it scarcely mattered. I had a tiny little deceit to confess.

Fletcher had *everything*.

16

I had never given any particular thought to romance beyond the arrival of a suitably extravagant bouquet of orchids designed to make a lady sigh with appreciation. But tonight there was something special, something wonderful, in the air between us. Romance was as good a word as any to describe it. And I did sigh.

Our hands met on the tabletop at dinner over and over, as if we were each reluctant to let the other go for so much as a moment. Still, the necessities of nourishment did need to be dealt with, and midway through the meal, I realized I was as famished as if I had not eaten for days. No doubt, the result of wanton, uninhibited lust. Apparently, all of one's appetites worked in tandem.

Everything seemed caressed by a touch of magic or perfection. Agostina's excellent food was tastier, if possible, this year than it had been last Christmas Eve. The wine was richer, the candles on the table burned more merrily and even the stars shinning on the bay shone brighter.

Perhaps, if we hadn't fallen into bed together the moment we'd seen each other, there might have been some awkwardness between us, but it was as if the time we'd spent apart had been no more than a day or two. Still, it was obvious from the casual nature of his appearance, as well as his demeanor, that much had happened in his life since last Christmas, and just as obvious, I feared, that nothing had happened in mine. It struck me now that I had done little more than mark time until I could return to Italy—return to him—even if I had not been willing to admit or accept it.

We spoke of everything and yet nothing of particular importance, as if we were each postponing more revealing conversation. He related stories about the affront to British sensibilities of living in a foreign land and the misadventures to be found in travel. I told him about my efforts to learn Italian and my aunt's continuing campaign to find suitable matches for the unmarried members of my family. She would have been annoyed to know how very amusing I made her sound. And we laughed a great deal. I was curious about the changes this past year had wrought in him, but not enough to break the spell of enchantment that had wrapped around us simply because we were once again together.

When dinner ended, Agostina and her husband bid us good evening and took their leave, accompanied by Margaret. Unbeknownst to me, Margaret too had studied Italian since our last visit. She told me pointedly, when I had at last appeared in my rooms, that she thought it was a skill that would come in handy for a lady's maid should she be seeking new employment. It was as close as she had ever come to threatening to leave my employ. Silvestro and Agostina had kindly invited her to join them, and Margaret informed me, in that lofty manner she had perfected, that she would be delighted to join a family for Christmas Eve, as she could not be with her own. Besides, it was the opportunity to try out her newly learned Italian.

Fletcher and I retired to the parlor as we had last year, once again blessedly alone, and he poured glasses of Strega.

"You didn't mention your aunt's efforts on your behalf. I assume, as you are here, that she has been unsuccessful this past year in finding you a suitable husband." He handed me a glass. "Unless I am mistaken?"

Thomas's face flashed through my mind, probably why I had failed to mention Aunt Helena's schemes in regards to my own marital prospects. I ignored it, as well as the guilt that came with it. "Don't be silly, Fletcher. While I may well join you for a week or two at Christmas, I would never betray a man to whom I had pledged my loyalty."

He chuckled. "I didn't imagine you would." He paused. "But it is good to know."

I stilled. "Why?"

"One never knows where the next path may lead us." He shrugged.

I wanted to ask more. *What path? Who does he mean by us?* I refrained only because I didn't know what I wanted him to say. How I might respond to his answers. I'd had a year to consider this very conversation, or one much like it, yet it did seem too soon.

Instead, I forced a light note to my voice. "And where has your path taken you since last year?"

He grinned. "Paris."

"Paris?" I stared. "You're no longer in India?"

"I am not." He sipped his liquor.

"Which explains your fluency in French." Paris was ever so much closer to England than India. Why, I knew any number of people who jaunted off to Paris on no more than a whim. If Fletcher now resided in Paris, well, it brought to mind all sorts of possibilities. Delightful possibilities that did not include waiting for Christmas. "You've been posted to Paris, then? How lovely. And my congratulations on what is obviously a promotion."

"Oh, I am no longer a member of Her Majesty's Foreign Service."

"You're not?" My mind raced. "Then what are you doing?"

"Painting." He raised his glass to me. "You are looking at a man who has followed his heart."

"I don't understand," I said slowly, although I thought I was beginning to. The enchantment of the evening faded.

"It's amazing how little one spends on necessities when one lives in a city like Calcutta. It's not at all difficult to save one's money. After I returned last year, I realized I had enough to sustain myself for at least a year in Paris. Long enough to determine if my work would provide a living income. Although . . ."

"Yes?"

"It hasn't. Not entirely anyway. At least, not yet." He grinned. "I find it amazing that that is no longer important."

"It isn't?" I said cautiously. "I would have thought making a living to be paramount."

He shook his head. "What is important is my work." He pinned me with a pointed look. "It's much better than it was last year."

"Oh?" I had no idea what to say. In spite of my efforts, it was obvious he had ascertained my opinion of his artistic skill. "I—"

He held up a hand to stop me. "No need to apologize."

"I had no intention of apologizing." I shrugged. "While last year I found your work intriguing, it was not entirely to my liking."

He stared at me, then laughed. "I have truly missed your candor, Portia."

"Thank you," I murmured and took another sip of the Strega.

I was not sure how to react to his news. The thought of him being closer to England was rather exciting, even if I wasn't sure what, if anything, it would mean to our odd relationship. But the idea that he had cast off the security of an acceptable position for something as absurd as art was most distressing.

"I have learned a great deal in the past year."

"How to paint well?" I asked in an overly innocent manner. I was still shocked at his revelation.

"Yes, in a way, I suppose I have," he said with a self-deprecating chuckle. "I have taken the opportunities Paris affords to study. That alone has been intoxicating. I had no idea how much I didn't know. But I have indeed learned much about technique and mastering the nuances of my craft. About style and expression and creating my own voice, if you will. More importantly, Portia, I have learned how to listen to my soul."

"You what?" It wasn't the most absurd thing I had ever heard, but it was certainly among them.

"When one is dabbling in art, as nothing more than a pastime, one cannot commit fully to the work. Only when one has shed the trappings of an ordinary life can one truly embrace the calling of one's soul." He raised his glass to me. "And that is where the essence of art is found."

"How utterly absurd." The words were out of my mouth before I could stop them. And I did wish I had stopped them, even if I had never spoken truer words in my life.

"Not at all. In fact, I think it's quite practical. Men always do better at something they love." He shrugged. "Or at least, they're happier."

I couldn't recall ever hearing anyone other than a woman speak of happiness that way. Oh, Julia or Veronica perhaps, but not a man. As if happiness was to be expected. Some sort of right, if you will. I was not so enamored of him that I could not see the fallacy of such a philosophy. "Am I to understand that you left your position, a perfectly good position, to starve in the streets of Paris?"

"I wouldn't put it quite that way, but yes." Laughter sparked in his eyes in a decidedly wicked manner. Unexpected desire shivered through me. It was all I could do to maintain my indignation.

"Fletcher, what were you thinking?"

"I was thinking about what you said last Christmas."

"What on earth did I say?" Surely this wasn't my fault. "Try as I might, I cannot recall saying, 'Fletcher, you should quit your respectable position with Her Majesty's Foreign Service and move to France where you shall willy-nilly slap paint on canvas in the hopes that someone will pay good money for the result.'"

His mouth opened, and his eyes widened. "Are you sure you didn't say that? I could have sworn—"

"Sarcasm, Fletcher, will serve neither of us well at the moment," I snapped.

"You're right, of course, but it was impossible to resist." He frowned. "And I did think you found sarcasm charming."

"Not in the least." I huffed. "Fletcher—"

"Portia," he said firmly, taking my glass from my hand and setting both mine and his aside. Then he pulled me into his arms.

"What are you doing?" I glared up at him, but I made no effort to pull away.

"Obviously, we need to talk." He settled his arms tighter around me. It was not conducive to rational thought. The man was trying to distract me. "And I much prefer to talk with you in my arms. Especially about topics not to your liking."

"I have no particular problem with the topic, in general. If someone I did not know ran away from his responsibilities to paint naked women in a city whose very name is synonymous with sin—"

He laughed. "I never mentioned painting naked women."

"Nor did you need to." I sniffed. "However, I was speaking in generalities. I was talking about *someone*, not necessarily *you*." I narrowed my eyes. "Are you painting naked women?"

"Only when necessary," he said in a somber manner, but those dark eyes of his twinkled with amusement.

"Fletcher—"

"Last year," he said, "you pointed out to me that I was wasting my life in a pointless government position—"

"I'm certain I never said pointless."

He ignored me. "In a futile effort to live up to society's expectations of what is proper and respectable. You, my dear Portia, pointed out that I was living in a box of my own making but not of my own choosing."

"Did I?" I asked weakly, but I vaguely recalled I might have said something along those lines. No doubt, a direct result of wine or Strega.

"You did, indeed." He nodded. "It lingered in my mind. Gnawed at me, really."

"My apologies," I said under my breath.

"Not necessary. It was what I needed." He nodded. "A month or so after I returned to Calcutta, the head of my department announced he was retiring and would be returning to England to spend the rest of his days. He confided in me, with pride, that he considered his years of service to Her Majesty to be the best of his life. It struck me then that, when

I had reached his point in life, I would prefer not to look back on a career of shuffling papers, dealing with correspondence and managing the minute details of policy that fell to men at my level, and think of them as the best years of my life. This revelation made me examine, for the first time, whether, as I did not have the familial contacts needed for advancement, I had the ambition required. The answer was no."

"No?" I said faintly.

"No." He shrugged as best he could with his arms around me. "I simply didn't care about the position, about a career doing insignificant work in an equally insignificant department. And the idea of residing in India for the next thirty years or so held no particular appeal."

"So you . . . resigned," I said slowly.

"In no uncertain terms." He chuckled. "Within a month of my decision, I was living in Paris."

"And it was wonderful, no doubt."

"Hardly. Indeed, it has been much more difficult than I had expected. But exhilarating nonetheless. Challenging in a way nothing has ever challenged me before." He met my gaze firmly. "I feel as if I am a different man altogether, Portia. As if I have been released from shackles I didn't know I wore."

"I see." I chose my words carefully. "And you are happy?"

"I am," he said as if he didn't have a doubt in the world. "Life is too short not to be happy."

I stared at him. "Are you dying?"

"Dying?" He frowned. "Why on earth would you ask that?"

"Just something my friends asked me when I was behaving irrationally."

He laughed. "I am not behaving irrationally."

"That does seem to be a matter of opinion."

"Perhaps." He grinned. "But the fact remains I have never been more satisfied with my life. And I have never been happier than I am now."

"Well, then . . ." I forced a smile and stared up at him. "I suppose that's all that really matters, isn't it?"

"Not all, but . . ." His gaze searched mine. "You're not at all pleased by this, are you?"

"You noticed that, did you?

"It was difficult to miss."

"My opinion really isn't significant, is it?"

"Of course it is." His brows drew together. "What you think is important to me."

"Why?" There was a challenging note in my voice that I did not intend.

"Because you matter to me." He stared down at me. "You matter a great deal."

Without warning, something very much like panic gripped me. I wasn't ready to throw my lot in with his. To declare my feelings. I had acknowledged in this year apart, or at least accepted the possibility, that I was in love with him. But was it enough? It was one thing to consider giving up my life for that of the wife of a respectable member of Her Majesty's government, and quite another to be the spouse of a struggling artist. Not that either of us had ever mentioned marriage. But I feared, in spite of my best efforts, my very proper background had, in the recesses of my mind, led me to contemplate marriage. Marriage was, after all, the goal of women like myself. I thrust the thought away and drew a bracing breath.

"If you're happy, then I am happy as well." I smiled up at him, belying the heavy lump in my chest where my heart had been, and slid my arms around his neck. "Now, kiss me, and then you shall have to tell me all about life in Paris."

"I can't think of a better way to spend Christmas Eve." He grinned, then pressed his lips to mine in a kiss that promised all sorts of things that would never come to pass.

For the next few hours, Fletcher and I sat on the comfortable parlor sofa, and he regaled me with anecdotes about life in the French capital. Even I knew Paris was the acknowledged center of the art world, and he spoke of artists he had met, none of whom I had ever heard of, but who, he assured me, would be well-known someday. He talked about the international aspect of the artist community. He was not the only Englishman to try to hone his skills in Paris. Fletcher had met a fair number of Americans as well and found them at once amusing and admirable. The more I listened to him talk, the more I realized that this decision he had made to uproot his life was right for him. As silly and irrational as I still thought it was.

"I have been talking all night," he said with a wry smile. "We've scarcely spoken about your year at all."

"As much as I hate to admit it, there has been little of note that has occurred in my life this past year." I thought for a moment. "Aside from evading Aunt Helena's matchmaking and a few improvements to my house and gardens, I have done nothing especially interesting. I have, however, attended a fair number of gallery exhibits—"

His brow rose. "Have you?"

"I do like to keep abreast of the latest in artistic endeavors."

"You do?" If his brow rose any higher, it would disappear into his hair. "I had no idea. Indeed, I had the distinct impression you preferred more traditional, established schools of art."

"Preferences change, Fletcher. I am not so rigid as to not be open to new ideas," I said, almost as if I believed it myself. "And I have been studying Italian."

He stared at me. "That is a new idea."

"Wanting to master the language of a country I enjoy?"

"No." He grinned. "You acknowledging that everyone does not speak English."

"Which does not mean I do not think they should," I said primly.

He laughed. I had forgotten how much the sound of his laughter warmed my soul. It was, as well, contagious, and I laughed with him, but, in truth, my heart was not entirely in it.

A few minutes later, I rose to my feet, and he stood with me. "I think I shall retire to my rooms for the night."

"I had hoped you would be staying in my room," he said slowly.

"It has been a very long day, Fletcher, and I find I am truly exhausted." I smiled. "I would prefer to sleep alone tonight. I daresay I shall be asleep before my head hits the pillow."

"As you wish." He studied me for a long moment. "You're not happy about my change in circumstances, are you?"

"I believe I've already answered that."

"I believe you avoided answering it."

I blew a resigned breath. "I suppose you want me to be perfectly honest."

He smiled. "Preferably."

"Very well, then." I thought for a moment. "In all honesty, I'm not sure how I feel. It does not strike me as a wise decision, but then, I have a tendency to be reasonable and rational, and I have usually done whatever was expected of me in this life."

"Portia—"

"Wait." I held up a hand to stop him. "I'm not finished."

"Go on, then."

"I knew the moment I saw you that something had changed. You are more . . ." I struggled to find the right word.

"I don't know, *alive*, I think, this year than you were last year. There is an air about you, a look in your eye of . . . self-worth perhaps. Or confidence."

He nodded.

"So, obviously, your choice was the right choice for you. The very thought of you someday looking back on your life and finding it lacking in some way . . ." I shook my head. "I could not bear that."

"Thank you," he said quietly, his gaze boring into mine.

I wanted to weep. To throw myself into his arms and cry until no more tears could come, even if I wasn't entirely sure what I would be crying about. He owed me nothing. And if my fickle heart had led me to believe there was more to our Christmas spent together than there was, it was my error. He had never made any promises to me. I had no right to be upset with him now.

I steeled myself and cast him a blinding smile. "Now, Fletcher, I believe we have some Christmas wishes to make, do we not?"

He considered me for a moment longer, then nodded. "Of course." He moved to a table near the far wall and returned with paper and pencil. He offered me a sheet of stationery and a pencil. "Did your wish last year come true?"

"Not really." I braced my paper on the wall and wrote the same wish I had written last year. It was entirely too good a wish to waste. "Did yours?"

"Yes." He scribbled on his paper and folded it.

"Oh? What did you wish?"

"I don't know that I can tell you." He shook his head in a somber manner. "I'm not sure what the rules are about telling a wish that has come true."

"If it's come true, it's no longer a wish." I folded my wish. "So, tell me."

"Very well." His gaze locked with mine, and that slow, wonderful smile of his spread across his face. "I wished to spend another Christmas with you."

My breath hitched, and I stared at him.

"Thank you for making my wish come true."

"Merry Christmas," I said, forcing a lighthearted note to my voice.

He took my hand, and we moved close to the fire and dropped our wishes in together.

"I hope your wish comes true, Portia."

"As do I," I said softly. But even as I watched the wishes in the fire turn to ash, I knew there were some wishes that were not destined to come true.

Even at Christmas.

17

I slept later than I would have preferred on Christmas Day, but then, it had been nearly dawn when I had at last fallen asleep. I had tossed and turned most of the night, and I had come to a decision.

Fletcher's life was Fletcher's life. He had not invited me to share it, and even if he had, I did not know if that was an invitation I could accept. I had no idea if his feelings for me equaled mine for him. Given his actions, I would assume so, but he had not declared himself. Nor had I. I was a coward, really. Afraid, not only of his feelings, but afraid of my own as well. And afraid of what acknowledging those feelings would cost.

It was for the best. We were from different worlds before he had left his position in government, and our worlds were even further apart now. I had no desire to break his heart, and I certainly did not wish for my own heart to be broken, although, in spite of my best intentions, it might already be too late to prevent that.

Still, it did seem to me the only sensible, logical thing to do was to make this Christmas, this time together, as wonderful as it had been last year and give no thought as to the future. This year, this Christmas, might be all we ever had. This—Fletcher, Italy, the villa—was my adventure, my first, and quite likely, my only adventure. I was determined to make the most of it.

Margaret fetched me a cup of hot coffee and the same kind of delicious fruitcake I had sampled last year. She helped me dress quickly, all the while regaling me with an accounting of Christmas Eve dinner with Silvestro and Agostina's family. Apparently, Agostina had a widowed brother who, according to Margaret's somewhat flustered description, was quite dashing and spoke English with a fair amount of fluency. It was obvious from what she said, what she didn't say and her suspiciously pleasant manner this morning that she was quite taken with the man. And wasn't that interesting?

I made my way downstairs, marveling at this change in my maid's demeanor. The very fact that she had allowed herself to be charmed by Agostina's brother—or any man—was startling. I would place the blame, or credit, on Christmas, although she had certainly not allowed the spirit of the season to influence her temperament last year. No, I blamed the villa for this. The Villa of the Enchanted Seas had cast its spell on Margaret, just as it had on me. It was a fanciful notion and yet . . . What better time than at Christmas to indulge in the fanciful, the improbable and all things connected with magic?

The enticing aromas of Agostina's cooking wafted around me as I descended the stairs. I closed my eyes for a moment and savored the mouth-watering fragrance. It struck me that, while the scent of roasted turkey and chestnuts had brought Christmas to mind for me in the past, I would never again smell the exotic blend of tomatoes and garlic and onion that permeated the air here without thinking of Christmas. I resisted the urge to wander into Agostina's domain and beg a sample. Not that I would ever go uninvited into my own kitchen. My cook would, no doubt, turn in her notice. I tried not to dwell on the fact that I had one servant who would not allow me entry to her domain and another who did not feel a cordial disposition to be part of her duties although, at the moment, I found it endearing of them. But this year, as last, I was not my usual self.

I entered the parlor, and my breath caught.

There, positioned between the French doors that led to the terrace, was the loveliest Christmas tree I had ever seen. It was tall and narrow, some sort of cypress, I thought, planted in a large, square stone pot set on wheels. I believed it was one of the potted trees that was usually on the balcony. Today it was covered with the most exquisite angels. Brilliantly colored, they perched on the branches as if caught in mid-flight. It was quite simply magic. "Well?" Fletcher appeared at my side. "Will it do, do you think?"

I swallowed against the lump in my throat. "Do you ever sleep on Christmas Eve?"

He laughed. "I knew you would be missing home, and I thought this might help."

"That was . . . quite nice of you." I moved closer to the tree to hide my face as much as to examine the angels. I didn't want him to know how very much his efforts had moved me, and I needed a moment to gather my composure. "This must have been a great deal of work."

"But well worth it. For you." His words were casual but underlaid with a meaning I didn't know how to interpret.

"These are remarkable." I leaned forward to examine an angel clothed in robes of blue and gold. Her face, hands and wings were terra cotta. Her robes were fashioned from stiffened fabric. I slowly circled the tree, entranced by every new celestial being. Each was unique, as if meant to depict real people. Or real angels. "Where did they come from?"

"Naples originally." He cleared his throat. "They belonged to my grandmother."

I peered around the tree at him. "And you brought them all the way here? For me?"

He paused. "I did."

I wasn't sure anyone, man or woman, had ever done anything quite so thoughtful for me. I studied a particularly exquisite angel, her painted face a study in serenity. "This must have taken you all night."

"Tradition, of course, demands a tree be put up on Christmas Eve and no sooner," he said staunchly. "I arrived three weeks ago, but while I did hope, I wasn't sure if you were going to be here. If what we'd said in parting was a true pledge to return."

I nodded.

"I didn't want to do this and then have it as a reminder if you did not come."

"I will be here every year if you will," I said without thinking, then realized what I had said. What had compelled me to say such a thing? I was on the far side of the tree and couldn't see his face. I held my breath.

For a long moment, there was silence.

"Is that a promise?" His demeanor was offhand, as if it was of no significance whatsoever. But it was, and we both knew it.

I stepped around the tree and met his gaze. "Yes, I believe it is."

"But is it a promise you can keep?" His tone was light, but there was a serious look in his eyes.

"I don't know." It certainly wasn't a promise I had intended to make. And yet, I had never made a promise I had more wanted to keep. I shrugged. "But I would try."

"I wouldn't expect you to come if you married."

I widened my eyes in feigned surprise. "I can't bring a husband with me?"

"Very well." He heaved an exaggerated sigh. "Bring him along if you wish."

"I don't know." I shook my head in a mournful manner. "It might be awkward."

"True." His brow furrowed, then he brightened. "I know. If you have a husband, I shall simply have to dig up a wife and bring her along."

I raised a brow. "Do you have someone in mind?"

He looked at me as if trying to decide what to say, then shrugged. "Not at the moment."

I brushed aside a stab of disappointment and turned my attention back to the tree. "I have no one in mind for a husband either. At least, at the moment."

"Good." He came up behind me and wrapped his arms around me. "Because you have just made a promise to me, and I intend to hold you to it."

"Oh?" I rested my head against his chest.

"I could never allow a friend to break a promise this important," he said firmly. "It is, after all, a Christmas promise. There is little else that is as sacred."

"I have already given you my word. I can't do more than that." I heaved an overly dramatic sigh. "And yet, I fear I'll be here all alone."

I heard the grin in his voice. "Are you asking for a promise from me?"

"It seems only fair. One sacred Christmas promise for another."

"Very well, then." He rested his chin on my head. "I promise you that I will be here every year for Christmas." He paused. "Barring circumstances beyond our control."

"I hadn't thought of that. Circumstances like marriage."

"I was thinking more along the lines of death and disease, but I suppose we can add marriage."

"So we each promise to be here for Christmas every year unless we are married or diseased or dead." I thought for a moment. "Much can happen from year to year."

"I am aware of that."

"But I can't think of anything else, can you?"

"Marriage, death and disease seem to cover it." He chuckled. "Although perhaps we should include volcanic eruption as well."

"Excellent idea." I shivered. "Do not expect to see me if Vesuvius is spewing molten rock."

He laughed. "Then we have a pact?"

I stared at the tree for a long moment. I didn't know what the future held for us, but on this Christmas, I knew I didn't want to spend any Christmas without him. If Christmas was to be all we had, then so be it. I nodded slowly. "We do."

"Good. Something to sustain me through the long year ahead."

"Don't expect my sympathy. You are living in Paris and doing exactly what you want to do." There was the tiniest edge to my voice. Was I envious of the freedom Fletcher had found? Or was it that he'd had the courage to, as he'd said, follow his heart and my heart had no idea what it wanted? "Most of us don't have that opportunity."

"You have to seize opportunities when they present themselves, Portia," he said mildly.

"Yes, well, the next time an opportunity wanders in my direction, I assure you I will seize it." I huffed. That wasn't entirely true. It had to be the right opportunity. Thomas had been an opportunity. "Given, of course, that it is an opportunity that is to my liking."

"That goes without saying." Amusement sounded in his voice. "Were you to have the opportunity to, oh, say, drive to the top of Vesuvius, I assume you would not—"

"That is not amusing, Fletcher." Although I could understand why he might think it was. "And I believe I owe you an apology."

"Oh?"

"You filled a tree with angels for me, and I don't have anything for you. It was quite thoughtless of me."

"Nothing?" Disappointment rang in his voice. "Nothing at all?"

"No, I'm afraid not."

"I do so love Christmas gifts," he said mournfully.

I twisted in his arms to face him and noted the laughter in his eyes. "I am sorry. I didn't decide to come until it was very nearly too late."

"And you are all I need," he said gallantly. "You are a gift, Portia. The perfect Christmas gift."

I narrowed my eyes. "You are even more charming this year than you were last year."

"I know. I have been practicing." He grinned wickedly and pulled me closer. "There a gift of sorts you can give me. Something I would very much like."

"I'm almost afraid to ask."

"I would be most appreciative."

"Very well," I said slowly. "What is it?"

"You could be my model as well as my inspiration."

"Goodness, Fletcher, we tried that last year, if you recall." An annoying wave of heat washed up my face. "You managed very little painting, and we both ended up with paint where it shouldn't be."

"It was fun, wasn't it?"

"Yes, I suppose it was, but—"

"This is important, Portia." He was abruptly serious. "I can't afford not to paint while I'm here, and painting a beautiful woman will add to my body of work."

Perhaps he hadn't been painting naked women in Paris, after all. "There is that charming manner of yours again."

"It comes in handy." He smiled down at me. "What do you say, Portia? Will you pose for me?"

"I warn you, I have never been good at sitting for a portrait. I am entirely too impatient, and I bore easily."

"I shall do my best to keep you entertained."

"Oh, that does make it sound worthwhile."

"Sarcasm, Portia." He shook his head in a chastising manner. "The least you can do to make up for it, as well as make up for that shocking lack of a pres—"

"Very well." And why not? He was so endearingly earnest, and it seemed little enough to do for a man who had gathered angels for me.

"Do you know what I wish to do now?" A wicked light flashed in his eyes.

"Yet again, I fear the answer."

"As well you should." He brushed his lips across mine. "As well you should."

18

"I think every Christmas should be like this," Fletcher said thoughtfully. His arms were folded under his head, and he gazed up at the ceiling.

I rolled over on my side and propped my head in my hand. "You mean doing nothing more than eating extraordinary meals created by Agostina followed by zeppole—"

He winced as if in pain. "I do love zeppole."

"And lying in bed for a great portion of the morning?"

"That lying in bed part does seem like a waste." He reached for me and pulled me to lay on top of him. "I can think of much better things we can do than just lying here."

I laughed, but then, I had laughed a great deal in the three days—three delightfully self-indulgent days—since Christmas. When I wasn't sighing with delight at Agostina's latest offering, I was sighing with an entirely different kind of delight. I wondered if lovemaking with Fletcher would ever grow old. Not that I would have the opportunity to find out. I pushed the thought out of my head. I was determined to live only in the present and not consider what might happen tomorrow. At least until I left Italy.

"Perhaps you haven't noticed, but I have been doing a great deal of work."

"It would have been difficult not to notice, as I have spent more hours than I can count watching you paint."

In spite of his revelation about his move to Paris, I had not entirely realized how committed he was to his work. He had returned to painting the day after Christmas. I had not yet posed for him, but I had indeed sat with an unread book in my hand, watching him apply paint to canvas. Watching the way his brow furrowed in concentration. Noting how he seemed to vanish into a world of his own when he worked. Studying the way he wielded his brush almost like a sword in battle. There was a passion about him that was irresistible and mesmerizing. And I couldn't pull my gaze away. It was as if I were storing up memories and images to sustain me when we were apart. I had planned to stay as long as he did, but we had not discussed how long that would be. Nor had we spoken again of our sacred Christmas promises, but they hovered between us nonetheless. A reminder, at least in my mind, that the days here were not endless. That this holiday, this respite, from the realities of my life, would soon be over. At the villa with Fletcher, it was easy to forget that the wanton, free-spirited creature I was here had nothing in common with the proper, strait-laced Lady Redwell.

"It is fun, isn't it?" He grinned, pulled me closer and kissed the tip of my nose.

"Oh my, yes," I said with feigned enthusiasm. "I can't imagine doing anything more exciting than watching you do something you enjoy."

"I knew it." He smirked. "You have to admit, you are liking my work."

"I refuse to answer that." I shook my head. "It will just make you arrogant."

"More arrogant, you mean?"

"Yes, but I was trying to be nice."

He laughed, tightened his arms around me and rolled over until our positions were reversed. He grinned down at me. "I can be nice." He nuzzled my neck. "I can be very nice."

"Have you given any thought to the possibility of a child?" I said abruptly. I hadn't intended to say anything on the subject at the moment, especially not this particular moment, but it had been in the back of my mind.

He raised his head and stared down at me. "What are you trying to say?"

"I'm not *trying* to say anything. I'm simply asking if you have given the possibility any consideration whatsoever."

"Actually, being the responsible sort I am, I have." He shifted to one side and stretched out beside me. It was so wonderfully decadent. "I have given a great deal of thought to it. Even concocted a somewhat twisted explanation for our hasty marriage."

"Marriage?"

"We would have to marry," he said firmly. "I would insist on it."

It was the answer I was expecting. Fletcher was an honorable man. Still, it was good to hear it aloud. "How *responsible* of you."

"Are you worried?"

"Not really. Women in my family tend not to have children before marriage. I'm not sure why."

"I suspect it's because women in your family do not have clandestine liaisons in foreign countries at Christmas."

"Or any other time." I thought for a moment. "At least as far as I know. I could be wrong, but—"

"Do you trust me?" His tone was abruptly serious.

"Should I?"

"Without question."

"Very well, then." I drew a deep breath and gazed into his eyes. "I trust you."

"Good." He kissed me quickly, then fairly leaped out of bed. "Are you coming?"

"Am I coming where?" I asked cautiously. Who knew what the man might have in mind?

"It's time to get to work."

As much as I did rather like watching him paint, today I was in no hurry to rise. Someone—probably Agostina—had tactfully left breakfast offerings outside our door this morning, so there was no need to leave Fletcher's rooms. Or his bed. I waved him off. "Do feel free to start without me."

"I can't." He pulled on his trousers. "Yesterday I finished the works I had started before you arrived."

"You finished the scene of the Roman villa clinging to the edge of the cliff?" I sat upright. "I love that painting."

"I know." He smirked.

The painting truly was remarkable, at least I thought so. He had been accurate enough in his depiction of the steep cliffs rising out of the sea and the ancient, nearly ruined building precariously perched as if it might tip into the water at any minute. But he had painted the scene as if one was looking at it through seawater or old glass. It had the overall effect of a dream or a vision. He was right. He had learned a great deal since last year. As had I. Thanks to my numerous gallery visits, I had knew enough to recognize that the blasted man really was respectably good by today's standards. The old masters,

Botticelli, Rembrandt and their friends, would probably disagree. But then, they were dead.

"You did promise to pose for me. I believe it's my Christmas gift." He nodded at the French doors. "On the balcony, with the bay in the background, you'll look perfect outside."

"A gift is a gift, I suppose." I wouldn't mind being immortalized by Fletcher. To be a part of his work and not just an observer. It was exciting, really. I swung my legs off the bed. "It will just take me a few minutes to dress."

He shook his head. "That's not what I had in mind."

I stared at him. "Surely you're not serious."

"I'm very serious."

"But I shall freeze."

"Nonsense, you're made of sterner stuff than that. Besides, the sun is shining, and it's quite pleasant today." He pinned me with a pointed look. "Last year, you said you would pose for me naked."

"That was last year." Now that the time had come to actually do the deed, I was not quite so flippant about it. "Now, however . . ."

"Now?" he said hopefully.

The look in his eye was impossible to resist. Besides, I had promised. "Very well."

I wrapped the blanket around me and stood up.

He smiled. "That's cheating, you know."

"Is it?" I glanced down at the blanket. "And I thought it was a compromise."

He laughed. "What it is, is a start."

"I'm not sure I like how that sounds," I said under my breath.

We had been lucky thus far this year. While it had rained a bit at night, the days were bright and sunny. He dragged a bench out onto the balcony and positioned me in a reclining position, facing the bay, the blanket draped artfully around me.

"Perfect." He nodded. "Especially the way Vesuvius is off to one side. It reminds me of something you said last year." He thought for a moment. "Ah yes, you said you didn't want to live in the shadow of a volcano. There was something profound about that."

"Was there?" I wrinkled my nose. "I thought it was nothing more than a desire not to be engulfed in flame and molten rock."

"There's much to be said for that too," he said absently.

I sighed and wished I wasn't quite so ill at ease. I was not completely naked, which suited my sensibilities, yet I did feel exposed. I tried reminding myself that I was revealing little more than I did when I wore a particularly daring gown. It did not help. Even so, there was a remarkable sense of freedom in being nearly naked under the Italian sun. I never would have suspected such a thing.

"In spite of my offer to pose sans clothing, I am not entirely comfortable with this," I said to him over my shoulder. "What if someone should happen along?"

"No one approaching the front of the house can see you here," he said absently, too concerned with the arrangement of his easel, paints, brushes and whatever else he deemed necessary. I had seen this before. It struck me as something of a ritual he performed before starting to paint. It was both intriguing and deadly dull. "Certainly if someone is on a boat in the bay, they might spot you, but unless they are very close, you will be no more than a pale pink blotch."

"How lovely," I murmured. "I have always wanted to be a pale pink blotch."

There was no response, and I realized his muse—that annoying tart—had already claimed him. I sighed and gazed out at the bay, trying very hard to stay still. It seemed the harder I tried, the more I needed to twitch, or shift, or scratch or just move. At last, I could take no more.

"Fletcher?"

"Yes?"

"I should like to take a break. Just for a minute. I'm really quite stiff." I rolled my shoulders. "After all, I've been quite dutifully sitting here for hours."

"Or eighteen minutes."

"Eighteen minutes?" I frowned. "Are you sure? Perhaps your watch has stopped."

"My watch is fine."

"Well, it feels like hours," I muttered. "I told you I bore easily."

Behind me, he heaved a resigned sigh. "Go on, then."

I gathered the blanket around me and rose to my feet. Apparently, my need to move was more in my head than anywhere else. I really wasn't at all stiff, not that I planned to admit it. "May I see what you've done?"

"You may, but you will be disappointed."

"Never." I came around him and studied the canvas. It was a bit disappointing. There was little to see, only a vague charcoal sketch of an even vaguer reclining figure. "You haven't managed much, have you?"

He cast me a withering look.

"Yes, I know—eighteen minutes." I winced. "I shall try to do better."

"I would appreciate that." He paused, then drew a deep breath. "Perhaps I haven't mentioned how important this is to me."

"You did say you wished to add to your body of work." I narrowed my eyes. "Is there more to it than that?"

"A bit more, yes." He ran his hand through his hair, and I realized he was far more concerned than he had let on up till now. "There is an art dealer in Paris who was quite taken with some of my work. He is willing to include five of my paintings in his next gallery showing, providing he likes them."

I was about to protest that I had no desire to have paintings of me at all, let alone without a stitch on, displayed in a gallery in Paris or anywhere. But Fletcher's style was such that I doubt anyone would ever recognize me. "I see."

"That's why I came here so early. This"—he waved broadly at the view beyond the balcony—"inspires me. As do you." He met my gaze, a hint of uncertainty in his eyes. "I need you, Portia."

I had never been needed before for anything beyond the mundane and ordinary. Oh certainly, I had been *needed* to manage a household, or *needed* to arrange a charitable event, or *needed* to do any number of other things all ladies were expected to do. And I had never been anyone's inspiration.

"Well, then, let's get back to it, shall we?" I kissed him lightly, then returned to my position. It was one thing to pose as a Christmas gift and quite another to do so as the inspiration for the man who had your heart.

And so the days passed, at once endless and all too finite. I found I was quite good at holding one position, when I set my mind to it. I had far more fortitude than I had ever imagined. We rarely spoke while he worked—he was too immersed in his own world, and I was too conscious of interrupting.

In many ways, I wished I had not agreed to assist him. When we were laughing or talking late at night in the parlor, or lying in his bed, it was impossible to think about anything other than that moment. Nor did I wish to. But in the long hours that I posed for him, my mind refused to think of anything but the future.

I knew it would be harder to leave him this year than it had been last year. I knew it with every day, every hour that passed. I knew as well that this world we had created in this enchanted villa would not last forever. And I realized, no matter how much I wanted to, returning here next Christmas would be a mistake. I could not live my life in a sort of limbo from one Christmas to the next. Still, I did not want this, this time, this Christmas, to end.

A few days after the new year, skies had darkened and a steady rain fell. I posed inside, fully clothed, curled up in a chair, my gaze focused on a book I held as if I were reading.

Fletcher had begun a half dozen or so paintings of me. One or two were nearly done, but the rest had nothing more on the canvas than preliminary sketches and dabs of paint. He said he would finish them in Paris.

"I have arranged your travel back to England," Fletcher said in a deceptively casual manner.

I jerked my attention away from the book in my hand. "You did what?"

"Tomorrow," he said. "You leave tomorrow."

"Why on earth would I leave tomorrow?" I stared at him. "I intended to stay as long as you do."

"I realize that, but—"

I drew my brows together. "Are you sending me away?"

"Absolutely not." He stood, crossed to me, took my hands and pulled me to my feet. "I'm leaving the day after tomorrow."

I considered him for a long moment. "The exhibit?"

He nodded, my hands still in his.

"I see." I wanted to offer to be there for him, but I couldn't bring myself to say the words. It would be a public acknowledgment of our—*my*—feelings. I wasn't ready to take a step I could not take back. And no matter how much I felt in my heart that he shared my feelings, he had been no more willing to declare his affection than I. Here, I was intrepid and daring. In the rest of the world, be it Paris or London, I was a coward. I adopted a brisk, no-nonsense tone. "I should start Margaret packing, then."

"Portia."

My heart skipped a beat. Would he ask me to stay with him? Accompany him to Paris? Share his life? "Yes?"

He considered me for a moment, then smiled. "I just wanted to thank you for assisting me in my work."

The most irrational sense of disappointment swept through me. "Think nothing of it, Fletcher. Why, I would do the same for any friend." I smiled and pulled my hands from his. "Now, if you will excuse me . . ." I grabbed my book and took my leave, forcing myself to maintain a sedate pace.

I wanted to flee, run down the hall and fling myself onto my bed and weep. It was absurd, of course. I hadn't wanted him to ask me not to go. To ask me to pledge myself to him. To declare his feelings for me. I wouldn't have known what to say. It would have been horrible and would have destroyed what we shared. Whatever that was.

I used the excuse of preparing to travel to avoid Fletcher for the rest of the day, but I did join him for dinner, a subdued affair with more attention paid to the food than each other. We tried, both of us, to attempt the kind of teasing banter we were so very good at and enjoyed so much, but it was to no avail. There was too much hanging in the air between us. Too much unsaid. Too much I—and, I thought, Fletcher as well—was afraid to say aloud.

And I did join him in his bed, because I couldn't bear not to. A voice in the back of my head kept whispering that this might be the last time I felt his arms around me or his lips on mine or the heat of his body pressed against me. As much as I tried to ignore the heavy feeling of finality, I was unsuccessful. The night was painted with a bittersweet brush. And neither of us slept.

19

"Have you decided which paintings you intend to offer for exhibition?" I asked lightly, in a desperate effort to say anything other than what was truly on my mind. Fletcher and I stood by the open door of the carriage that would take me to Castellammare and beyond, to home. Margaret was already seated inside.

"Not yet." He shook his head. "I suspect I will choose some of the ones of you, if they turn out as well as I think they will."

"I wish you all the best, then." At once it struck me how final my words sounded. As if I were saying farewell forever. Perhaps I was.

"Portia, I have been thinking," he said slowly. I don't know if it was the tone in his voice or the look on his face, but my stomach clenched.

"I thought we had agreed, no good can ever come of that," I said in a teasing manner, belying the dread settling around my heart.

"It never does, does it?" He smiled wryly. "I will not hold you to your promise."

"My promise?" I knew exactly what he meant, but I wanted him to say it.

"Your promise to return next year for Christmas."

"Oh, that promise." I waved off his words as if we were discussing nothing of particular importance, but we were and we both knew it. "We agreed that any number of things could happen to keep me—either of us—away."

"In spite of our pact, while I will be disappointed, I will understand if—for whatever reason—you don't come."

"Goodness, Fletcher, if I don't come, or if you don't come, for that matter, neither of us will ever really know the reason why, will we?" I had intended my words to be flippant, lighthearted, but they carried the weight of truth nonetheless.

"You have me there." He chuckled in an oddly mirthless sort of way.

For a long moment, we stared at each other. There was so much we should say, so much we needed to say, yet neither of us had the courage or the strength or the confidence, perhaps, to say anything of importance. In spite of my doubts and my desires, I would not make a decision here and now about next Christmas. About the rest of my life. Here and now was Fletcher.

Here and now was magic.

At last, I drew a deep breath. "We should be off if we are to make the train to Naples."

"Of course." He nodded and took my hand to assist me into the carriage.

"Fletcher." I paused on the step and looked at him.

"Yes?"

I gazed into his dark eyes and saw my own regret mirrored there. At what could have been, perhaps. Or what might never be. "It was a remarkable Christmas."

He squeezed my hand. "Indeed, it was, Portia. I shall never forget it."

"Nor will I," I said softly, fighting to control emotions that threatened to overcome me. "Safe journeys to you, my dear Fletcher." I released his hand and hurried to take my seat.

"And to you, Portia," he said quietly. He said something else, but the driver shut the door and I didn't hear it. It didn't matter, really.

I stared out the window as the carriage pulled away from the Villa Mari Incantati, not daring to look back to see if Fletcher watched as my carriage disappeared in the distance. I was afraid that if I looked back, looked at him, I would never leave. And afraid, as well, that he had not watched me go but had already returned to his life. As I would return to mine. The carriage went around a curve, and the opportunity to look back was lost. Probably for the best.

The farther I got from the villa, from him, the closer I came to home, the more I accepted the fact that this Christmas might well have been our last. After all, I was not the kind of woman to carry on a secret affair with her artist lover year after year on the coast of Italy. At least, I never had been. But the Portia who lied about her real name and posed nude on a balcony overlooking the sea with a volcano rising in the distance had little in common with the very proper Lady Redwell who had very nearly always done exactly what was expected.

I was almost home when I accepted that I'd had my adventure and it was past time to move forward. I certainly couldn't imagine spending the rest of my life counting the days between one Christmas and the next. It might have been different if Fletcher had declared I was his one true love and he couldn't live another day without me. Or if I had said something of my feelings and what I wanted, but that was the problem. I didn't know what I wanted. And what I was willing to sacrifice for it. I resolved to put him firmly out of my head. And ignored the distinct crack somewhere in the vicinity of my heart.

I had thought I was not the kind of woman to disregard everything she believed about what one was and was not expected to do in life simply because she fell in love. That I did not have the kind of courage it took to abandon everything for love.

But I'd never been tested.

He had never asked.

Part Four

1887 England

20

Fletcher Jamison would not let me rest, no matter how hard I tried to push all thoughts of him out of my head.

The man haunted my dreams and hovered constantly on the fringes of my waking thoughts with his wicked, dark eyes and his infectious laughter. Blasted, inconsiderate, selfish beast that he was. Certainly a rational observer might argue that he had done nothing whatsoever to warrant such a title. Although an equally rational observer, a female observer perhaps, would point out that the very fact that he had done *nothing* was exactly the problem. He had not stopped me from leaving. He had not asked me to join him in Paris. He had not declared his undying love. No, he had done *nothing* beyond waving farewell, and as I had not looked back at the villa, that was no more than an assumption on my part. That I had no idea how I would have responded to any of those things he had *not* done was beside the point.

I'd thought, when I returned to England, I could put him behind me. As one might place a souvenir of travel on a shelf and then forget about it. It was proving to be more difficult than I had expected. Frankly, it was affecting my life in ways I had not imagined. Why, I was hard-pressed to maintain my usual pleasant nature. Which might well explain why neither Julia nor Veronica inquired as to what had had happened at Christmas. Obviously, there was something in my demeanor that told them without words that Christmas was not a subject I wished to speak of. Something that indicated it had not gone well.

Which was absurd, of course. My stay at the villa had been nothing short of magical.

By the end of January, I assumed I simply had not had enough time to fully put all thoughts of Fletcher aside. I decided I needed something else to occupy my mind. I turned in earnest to the study of French. My French was no more than adequate, and as I was well on my way to the conquering of Italian, it seemed rather clever to turn my attention toward French as well. I wasn't sure why.

In February, I reluctantly attended a Valentine's Day ball. As did nearly everyone I knew, including my aunt and no less than four prospective husbands. I was not inclined to look favorably upon men in February. I feared they noticed. My attitude did not change significantly in March. Especially when Margaret confessed she had left a pair of my gloves at the villa and perhaps it would provide an excuse for someone to return them. I was concerned about Margaret. She had become almost pleasant, and she hummed a great deal.

In April, I considered a trip to Paris. Not to seek out Fletcher, of course, but it had been some time since I had paid Mr. Worth a visit, and my wardrobe was sadly out of fashion. I had told neither Veronica nor Julia about Fletcher's move to France. They certainly would have advised me against going for that reason alone. One never knew who one might bump into on the street. Even so, Veronica, who was always inclined to travel, especially to spend exorbitant amounts of money, pointed out it was entirely too late in the season to commission a new wardrobe, my current wardrobe was not the least bit dated, and most important, leaving now meant I would miss a fair number of events leading up to this summer's celebration of Her Majesty's Golden Jubilee, including our own next month. It did not help to know that she was right.

Everyone who was anyone had some sort of gathering in honor of the queen. Parties had begun in earnest with the warmer weather and continued to grow in frequency—and extravagance—the closer we came to the official celebration in June. Veronica, Julia and I joined in hosting a small ball at the Explorers Club. Her Majesty was expected to make an appearance, but one never knew if she actually would. I would have wagered against it.

The evening, however, was very nearly perfect. Spring was at its height. Flowers bloomed uncontrollably everywhere one looked. The day had been mild and sunny, the night was cool but not uncomfortably so. And I, for the first time in a long time, felt rather like my old self.

"You look lovely tonight, my dear Portia." Cousin Sebastian took my hand.

I narrowed my eyes. "Did Veronica tell you to say that?"

He looked genuinely surprised. "My wife tells me to do many things, but she did not prompt this particular comment. Nor did she need to." He studied me for a moment. "You look . . . like spring, I think."

I laughed. "What a perfectly charming thing to say, Sebastian, even if it makes no sense. I'm not quite sure what spring looks like."

"It looks like a new beginning," a familiar voice said behind me. "A fresh start, if you will."

Sebastian's gaze shifted from me to the owner of the voice, then back, and he grinned. "And I believe my wife is looking for me. So if you will excuse me. Portia. Lindsey." He nodded and took his leave.

"I wasn't sure I would ever see you again."

I smiled and turned. "Goodness, Thomas, I am where I always am."

"Your cousin is right." Admiration shone in his blue eyes. "You look well."

"Thank you, Thomas, as do you." He did indeed look well. Healthy and fit, with a cast of color in his face as if he had spent time in sunnier climes. "Have you been traveling?"

"I am very nearly always traveling these days." He paused. "I am glad we happened into one another."

I tilted my head and considered him. "You would have been hard-pressed to miss me here. I am one of the hostesses tonight."

"Yes, of course. I knew that." I don't believe I'd ever seen him uncomfortable before, yet it was obvious that he was. He grimaced. "I believe I owe you an apology."

I wasn't sure what to say, so I wisely, for once, said nothing.

"I had no right to issue ultimatums. You never led me to believe there was more between us than there was," he said in a measured tone. "I made assumptions based on nothing more than what I wanted."

"I am sorry, Thomas."

"I know you are, but you have nothing to be sorry for." He paused. "Here's the, well, problem I suppose is the only word for it. I miss you, Portia. I miss our friendship."

"Thomas, I—"

"I'll ask for nothing more than occasional companionship. And if someday your feelings change, I would welcome that, but I would be happy with nothing more than your friendship for the rest of my days."

"Oh, Thomas." I stared at him. "I would wish you a better fate than that."

He laughed. "It doesn't sound as bad to me as it obviously does to you."

"Oh, it doesn't sound bad. But it does sound horribly unfair." I thought for a moment. "However, I will accept your friendship, and as any good friend should, I will make it a point to introduce you to every marriageable woman I know."

He groaned. "How very *fair* of you."

I laughed. "I have missed you too. But I'm still not sure this is a wise idea."

"The only one risking his heart is me." He grinned wryly. "I'm willing to take that risk."

I considered the idea. It had a great deal of appeal. "You're quite wonderful, you know."

"I am glad you realize it. Not that it has done me much good."

"I daresay you'll get your reward in heaven."

"Something to look forward to, then." He offered his arm. "Shall we dance?"

"I would be delighted." I took his arm, and he led me onto the floor. And indeed it was delightful to dance with him and be with him again.

We began spending a great deal of time together. I enjoyed his companionship and, I believe, he enjoyed mine. He kept to his word and did not push me for more than I was willing to give. I did feel occasional twinges of guilt, as he so obviously felt affection for me that was beyond friendship, but I assuaged them by introducing him to one eligible lady after another. Thomas, however, was every bit as particular as I when it came to prospective spouses. Although my offerings were far better suited to him than any Aunt Helena had produced for me. I believed Aunt Helena still held out hope for a match with Thomas, as her efforts to find me a new husband eased.

June and July were filled with a plethora of festive events commemorating the queen's fifty years on the throne. Not a day went by that I did not attend a soiree, a garden party, a ball or a dinner with endless toasts to Her Majesty's continued good health. I daresay London had never seen quite so many heads of state, kings and maharajahs, queens and grand dukes, princes and princesses from throughout Europe and the Far East. Thomas and I joined my family to attend the queen's garden party at Buckingham Palace. It was an intimate affair with Her Majesty and thousands of her subjects. Nonetheless, it was not to be missed.

But for the Hadley-Attwaters, the most important event of the summer took place at Fairborough Hall in the country, where my cousin Miranda wed Winfield, Viscount Stillwell. The ceremony was held out of doors, the happy couple saying their vows in a Grecian temple, a folly, built some two hundred years ago as a gift of true love. It was quite simply perfect, and even the most cynical among us sniffed back a tear when Miranda and Winfield vowed to love each other for the rest of their days. And when Thomas took my hand in his, I did not pull away. We both knew that was attributable to nothing more than the romance of the day, and I was grateful for his company. Still, it did strike me at moments like this to wonder if I was saving Thomas as some sort of insurance against the day that I decided I could accept *content*. It was a terrible thing to do, and yet I was afraid to completely push him away. At those times, I reminded

Thomas of the unfairness of our relationship as well as renewed my efforts to find him a perfect match.

Autumn came and, in spite of my best intentions, with the falling of the leaves, my thoughts inevitably turned to the months ahead and Christmas. I added the study of Spanish—my Spanish was little better than my French—to French and Italian. If nothing else, I should one day be able to travel the world with the understanding of what was being said to me. Besides, the study of languages—in addition to my charitable work and social activities—kept me far too busy to dwell on matters like Christmas and Italian villas, threatening volcanoes and dark-eyed artists. Some nights, I was almost too tired to sleep. Which was not at all a problem, as my dreams about villas, volcanoes and artists seemed to have increased in intensity.

In mid-October, Thomas accompanied me to the opening of Mr. Terry's new theater in the Strand, reputed to be the safest from fire ever built. He was oddly pensive during much of the evening, as if his mind was occupied by something other than the moderately amusing play on stage.

Afterward, we retired to my house for brandy in the parlor. It had become a custom of sorts, to discuss whatever event we had just come from, who we had spoken to or observed and whatever interesting bits of news or gossip that had come to our attention. In some ways, Thomas and I were as predictable as a couple who had been married for twenty years. We shared common interests, we were comfortable together and, yes, we were content.

I took a sip of brandy and adopted a casual manner. "What did you think of Mrs. Portman?"

Thomas leaned against my fireplace mantel and considered me thoughtfully. "The pretty blond widow you introduced me to before the play began tonight?"

"You thought she was pretty?" I asked with a satisfied smirk.

"She is pretty." He took a sip of his brandy. "She also taps."

"What do you mean—she taps?"

"I mean, she taps her foot. Like this." He tapped his right foot. "Or something like that, although she does seem to have excellent rhythm."

"That's ridiculous. I've known Jane Portman for years, and I've never seen her tap her foot, rhythmically or otherwise." Although that might explain why she was close to my age and had never wed.

"Admittedly, she didn't tap at first. It wasn't until you wandered off to chat with someone—"

"Thus cleverly leaving the two of you alone."

"—that the tapping began in earnest."

I stared in disbelief. "Really?"

"Oh." He shuddered. "Yes."

"Goodness, Thomas, I can't leave you to your own resources for a minute. It's painfully obvious"—I pinned him with a firm look—"*you* make her tap. How could you?"

"I'm not doing it deliberately. In fact, I have no idea what I'm doing, but you're probably right. Every time I asked her a question, or merely commented on something she said, the tapping increased. I began wondering if she was impatient or was tapping to a particular tune." He lowered his voice in a confidential manner. "I would never admit this to anyone else, but I began to find her tapping quite fascinating."

"You didn't!"

"Wicked of me, I know, but I did, indeed. I even found myself trying to figure out the tune." He shook his head in a mournful manner. "I thought she might add gestures, begin humming and tap her way right out the door."

"Thomas!" I tried very hard not to laugh. "What an awful thing to say! You are a terrible, terrible man!"

"It's a burden I bear." He shrugged. "But I don't tap."

I laughed in spite of my best efforts, although it sounded more like a snort than a laugh.

"Do you plan to go to Italy for Christmas?" he said abruptly.

I stared at him. "What on earth brought that to mind?"

"You."

I drew my brows together. "You will have to be more specific than that."

"Your"—he searched for the right words—"demeanor of late, your mood, if you will, you're not your usual self. You're restless and preoccupied."

"Nonsense." I waved off his comments. "I'm simply busy. My life is extraordinarily full."

"There are only so many languages you can learn, Portia."

"There is nothing so fulfilling as broadening one's mind," I said in a superior manner.

He studied me for a long moment as if I were an insect pinned to a board under glass. I resisted the urge to squirm. "Your manner was exactly the same at this time last year."

"Don't be absurd," I said with more conviction than I felt, given that he was probably right.

"Are you going to Italy this year?" he asked again.

"I haven't decided." Although, hadn't I decided not to go? To put Fletcher in the past? To move forward with my life? Then why couldn't I say so?

"I see," he said thoughtfully. "You should know, as your friend, I think it's a mistake."

"I appreciate your concern, but you really know nothing about it."

"True enough." He nodded. "All I know is that you spend Christmas somewhere in Italy. And, as you did not deny it last year when we spoke of it, I assume there is a man involved."

"I find this discussion extremely awkward." My voice hardened. "And I'm not sure what you want me to say."

"I want the truth, Portia. More than that, I want you to trust me. If we are truly friends, I deserve your trust."

"I do trust you. You're the most trustworthy man I know."

"Lucky me," he muttered. "Portia." He crossed to my side, set our glasses down and took my hands. "I don't want to see you embroiled in some sordid scandal, and you have avoided it thus far. But more than that, I don't want to see you hurt."

I tried to pull my hands free, but his grip tightened. "Thomas, I-"

"I say this only as your friend, and I would say the same to any friend." He met my gaze directly. "You are taking a huge risk. Nothing in this world remains secret forever. You would be ruined if any of this became known. Ostracized from society. Your life in London—in England—would be over."

"I am well aware of that."

"Are you in love with him?" he asked without warning.

"I . . ." I shook my head and shrugged helplessly. It was not something I wished to admit aloud, especially not to Thomas.

"Is he in love with you?"

"I don't know that either."

"Portia, I am ill-suited to give advice on matters of the heart, but I do think you and I have come to know each other fairly well. I strongly urge you to put all this behind you. For your own sake, do not go back to Italy this Christmas."

"I'm touched by your concern, I really am." I drew a deep breath and made a decision. "But I do plan to return to Italy for Christmas."

Last year, I simply needed to know if Fletcher was there, if he cared enough to return. This year, I needed to know what being there meant. To him and to me.

He heaved a resigned sigh. "Very well."

"Is this the point where you threaten not to be here when I come back?" I attempted a teasing tone.

"No." He smiled in resignation. "That did not work, if you recall. I'll be here for you." He released my hands. "Always."

"Thomas—"

"Do not take that sympathetic tone with me, Portia. I am quite all right. I am simply doing what I think is in the best interests of a friend. That my feelings go beyond friendship has nothing to do with it." He picked up his glass and tossed back the rest of his brandy. "However, the hour is late, and I should be on my way." He nodded and started for the door.

"I do appreciate your concern on my behalf," I said weakly, wishing I had thought of something not quite so inane to say.

"I know." He pulled the door open, then looked at me. "You do what you have to do, Portia, and I shall do what I have to do." He nodded. "Good evening." He took his leave, shutting the door behind him.

For a long moment, I stared after him. What on earth did he mean by that? What did he have to do? The question bore further examination but was eclipsed by a more important realization.

I was going to Italy for Christmas.

21

I Am Going to Italy for Christmas!

For the first time in a long time, I awoke in the morning refreshed and with a renewed sense of purpose.

Now that I'd made the decision, it was as if a weight had lifted off me. I was indeed going to Italy. If Fletcher was not there, then whatever we had was at an end. And that would be that. But if he was, it was time—past time, really—to decide, or perhaps admit, exactly what we meant to each other. And where we were going to go from here. This would, after all, be our third Christmas. I had no intention of spending another Christmas in a mindless blur of heated flesh and denial. Although the heated flesh part was quite wonderful, and I certainly did not object to that. But this year, it would not be enough.

I could no longer live my life from Christmas to Christmas. I needed more than that. And perhaps, at last, I was willing to make the sacrifices necessary. It was quite simple when one thought about it. I was not happy without him. And I deserved to be happy, even if there was a high price to pay. If I had to give up my position, my expected place in the world, to be with him, well, so be it. It was not as if we would be poor. I had more than enough money. Most men wanted a wife with a tidy fortune, although I did rather hope he wasn't one of them.

Perhaps I shouldn't wait for Christmas? Perhaps, I should go to Paris? If I was prepared to toss a lifetime of living by the rules of society aside, what was I waiting for? Apparently, I did have the courage required to throw away everything in the name of love. And why not? I was a woman of adventure, after all. It just took me some time to realize it.

Aunt Helena called on me late in the day to allegedly join me for tea, but I was certain she had come to, again, encourage a match with Thomas. She did so at least once a month. One did wonder if a mere month was the limit of her ability to mind her own business.

Tea had been served, and Aunt Helena waited for the kitchen girl to leave the parlor before saying anything beyond pleasantries.

"I ran into Lord Lindsey today," my aunt began. "Lord Lindsey? Thomas? You remember him?"

Good Lord, she hadn't spoken to me like that since I was nine years old. A weight settled in the pit of my stomach. I blamed it on the biscuit I had just eaten. Not one of my cook's better efforts.

"Don't be silly, Aunt Helena," I said smoothly, filling her teacup and mine. "Thomas and I went to the theater together just last night."

"Yes, I believe he mentioned that." She paused, and I braced myself for whatever was next. "He also mentioned you were planning to return to Italy for Christmas."

"Oh?" This was not what I had expected.

"He suggested I might wish to speak to you about it."

"Did he?" I handed her a cup. No, this was far worse. "And where, precisely, did you run into Lord Lindsey?"

"My parlor."

"I see." This was obviously what Thomas had meant by *doing what he needed to do*. He'd wasted no time in telling tales to my aunt. In the spirit of friendship, no doubt. I was not happy about it, but I did understand. I might well have done the same in his place.

"He seemed quite concerned, although he did not give me any specific reason for that concern." Her eyes narrowed. "Do you know why he would be worried about an innocent trip abroad?"

"No idea," I lied.

"I thought not." She sipped her tea, never taking her steely-eyed gaze off me. "You—of all my children—are the one I always thought least likely to court scandal."

I wasn't sure exactly what she knew—or what she thought she knew—but I was not about to blurt something out and give her more information than she already had. "Am I?"

"You *were*." She paused. "As Lord Lindsey revealed no solid information, I paid a call on Lady Mountdale."

"How is Julia?" My smile never slipped.

"Evasive." Aunt Helena's fingers absently tapped the sides of her cup. It was a very bad sign. "And she does not lie well. Oddly enough, she barely waited for me to take my leave before she too left. I suspect she was off to see my daughter-in-law. They have always been as thick as thieves."

"Julia is always dashing off to Veronica's." Exactly how much did she know?

She squared her shoulders. "It's a man, isn't it?"

"Did Julia tell you that?" I asked cautiously.

"Lady Mountdale would not answer my questions, which told me all I needed to know."

Then she really didn't *know* anything. At least not for certain. "Really, Aunt Helena, you know how scattered Julia can be. And, frankly, I think Thomas's imagination has simply run amok."

"This is not Thomas's imagination speaking now. This is your aunt. The woman who raised you." She leaned forward slightly. "I know you. I know everything about you. I simply put the pieces together."

"Well done," I murmured.

She heaved a disappointed sigh. "Oh, Portia, how could you?"

I sighed and surrendered. "I really don't know."

"And for two Christmases?"

"The first was . . . unexpected."

"You were discreet, I'll give you that. I suppose if someone is going to have a . . ." She closed her eyes for a moment, as if asking for divine help.

"Holiday?" I suggested brightly.

"Yes, that will do. If someone is involved in a *holiday*, at least having said *holiday* in a foreign country, at Christmastime, is probably the most inconspicuous way to do it."

"Thank you," I said, then immediately regretted it. Not my wisest response.

"That was not a compliment, simply gratitude." She blew a resigned breath. "So, you're off to meet this man again this year?"

"I'm afraid so."

"Is there any possibility that a marriage will come of this?" A spark of hope shone in her eyes.

"I don't know."

Her brow furrowed. "Don't you think you should find out?"

"I intend to." I summoned my firmest tone. "In fact, I have this well in hand. Why, I am only going to Italy at all to . . . to settle things." The more I talked, the better it sounded. As if I really did know what I was doing. "To find out what he wants and what I want . . . and, well, you understand."

"Not in the least. Good Lord." Aunt Helena groaned. "Your mother would have loved this," she added under her breath.

"My mother?"

She shook her head. "She had a dreadful adventurous streak and a flagrant disregard for the rules of society."

Surprise coursed through me. "*My* mother?"

"Oh my, yes. She did try to conquer that tendency in herself, but she was never able to do so completely. She was free-spirited, you see, and saw nothing wrong with following your own path." She sighed. "I do so miss her."

"I had no idea." I stared in disbelief and a bit of shock. "I always thought she was utterly proper and rather perfect."

"Not at all. Completely imperfect, really." Aunt Helena smiled wistfully. "But it was part of her charm. Who she was, if you will. And why she was so loved, I suppose."

"You never said anything at all to imply my mother wasn't perfect." Accusation rang in my voice, as well it should. I had lived my entire life under a mistaken belief as to what my mother would have thought of my behavior, of my every action, my every word. "I always assumed she was the type of woman who demanded perfection from others. You never even hinted otherwise."

"One always puts those who have gone before in the best possible light. One does not speak ill of the dead, dear." Aunt Helena sniffed. "And one certainly does not enumerate their many faults. That would be wrong, as the dead cannot defend themselves. She was my sister, after all."

"I see." But I really didn't. Worse than knowing I had been wrong for much of my life was the realization that I now had no idea who that voice of propriety in my head was. Although, admittedly, it would now be much easier to ignore.

"Your mother would tell you to follow your heart."

"Are you telling me that?"

"The last thing I want is for you to be unhappy," she said reluctantly. "You weren't particularly happy with David."

"I wasn't unhappy."

She cast me a skeptical look.

"I was quite content with David," I said staunchly.

"No doubt." She considered me for a moment. "I cannot condone the immoral nature of your previous illicit liaisons with this man you plan to meet in Italy, whoever he is. However, as your intentions now are to resolve matters between you, we shall simply forget that I know anything about last Christmas or the Christmas before."

"I don't think—"

She held up a hand to stop me. "I assume you think I will judge him because of what his name is or who his people are? Because he might not be of our social standing?"

"Not you, but—"

"And that, my dear girl, is the problem." She drew a deep breath. "It's my duty to tell you exactly what you will give up by following your heart. When your association becomes public, even if marriage is involved, there will be an enormous scandal."

I nodded. "I know."

"First of all, you will not be accepted into polite society again. People you thought were your friends will no longer acknowledge your existence. You will not be invited anywhere, and you will be welcome nowhere. Do you understand?"

My stomach churned. "I'm afraid I do."

"Living in London will be impossible for you. Or, at the very least, extremely awkward."

"I realize that as well."

She paused. "I hope you also realize your family will stand by you, regardless of what happens."

"I am very grateful for that."

"That's what love means, dear." She patted my hand. "Unquestioned support, even if we think one is making a dreadful error in judgment. You will have that, at least. There is nothing in the world greater than the courage one derives from love."

"Aunt Helena, I—"

The parlor doors slammed open. Veronica and Julia burst into the room.

"Portia! You will not believe what—" Veronica pulled up short at the sight of her mother-in-law. Julia nearly stumbled into her. "Oh, Helena. What a lovely surprise."

"Yes, I can imagine." Aunt Helena peered around Veronica. "And good day to you again, Julia."

"Good day," Julia said weakly.

Veronica's gaze shifted from my aunt to me and back. "Helena," she said with a pleasant smile. "Would you mind giving us a moment alone?"

"Gladly." Aunt Helena threw her hands up and huffed. "I've already learned entirely too much. I don't want to know anything more than I already do. It's very hard to pretend ignorance when one isn't, you know." She started toward the door on the far side of the parlor. "I shall wait in the other room. Portia, we will continue our conversation when you and your friends are finished." With that, she swept out of the room.

"She's far more devious than I ever suspected." Julia shuddered.

"Deceptive, isn't she?" Veronica shook her head, then turned her attention to me. "We have a great deal to tell you."

"Now?" I glanced in the direction my aunt had taken. I had no idea what was left to say, but I would rather be done with it now than put it off until tomorrow. "Another time would be better."

"No," Julia said sharply. "This cannot wait." She glanced at Veronica. "We know about Mr. Jamison."

"Of course you do," I said cautiously. I suspected I was not going to like this. "I told you about him."

"No." Julia shook her head. "We know *all* about him. *Everything* about him."

"I had him investigated," Veronica said bluntly.

"You did what?" Although I should have suspected they would do something like this. My stomach twisted. "Go on."

Julia traded glances with Veronica. "As you are our dearest friend, we thought it would be wise to retain the services of Mr. Phinneas Chapman."

"Did you?" Phinneas Chapman was well-known among the upper classes for his skills at detection and, more important, his absolute discretion.

My friends probably did indeed now know all there was to know about Fletcher, no doubt more than I did. And my aunt now knew far more than I would have liked her to. I did wish I was the type of woman to faint when confronted by adversity. It would have been most convenient.

"We had him look into Mr. Jamison's life," Veronica said.

"And we do apologize for that," Julia added quickly.

"I don't." Veronica shook her head. "I realize it was a terrible violation of your privacy, but this whole adventure was so unlike you, and—"

"We were worried," Julia said. "Extremely worried."

I glared at them. "I'm not sure I fully appreciate your concern."

Julia waved off my words as if they were of no significance whatsoever. "Nonetheless, we do know about his painting, and we know he's living in Paris, and we know about his family, and we—"

"More importantly," Veronica said with an impatient huff, "we know he's here."

"Who is here?" I asked slowly, although I was afraid I already knew the answer. "And where precisely is *here?*"

"*Who* is Mr. Jamison, of course." Veronica drew a deep breath. "And *here* is London. More precisely, earlier today, *here* was my house."

"What?" My mind was racing, and yet I couldn't seem to formulate a single coherent thought.

"As I was saying, earlier today—"

"She needs to hear it from the beginning," Julia said firmly. "You might already know this but this afternoon, your aunt paid me a visit. She has it in her head that you have been spending Christmas in Italy with a man." Julia lowered her voice. "In spite of your aunt's claim not to wish to know more, do you think she's listening?"

"I would wager on it." Veronica shrugged. "I would be."

Julia raised her voice. "I said I had no idea what she was talking about and that the very thought was absurd." She grabbed my elbow and steered me toward the open door to the hall, as far away as one could get from the door Aunt Helena had taken. Veronica trailed behind. "Then I went to Veronica's, intending to bring her to your house with me."

"We thought you should know about your aunt's"— Veronica glanced at the far door and spoke a bit louder— "unfounded suspicions." She nodded and continued quietly. "We were just about to leave to come here when I learned I'd had a gentleman caller while I was out this morning. My butler said the gentleman had a pair of gloves, belonging to Lady Smithson, that his great-aunt wished him to return." Veronica stared at me, her mouth set in a grim fashion. "Gloves she had left in Italy last year."

"Oh?" There wasn't much more that I could say. Denial seemed pointless.

"Imagine the gentleman's surprise when he was informed— not only had Lady Smithson not been to Italy in years—but she has not been Lady Smithson since her marriage more than a year and a half ago. I realized immediately who the gentleman was looking for and who he was." Veronica paused, no doubt to maintain control. It was obvious she was not happy about my borrowing her name. "I must say, I'm thrilled that you chose to besmirch my reputation instead of your own."

"Yes, well . . . I do apologize for that." I cringed. "Yours was the first name that came to mind."

"It would by my first choice," Julia said under her breath.

"I shall take that as a compliment." Veronica huffed. "From both of you."

"I am truly sorry." I shook my head. "That might have been an error in judgment on my part."

"Do you think so?" a male voice said from the shadows of the entry beyond the open doors.

My heart lodged in my throat, and for a moment, I couldn't breathe. I peered around Veronica.

"A mistake perhaps?" The owner of the voice strode into the light. "Or possibly a misstatement?"

Fletcher?

"Lord Castleton?" My aunt stepped forward from behind me.

"Oh, this is good," Veronica said in a quiet voice, for my ears alone.

I had no idea when my aunt had joined us or how much she had heard. She glanced at me. "I couldn't hear a word so I decided I might as well go home."

Julia and Veronica traded uneasy looks. Aunt Helena directed a smile at Fletcher. "I didn't know you knew my niece, Lady Redwell?"

"I don't know Lady Redwell," he said smoothly. "But after I called on you today and you suggested the gloves I had found might belong to your niece, as she had stayed at my great-aunt's villa the Christmas before last, I decided the least I could do was return them in person."

I turned to my aunt. None of this made any sense to me. "He called on you?"

"Earlier today, before . . ." Aunt Helena waved off the rest of her explanation. "Well, that's of little importance now." She cast Fletcher her most charming smile. "He said he remembered my name from correspondence he saw the last time he was at the villa." She glanced at me. "Wasn't that clever of him?"

I nodded. I'd forgotten Silvestro had Aunt Helena's name even if he did not have mine. So much for my attempt at a disguise.

"Allow me to introduce you," she continued. "These are my niece's dear friends. This is Julia, Lady Mountdale."

Fletcher nodded at Julia, who responded with a stunned nod of her own.

"And Veronica, Lady Hadley—Attwater."

"How very nice to meet you," Veronica murmured.

"My apologies, but I thought it was Smithson," Fletcher said politely.

"It was," Aunt Helena answered before Veronica could get a word out. "But Veronica married my son, oh, it will be two years ago this coming January."

"That long," he murmured.

Veronica shot me an uneasy look.

"And, of course, this is my niece, Lady Redwell," Aunt Helena said with a flourish. In spite of our discussion, and my determination to return to Italy, it was obvious that she saw this newcomer as a prospective spouse. A man to rescue me from the clutches of an inappropriate stranger on the coast of Italy. Thank God I had not given her his name. "Ladies, this is Lady Wickelsworth's nephew—"

"Great-nephew, actually," he said politely. "My grandmother on my mother's side was her sister."

"Yes, of course—her great-nephew," Aunt Helena continued, "Lord Castleton."

"*Lord Castleton?*" I said without thinking, and then hurriedly extended my hand.

The moment his fingers met mine, my pulse quickened and I wanted to throw myself into his arms. I didn't, of course. He raised my hand to his lips, his dark gaze locking with mine.

"It's a very great pleasure to meet you. Your aunt speaks quite highly of you."

I couldn't stop staring. "How very kind of you to say."

The moment between us lengthened. There was so much to say, but I had no idea where to start and no desire to say anything of significance with my aunt, and my friends, as witnesses. Worse, whereas I had often been able to look into his blue eyes and read his thoughts, his gaze now was shuttered and revealed nothing. A cold chill shivered up my spine.

"Helena," Veronica said briskly. Fletcher released my hand, and I cast her a grateful look. "You said you were leaving, and we are as well. We should be on our way."

"But he hasn't given her the gloves," Aunt Helena said pointedly, as if returning a pair of gloves was the traditional start of any courtship.

"And that is my purpose here." Fletcher patted his waistcoat pocket, then frowned. "Unfortunately, I seem to have left them in my carriage." He offered his arm to Aunt Helena. "Allow me to escort you out, and then I will fetch the gloves and return them to their rightful owner."

Aunt Helena took his arm and gazed up at him as if he were indeed the answer to her prayers. "How very thoughtful of you to offer." She glanced at me. "Portia, I shall expect you to call on me tomorrow so that we may finish our discussion."

"I look forward to it," I said faintly.

Fletcher escorted my aunt out of the parlor, my friends close on his heels. Julia cast me a look of support, and Veronica squeezed my arm when she passed by me. A moment later, I was blessedly alone.

I sank down onto the sofa and buried my face in my hands. So much had happened in the last few minutes I couldn't quite sort it all out.

First, my aunt knew how I'd spent the last two Christmases and had revealed my mother was far less perfect than I had thought. And then my friends had taken it upon themselves to investigate my—I flinched at the word—*lover* and now knew more about him than I did. If they knew about his family, it was obvious they knew about his title as well. At least they'd shown no particular surprise when he was introduced. Fletcher had never given me any indication that he was heir to a title. Nor had he so much as hinted at his relationship to the owner of the villa. It explained a great deal. But then, even last Christmas, we'd been too immersed in each other to so much as think about the myriad details of our lives away from each other.

Most important, and the only revelation of all of those of the past hour that truly was important, was that Fletcher was here. Here, in London, at my house. That fact alone was difficult to grasp. I was at once thrilled and completely terrified. He obviously already knew about my use of Veronica's name.

I blew a long breath. I had thought, the next time I saw him, it would be no more than a few moments before we were wrapped in each other's embrace. However, I had not envisioned our next meeting taking place in front of my aunt and dearest friends. In addition, the look in his eyes had not been one of joyous reunion and barely restrained passion. Even if we'd been alone, I feared it would not have been the greeting I had imagined.

Now, I was caught off-guard and unprepared. I stood and headed for the table bearing the brandy decanter. Brandy seemed like an excellent idea, and I poured two healthy glasses. I suspected Fletcher might need one. Given that my hand trembled when I filled the glasses, I certainly did.

"You lied to me."

I took a fast swallow of brandy, then turned toward him. The last time I'd seen him, he'd been slightly unkempt but charmingly so. Lighthearted and mad with passion, for his work and for me, he'd been completely irresistible and the tiniest bit dangerous. Today, he was the perfect embodiment of the perfect English lord. His clothes were well tailored and impeccable and obviously expensive. Not a hair on his head was out of place. Utterly, completely perfect. It was little wonder that Aunt Helena thought he would be completely perfect for me.

"Is that for me?" He nodded at the glass in my hand.

"No." I took another swallow. "I poured one for you."

He crossed to my side and took his glass, tossing back half the contents. I resisted the urge to take a step away.

He glanced at me. "Why?"

"Why what?" I said cautiously.

"Why did you lie to me about who you are?"

"Oh, that," I said, as if it wasn't the least bit important. "Quite honestly—"

He snorted.

I ignored him. "It seemed like a good idea at the time. After all, I didn't know you. And the situation itself was fraught with the possibility of scandal. It wasn't something I planned, you know. When we introduced ourselves, the name that came out"—I winced—"wasn't mine."

"It's understandable you were simply being cautious. As you said—you didn't know me." His gaze bored into mine. "Last Christmas, however, you knew me. Quite well, I would say."

"Yes, well . . ." I struggled for something to say, some explanation that would sound plausible. I had nothing but the truth. "I wanted to. Indeed, I intended to, but the moment was never quite right. And the longer I let it go on, the harder it was to say anything."

"I thought you trusted me. I thought we trusted each other." He ran his hand through his perfect hair, disturbing it just enough to make my heart flutter and my stomach clench.

"I did trust you. I do . . ." A thought struck me, and I paused.

"What?"

"I do trust you, Fletcher." I chose my words with care. "However, I'm not sure you can say the same about me."

He scoffed. "I trust you."

"Do you?" I studied him intently. "Then why did you never tell me about your family? Or that you are the heir to a title? And obviously—looking at you—significant wealth along with it?"

"You didn't tell me about your family either," he said sharply.

"I never used anyone's name, but I told you a great deal about my husband and my aunt and the rest of my family. And I never led you to believe I was anything other than what I am. My name is the only thing I misstat—"

"Lied."

"Fine," I snapped. "*Lied.* My name is the only thing I *lied* about. Whereas you made me think you were poor!"

"I *was* poor!"

"Hah!" I waved at his clothes. "Those are not the clothes of a poor artist."

"I'm not poor *now. Now* I have a fortune." He refilled his glass. "And your observation was correct about the significance of it."

"How fortunate for you. My aunt was certainly impressed."

"Are you?" His eyes narrowed.

I shrugged. "I have always appreciated good tailoring."

"I'm glad I now come up to your standards."

"Indeed, you're more than suitable now," I said without thinking.

"Suitable to marry, you mean." A hard note edged his words. "Now that I have a title and a fortune, you'd marry me."

"Because that's all I look for in a husband? Wealth and position?"

He shrugged.

"I might have married you before," I said in a lofty manner. "Thrown aside everything for love. You've heard that story. It's as old as time."

"What stopped you?"

"You." I leaned closer and gazed into his eyes. "You never asked."

"Because I knew the answer."

"You, Fletcher Jamison, Lord Castleton, are truly the most arrogant man I have ever met. You don't know anything about me." I fairly spit the words. "Anything at all."

"I know *Lady Smithson* would never have agreed to marry a lowly civil servant or a struggling artist."

"You're so sure of yourself, are you?" Now was not the time to tell him I had planned to abandon everything for him. For love. Stupid, stupid woman that I was. "As I said, you never asked."

"No, but . . ." For the first time, the tiniest glimmer of uncertainty shone in his eyes.

"You never asked me anything." I hadn't realized how much this had bothered me, but it did seem once I started, I couldn't stop. "You never asked me to stay in Italy with you. You never asked me to join you in Paris. You never even asked me to come back for Christmas."

He glared. "We had a pact."

"A pact I initiated, not you." I shook my head. "Aside from the possibility of a child, we never talked about marriage. We never talked about the future."

"Perhaps we should have."

"Perhaps, but we didn't." I cast him a scathing look. "You had the courage to give up everything to follow your dreams to Paris. You made all those grand speeches about refusing to live your life trying to live up to society's expectations of what was respectable and proper. But when it came to me, you never even considered disregarding expectations and propriety and respectability. You never had the courage to ask me to join you."

"Would you have?"

The question hung in the air between us. I couldn't answer him, because I didn't know what I would have said if he had asked me to stay with him last Christmas or the Christmas before. Indeed, it was only today that I had at last realized I was willing to give up everything for him. I had planned to go to him, tell him of my feelings and demand to know if he felt the same. Now, fear, or possibly pride, held me back.

I lifted my chin and gazed into his eyes. "Does it matter now?"

"I suppose . . . no." He stared at me, and again, I could read nothing in his eyes. Not regret, not hope, not love. My heart sank. "Probably not." He finished his brandy and set his glass down. "I should be going." He nodded, strode to the door, pulled it open, then paused and turned back to me. "One more thing." He started toward me.

"Yes?" I took a step forward, my heart thudding in my chest.

He reached me and stared into my eyes.

"Yes?" I tried and failed to hide the note of ragged hopefulness in my voice.

"I nearly forgot." He reached into his pocket and pulled out my gloves. "I believe these are yours."

I forced a smile and took the gloves. "Thank you for returning them."

"It was good to see you again." He stared a moment longer, then nodded. "Good day, Portia," he said, but it sounded more like farewell. He turned and took his leave.

For a moment, or a lifetime, I stood frozen, gazing after him. I feared when I moved, when I so much as took a single step, I would collapse into a quivering mass of despair. How could I let him go? How could he leave?

I'd found the courage to follow my heart back to Italy, back to him. He'd had the courage to give up his position and follow his muse to Italy. But he'd never had the courage to ask me to be with him. Perhaps it made a fair amount of sense.

After all, of all the things he'd never done, he'd never said he loved me either.

22

My Dear Lady Redwell,

You have my utmost apologies and deepest regrets for our ill-advised words yesterday. Please allow me the opportunity to make amends.

I have been invited to a ball in honor of the Queen's jubilee at the home of the Duke and Duchess of Roxborough. I would be honored if you would accompany me. I believe we still have a great deal to discuss.

I am currently residing at the Langham Hotel and may be reached there. I shall send a carriage at eight o'clock if this is amenable to you.

Yours,

Fletcher

I stared at the note that had arrived early this morning, long before I came downstairs. But Fletcher never did sleep when he was involved in something, and apparently, today that something was me. And I never slept well when he was on my mind. Admittedly, I was surprised by his invitation. I had doubted that I would see him again after yesterday. Our words had created a rift that would never heal. I wasn't sure what the point was of accepting his offer. It seemed to me there was nothing left to say, and it would probably be wiser simply to move on from here.

Besides, I ached with an empty, hollow sort of pain. I'd never felt—never imagined—pain like this. I'd never suspected a broken heart would feel as if my heart had been physically wounded. As if it had been stabbed or shredded. I wanted nothing more than to crawl back into my bed, curl up in a ball and pull the covers over my head until I could breathe again. And I wanted to weep.

But Hadley-Attwaters were made of sterner stuff. Even though I wasn't a Hadley-Attwater by blood, I was by upbringing. I would not cower, I would not hide, and I certainly would not allow anyone to know how I ached. Besides, wasn't I an adventuress? Apparently, pain was the price one paid for adventure gone horribly, horribly wrong.

I would like to think I had no interest in hearing whatever it was Fletcher thought we still had to say, but I thought lying to oneself was always a mistake. I was glad that he felt badly about our talk yesterday—I certainly did. There was, as well, a vile part of me that hoped he was as miserable as I was, but—as he had never given me any clear indication of how he felt—I had no idea if that was possible. Still, quite aside from the turmoil of my emotions, I had more than a few questions I would like answered.

Dear Lord Castleton,
I regret I must refuse your offer of accompaniment as I have already agreed to attend the ball in the company of a dear friend.

However, I would not be averse to sharing a dance or a refreshment.
Cordially,
Portia Redwell

I had indeed agreed to accompany Thomas to the Roxborough ball at Effington House, and it would have been rude to abandon him in favor of Fletcher. Even though I was not happy with Thomas's discussion with my aunt, I was not above allowing Fletcher to think what he might about my *dear friend*.

I sent my response off to Fletcher and penned a note to Aunt Helena to inform her that, upon further consideration, my plans for Christmas had changed, and I would not be calling on her today. Not that I expected her to accept that, but I did hope she would at least give me a day or two to pull myself together. I would prefer that no one knew of my heartache.

"I feel I owe you an apology," Thomas said almost immediately upon his arrival at my house.

"For running to my aunt and telling her of my plans?" I cast him a pleasant smile.

"Well . . ." He grimaced. "Yes. Your business is your business, and it was not my place to intrude."

"No, it wasn't." I kept my smile firmly on my face. "But as you did so out of concern for my welfare, I would be hard-pressed not to forgive you."

"Do you forgive me, then?" Hope lit his face.

"Oh, not today. But I'm sure I will. Eventually." I nodded toward the door. "Shall we go? It's impolite to arrive too late."

"We wouldn't want that," he murmured and escorted me to his waiting carriage.

The ball was all that a successful ball should be: too warm, too loud and entirely too crowded. A place where everyone knew nearly everyone and it was all quite pleasant. If expected. Aunt Helena greeted us as if nothing untoward had happened between us, and I was grateful for that. Thomas and I fell into our usual comfortable manner with each other, although it struck me as somewhat forced. He was a bit tentative, as if he were walking on eggshells. He could be quite perceptive. I was certainly preoccupied, which I assumed he credited to my legitimate annoyance with him and not the fact that I was apprehensive about an encounter with my Christmas affair.

An hour or so after we arrived, we were in the midst of a waltz when he indicated a point across the room. "Do you see that gentleman over there?"

I followed his gaze, and my heart stopped. Fletcher stood on the other side of the ballroom, engaged in conversation with a couple I didn't know. I nodded.

"That's the new Earl of Castleton."

"Oh?" I said coolly. "I was not aware there was a new Earl of Castleton."

"I think his name is James—no—Jamison. The previous Lord Castleton died in a boating accident several months ago."

"I might have heard something about that." It did sound vaguely familiar, but as I did not know Castleton or his family, I'd paid no real attention at the time.

Thomas continued, not noticing I was hanging on his every word. "From what I've heard, Jamison was never expected to inherit the title."

"He wasn't?" And wasn't that interesting?

"Not at all. The previous lord was quite young, and his death was unexpected. Jamison was a fairly distant cousin. I understand he'd been living abroad. Now he has the title, rather extensive property and"—he chuckled—"considerable wealth."

"He does look well-tailored," I murmured.

Thomas laughed and led me through the intricate steps of a turn. My gaze strayed back to Fletcher and caught with his. I nearly stumbled and I never stumble.

"Are you all right?" Thomas frowned down at me.

"Just a bit fatigued, I think." I shrugged. "Perhaps some refreshment is in order."

"Excellent idea." Thomas steered me off the floor. "Besides, I noted some gentlemen I need to speak with near the refreshment table. If you don't mind, this might take a few minutes."

"Goodness, Thomas." I raised a brow. "This is not the first time I have been alone at a ball, and I daresay I won't be alone for long. I'm acquainted with half the people here and no doubt related to the other half."

"Very well." He grinned. "I'll try to be quick as possible, but—"

I waved him off with my fan. "Go."

"I thought he'd never leave," Fletcher said behind me.

I closed my eyes against a wave of longing, drew a calming breath and turned. "Why, Lord Castleton, what a delightful surprise."

"I thought it might be." He offered his arm. "Would you do me the honor of this dance?"

I hesitated. I wanted nothing more than to be in his arms, but I feared it might be my undoing.

He leaned closer. "Come now, Portia, we have never danced together before."

"No, I don't suppose we have," I said and surrendered.

He led me onto the floor, and I stepped into his arms. The music began, and we danced together in perfect step with each other. As if we had indeed danced together before. As if we had danced together always.

For a few minutes, neither of us said a word. There was so much to say, and yet I didn't know where to begin.

"How was your exhibit?" I asked at last.

He looked startled. "That was not the first question I expected."

My jaw tightened. "What did you expect?"

"I don't know, but . . ." He drew a deep breath. "The exhibit went well, better than I'd hoped. In fact, my work has been very well received. I've exhibited and sold nicely. I've already made something of a name for myself."

"Won't that be awkward for the Earl of Castleton?" Society, being what it was, might well buy art, but an artist in its midst would never be tolerated.

"Fortunately, I was clever enough not to use my real name."

"My, that was clever. Not using your real name, that is. I can see where that might make things significantly easier." The words came out faster and harder than I had intended, as if of their own accord. I struggled to keep my voice low. "Avoid scandal and all that. After all, you never know what might happen if you were to use your *real name*. Why, you were just being cautious. Prudent. One might even say wise. And I say bravo, Fletcher, for being so clever."

"Stop it, Portia," he said through clenched teeth. "And try not to look as if you're about to rip my head off. We'll attract attention, and I don't think either of us wants that."

I summoned my most brilliant smile. "No, we do not. Of course, it would be hypocritical of us to pretend to be having a lovely time when we're not. Nearly as hypocritical as being outraged over someone lying about their name when you did the very same thing yourself."

He cast me a blinding smile. "It was not at all the same thing. I painted under a false name to protect my family from scandal."

"It's exactly the same thing." I struggled to keep my smile in place.

"You lied to me about your name. How do I know you didn't lie to me about everything else?" He led me through the steps of a turn a bit faster than I was used to, but apparently, outrage had its benefits. I was flawless.

"What everything else, Fletcher?"

A muscle in his jaw tightened. "I don't know, but—"

"You asked me to trust you, and I did. Unfortunately, I never asked you to trust me. I simply expected it."

"This is a mistake. We shouldn't be talking here." His eyes flashed with anger, but his smile remained.

As did mine. "Not our first!"

He drew to a stop near the edge of the dance floor. "Come with me."

"I don't think that's wise."

"We've never been especially wise, and we need to talk." He took my elbow and steered me out of the ballroom.

"We have talked." I sniffed.

"Not enough."

"I'm not sure we have anything left to say," I said under my breath. Nonetheless, I did not pull away. "Have you ever been here before? Do you know where you're going?"

"Somewhere private."

"The library, then." I nodded at a doorway a few feet farther down.

"Excellent." He cracked open the doors and peered inside. "This will do." He waved me to enter in front of him. We were lucky. During a ball, the Effington House library was frequently occupied by those seeking a respite from the festivities or those wishing privacy. On more than one occasion, I myself had sought refuge here from my aunt's attempts at matchmaking. Fletcher closed the doors behind us.

I folded my arms over my chest. "What did you wish to say?"

"There are things I need to explain." He thought for a moment. "I didn't tell you everything about myself and my family, but you didn't tell me everything either."

"I told you a great deal."

"What do you want to know, Portia? I assume you have questions."

I stared at him for a moment. "I understand you were never expected to inherit the title."

"No, I wasn't." He shook his head. "My cousin's death came as quite a shock, although I barely knew him." He paused. "So you see I never lied about that."

I would give him that. "No, I suppose you didn't."

"When my cousin died and I came to London to see to his affairs, I was hoping that, now, you and I might see one another. Publicly."

"When your cousin died?" Hadn't Thomas said the previous Lord Castleton had died some time ago? "When was that?"

He thought for a moment. "Summer. June."

"And that's when you came to London?" I said slowly.

The import of what he'd just admitted showed on his face. "I did intend to call on you."

He had waited months to see me? *Months?* "It's mid-October. June was four months ago. Or did you just plan on waiting until Christmas?"

"Bloody hell, Portia, it's not easy to completely change one's life." He blew an exasperated breath. "Without warning, I had obligations, here and in the country and in Paris as well. New responsibilities and expectations. I wasn't prepared for any of it. I needed to get my life in order, and I needed to make some decisions. I fully intended to call on you. The right opportunity never arose."

"Did you think about me at all?"

"That's not fair, Portia."

"Isn't it?"

"I was afraid," he said sharply. "I didn't know what to do about you. So I put off seeking you out, and every day that went by, it was harder to explain why I didn't. It occurred to me that it might be easier to tell you everything if indeed I waited until Christmas."

"Easier?" I stared. "For whom?"

"I didn't want you to want me only because I am now Lord Castleton."

I sucked in a sharp breath. "Do you think so little of me?"

"Quite honestly . . ." His voice hardened. "I don't know what to think."

"I thought we knew each other better than that." I clasped my hands together to keep them from shaking.

"Do we?"

"Perhaps not." I drew a deep breath. It didn't help. "You could have used my gloves as an excuse anytime. Why did you decide to call on me yesterday?"

He hesitated, and I knew this was not going to be good. "I had a matter that I wished to discuss with you."

"Go on."

"My great-aunt had every intention of leaving the villa to me when she died, but she has decided she no longer wants the responsibility for it. So she is deeding it to me now."

"When you said you spent Christmases with your grandmother and her sister in a house overlooking the sea, it was the villa, wasn't it?"

He nodded. "I have always tried to go back for Christmas."

My heart caught.

"However . . ." He paused, and I braced myself. "A gentleman who has let the villa every spring for years is now interested in purchasing it. I am inclined to accept his offer and turn over the villa in the new year."

I started as if I had been slapped. "My God, Fletcher, you can't sell the villa! It would be like selling your soul. Some of the best times of your childhood were spent there. It's part of your history, your past. There are memories there that will never come again."

"Too many, I think." His gaze bored into mine, and I realized we were no longer taking about childhood memories.

"It's magic, Fletcher." I stared up at him. "You don't sell magic."

"I suspect the magic might be gone. I would imagine magic works only for so long. We accept that and move on." His gaze searched mine. "But it was good."

"Yes." My throat clogged. "It was."

"I'm returning to Paris in a few days," he said abruptly.

"Are you?"

"I have matters I need to resolve. I—" He nodded. "I just wanted you to know. About the villa, that is."

"And now I do." I summoned all the calm I could manage. I had no idea how. "If that's all, we really should return.

We don't want Lord Castleton to be the subject of gossip." I turned to go, then turned back. "Is there anything else you wish to say to me?" The oddest note of desperation sounded in my voice. I didn't care. I didn't know exactly what I wanted him to say, but I held my breath.

"I shall miss you." He smiled. I wasn't sure I had ever seen a smile quite so sad before. I swallowed against the lump in my throat. It didn't help. "Especially at Christmas."

For a long moment, we stared at each other. It occurred to me that I should be blunt and ask him directly what his feelings were for me. That I should fight for him. But I was the worst sort of coward. I didn't think I could bear him telling me that he didn't care for me. That he didn't love me.

It was painfully clear that—beyond a few weeks at Christmas—I was not what he wanted. If I was, surely he would do something more than merely say he would miss me. Obviously, my feelings were not returned. It struck me that this must be how Thomas felt. Poor, dear man.

I raised my chin and mustered a polite smile. "I shall send you a card." I nodded, turned and left the library before he could say a word. Before what little courage I had failed me completely.

A lady does not chase after a man who does not want her, a voice whispered in my head. I knew now it wasn't my mother's. It was mine.

And it was right.

23

It appeared a broken heart was very much like any seri-ous wound. The edges mended slowly, and just when you thought you were fully healed, there would be a twinge or a moment, a sight or a sound or a scent, and the crushing pain would return.

My life was as full as it had always been. I had my friends and my family and Thomas, although we did not see each other as often as we had. I continued my study of languages and all the other things I had cultivated to fill my empty days. And yet, they were still empty. Or perhaps it was simply my fickle heart that refused to accept that whatever Fletcher and I had shared in that villa overlooking the sea was over. Still, I had the oddest sensation I was waiting for something. I tried to blame Christmas. Wasn't everyone always counting the days until Christmas? But I knew that wasn't it.

October turned to November, and then it was December. Christmas was mere weeks away, and with every day closer, a horrible sense of dismay grew within me. As if, when

Christmas came, what Fletcher and I had found would finally, irrevocably be over.

As much as I tried to hide it, Veronica and Julia were well aware of my melancholy. I had told them all that had happened with Fletcher. They were appropriately sympathetic and righteously indignant on my behalf. They agreed that I was right not to fight for him, as there was nothing to fight for. And they took it upon themselves to improve my disposition. I believe they saw me as this year's Christmas charity.

"We have something we want to show you." Julia swept into my parlor, where I was dutifully conjugating Latin verbs.

Veronica was by her side. "Something you will want to see."

I cast them an annoyed frown. "Do the two of you realize that I do have a butler whose duties include announcing visitors before they invade my privacy?"

"We told him you wouldn't mind," Veronica said, "and that we would just come right in."

"He did not seem inclined to stop us." Julia grinned.

"He wouldn't dare." I narrowed my eyes. "I'm not sure what you've done to him, but you have the poor man terrified. Not individually, but when you are together, he quakes like a frightened bunny."

"Then you need a butler who is made of sterner stuff." Veronica thrust my hat and cloak at me. "Now then, let us be off."

I stood and reluctantly accepted the garments. "Dare I ask where?"

"No," Julia said firmly. "It's, well, it's a surprise."

Veronica snorted.

"Am I going to *like* this surprise?" I asked slowly.

My friends exchanged cautious glances.

"We don't know." Veronica shrugged. "We thought it was rather impressive."

"Extremely impressive." Julia nodded.

I looked at the two of them and understood there was no escape. "Very well, then. Let's go see this impressive surprise."

Some twenty minutes later, they ushered me into the Rossier Gallery.

"Art?" I glared at them. "I am in no mood to view an exhibit."

"Oh, you might like this one." Julia steered me around false walls arranged so as to display more paintings.

"Or you might not," Veronica said in a determined voice. "But you do need to see it."

The gallery was busy but not overly crowded. Indeed, at another time, I might have enjoyed wandering through the room. If my relationship with Fletcher had done nothing else, it had awakened me to the world of contemporary artists. We turned a corner, and my friends stopped.

"This is what you need to see," Veronica said quietly.

I sucked in a sharp breath.

There, displayed for all the world to see, were a dozen or so paintings, all obviously by the same artist. They were quite impressive, with colors that were at once vivid and yet muted, as if the scenes depicted on canvas were illusions or fantasies and had nothing to do with the reality of life. And fully half of them featured a dark-haired woman in various states of dress and undress. There was little flesh exposed, but the suggestion of nudity, together with the dream-like essence of the works, combined for an eroticism that fairly pulsed with desire.

I knew without question these were Fletcher's works. And I was the woman.

"Bloody hell," I murmured.

"That was our reaction," Julia said in a low voice.

I glanced around. "Do you think anyone—"

"Would know it's you?" Veronica shook her head. "I doubt it. We wouldn't have known if it hadn't been for the setting and, of course, the volcano."

"He's done a remarkable job of disguising and yet revealing you at the same time." Julia studied a painting of me with a book in my hand. At once I was back in the villa on the day Fletcher said I was leaving. My heart shifted in my chest.

I drew a breath to steady myself and glanced at the signature. "James Florian. Interesting choice."

"His grandmother's maiden name," Veronica said. Yet another reminder of how much I didn't know about this man.

My gaze slid from one painting to the next. Some of them I had posed for, others came from observations or his own imagination. No, I didn't think anyone who didn't know about our Christmases together would ever imagine the woman in these works was me. She looked so ethereal and serene and . . . happy.

"This is my favorite." Veronica pointed out a painting of me clad in nothing but a long scarf draped seductively from my shoulder to my feet. One had the impression that the scarf would slither to the stone floor with no more than a breath of air. I leaned against an archway, gazing out at the sea and the volcano beyond. I remembered the day I posed for this and how happy we had been.

"The collection is called Shadows of Paradise." Julia sighed. "I've never seen anything like them."

"They just reek of . . . passion." Veronica blew a long breath. "And love."

"Love?" I jerked my gaze to hers.

"Without doubt." She nodded

I turned my attention back to Fletcher's work, and Veronica continued. "The ones without you are very good." She studied them closely. "But the ones with you are remarkable."

She was right. It was apparent in very brushstroke, obvious in every swath of color and light. It was clear as well that not only was the artist in love with his subject, but he had captured the love she felt for him.

The man had never told me of his feelings. He'd never said he loved me. Yet here, on the walls of this fashionable gallery in London, here he said all he'd never said with words.

I was quiet in the carriage on the way home. Julia and Veronica knew me well enough to know I did not wish to engage in conversation. They followed me into my parlor.

I pulled off my glove. "I'm going to Italy."

"What?" Julia stared.

"Why?" Veronica asked at the same time.

I looked at Julia. "I'm going in hopes Fletcher will be there. Besides, I made a pact." I shrugged. "As for the why . . ." I met Veronica's gaze. "If indeed he sells the villa, I know he will want to spend one final Christmas there. Which means this is the last Christmas. And, more than likely, our last chance. I can't live the rest of my life wondering what I might have missed—what I might have lost—by not going to the villa. And I won't."

My friends exchanged worried looks.

"The man broke your heart," Veronica said slowly. "How can you go after him?"

"Because he loves me." I pulled off my other glove. "You said it yourself. The paintings that were landscapes or still lifes were quite nice, but the ones of me were remarkable, awash with emotion and love. His heart and soul are in those paintings, and his passion. I am not an expert in art, but those works were painted by a man in love. The man I love." I clenched my jaw. "And I am not going to let him out of my life without so much as a strongly worded protest."

"You said you weren't going to fight for him," Veronica pointed out.

"Actually, I believe I said I didn't have the courage to fight for him. And I didn't when I didn't think there was anything worth fighting for. Now, it's obvious that there is."

"Do you think this is wise?" Julia asked. "It doesn't seem like a very good idea to me."

"To *us.*" Veronica nodded.

"You're right, both of you. It's not a good idea." I scoffed. "It's a dreadful idea. And if either one of you were considering something so absurd, I wouldn't hesitate to tell you what a bad idea it was."

"Then we don't have to tell you how much can go wrong," Veronica said slowly.

"No, you certainly don't." I shook my head. "I'm fairly sure all the possibilities for utter disaster have filled my head since I realized what I need to do. I have been so angry at him, and so hurt, that I forgot that I never truly gave him any indication as to my feelings. The fault here is as much mine as it is his." I thought for a moment. "I followed all those rules about how women are and are not expected to behave. Our role has always been to wait. I am tired of following rules I had no say in making. That first Christmas, when I decided to go on to Italy without my aunt, was my first step toward being an independent woman. Toward making my own decisions. But when it came to Fletcher, I fell back into the habits of a lifetime.

"For good or ill, I can make my own decisions. I can direct my own life. And I will not let this man walk out of my life without knowing I did everything I could to stop him."

"Even so," Veronica said in a cautious manner, "you might want to reconsider—"

"Come now, Veronica, you are on your second husband, but you are still the most independent woman I know. And Julia was forced into independence, but she took to it nicely. It's past time I tried it. Nothing else seems to have worked all that well."

"But what if—" Veronica began.

"It doesn't matter," I said firmly. "My mind is made up."

"We can see that, but . . ." Julia met my gaze directly. "Didn't he say the magic was gone?"

I chose my words with care. "Isn't it possible that magic, like very nearly everything worthwhile in life, requires effort? And work? And faith?" I straightened my shoulders. "This may well be a mistake, but I refuse to spend the rest of my life wondering what might have been if I had had the courage to . . . to ignore the restrictions of the box that is my life. To follow my heart."

"It might well be broken again." A warning sounded in Veronica's voice. And sympathy.

"Indeed it might, but at least I will have no regrets."

"What will you do about Thomas?" Julia asked.

"I don't think Thomas will be surprised by this."

Thomas knew nothing of what had transpired between Fletcher and me. It had added to the distance between us. That and the nagging suspicion I had that he would always try to control my life. David had done that, and not only had I allowed it, I hadn't noticed. But I had changed since David's death. And as much as I considered Thomas a dear friend and as much as I enjoyed his companionship, I could not go back. I didn't love Thomas, and that was a sacrifice I could not make.

"I will write him a note. I should write to Aunt Helena as well. If one of you will be so good as to have them delivered for me." I paused. "Tomorrow is soon enough, I think."

Veronica grinned. "Excellent plan."

Without thinking, I reached out and took Julia's and Veronica's hands and smiled at these women, my closest friends. The sisters of my soul. No matter what I did, I knew without question or doubt that they would stand behind me. As would my family. Aunt Helena was right. There was nothing in the world greater than the courage one derived from love.

"If I leave tonight, I can be at the villa for Christmas Eve."

24

I sent a silent prayer heavenward and reached for the door knocker. The ornate design was that of a woman's face. Her expression had always struck me as tentative, as if she didn't know if you were friend or foe. I let the knocker fall and waited for the door of the villa to open. And hoped I wasn't too late. The sense of dread that had settled as a heavy weight in my stomach three days ago had only increased. Weather had delayed my ship and put it two days behind schedule.

Christmas was yesterday.

Still, I had come this far, and I was not willing to give up. Not now and not ever. I had made the decision to pursue what—or, rather, who I wanted. I still wasn't sure as to the wisdom of it, but I was certain I had no real choice. I would not live the rest of my days regretting that when life demanded I do something, I didn't. Even something wrong was better than nothing at all.

Silvestro rarely took longer than a minute or two to open the door. I waited for at least five before I tried the door. The villa was never locked. I grasped the handle and pushed the door open.

It was the middle of the day, yet shadows hung over the room. I stepped inside, the ever-faithful Margaret preferring to stay behind in our hired carriage. It wasn't until I made my way to the parlor that I noticed that much of the furniture was missing and sheets covered most of the rest.

My heart twisted.

I was indeed too late. The house was empty and, apparently, in the midst of being sold. I walked slowly to the doors leading out to the loggia. The view was as beautiful as it had always been. The bay as deeply blue. Vesuvius as threatening. I believed I was too stunned to do more than stare unseeing, although I should have been prepared. With every hour my ship had been delayed, my hope that I would be here for Christmas dimmed.

I heard a footstep behind me. I didn't dare to turn around.

"Portia?" Thomas said.

I swallowed against the lump in my throat and forced a calm note to my voice. "I believe, in the note I sent you, I specifically asked you not to follow me."

He paused. "I must have forgotten to read that part."

I turned toward him. "Why did you come?"

"For a number of reasons. One is that I have been giving this—giving us—a great deal of thought in recent months. Apparently"—he looked me straight in the eye—"we are not meant to be. At least, not at this time." He shrugged. "Do not take this to mean I am giving up. One never knows how all might turn out in the end." He cast me a wicked smile.

I did so wish I loved him.

"But most importantly, I came because I have vowed to be your friend."

"And you are here to support me in my time of need?" I attempted a lighthearted laugh that—even to me—sounded forced.

"I am. And I hope you'll allow me to do so." He moved toward me. "I don't know the details of your Christmases. I only know that two months ago, you were determined to come here, and then abruptly you changed your mind. You have not been your usual self since."

"You are perceptive, I'll give you that."

"It's a gift." He grinned.

I almost laughed. "Did you think I would crumple to the floor in despair?"

"No, of course not. You're made of sterner stuff than that. I was simply being prepared." He paused. "I was prepared as well to intrude upon a joyous reunion, which would have been most awkward for all of us."

"Well, then, we should be fortunate it did not happen." I turned around and directed my gaze back toward the bay. As much as I was grateful for his thoughtfulness, I would have preferred to be alone. If I was going to say farewell to the Villa Mari Incantati, I would rather do it by myself. Thomas was out of place here.

Here was magic. Here was Fletcher.

I shook my head. "You really shouldn't have come, Thomas."

"She's right, Thomas," a familiar voice said behind me. "You shouldn't have come."

My breath caught and I turned on my heel.

"Fletcher?" I said softly, unable to believe my eyes.

The corner of his mouth quirked upward. "Portia."

"Lord Castleton?" Thomas's eyes widened.

"Lord Lindsey." Fletcher nodded, his gaze still locked with mine.

He looked haggard, as if he hadn't slept well, or at all. As if he were miserable. I'd never seen anything quite so wonderful. "You look dreadful."

He shrugged. "I had a . . . difficult Christmas." He turned his attention to Thomas. "As we all agree you shouldn't have come in the first place, now would be an opportune time to take your leave."

"Oh, I don't think so." Thomas crossed his arms over his chest. "I should leave Portia's fate in the hands of some man who was not smart enough to realize she was in love with him?" He snorted. "Not bloody likely."

I stared at him in surprise.

"Good Lord, Portia, I knew you were in love with someone. That your Christmas trysts were more than insignificant flings. The best I could hope for was to be there for you should you need me."

"And you have been, Thomas." I laid a hand on his sleeve. "You have been the very best of friends."

"Lucky, lucky me," he said wryly.

"And I do hope we can remain friends."

His gaze shifted to Fletcher. "I suppose that depends on what happens now."

"Now?" Fletcher considered him for a moment. "Now, in spite of the fact that you insist on remaining here, I intend to confess all to Lady Redwell. I had time in my carriage on my way back here to determine exactly how to say what I need to say. Although that really wasn't necessary." He grimaced. "I had all day Christmas to decide what I needed to do, as well as the last few months."

"And what did you decide?" I stepped toward him, my heart thudding in my chest.

"Any number of things. I've been a coward and an idiot, you see. For that I am truly sorry." Regret sounded in his voice. "I've been in love with you since our first Christmas. Probably since the first moment you indignantly informed me, in a very poor attempt at Italian, that this was *privato propertyo*."

"That means private property," I said in an aside to Thomas.

His brow furrowed. "No, it doesn't."

"But I was a mere civil servant, admittedly from a respectable family, but with no true prospects." Fletcher shook his head. "I couldn't ask you to throw your lot in with mine. In spite of my fine words, I still lived by all the expectations laid upon a man of my position. Besides, I feared what you might say. I don't think I wanted to know if you didn't share my feelings."

"So you made a Christmas wish."

"I did. It was the best I could hope for, really. That you'd return for another Christmas." He smiled. "And you did."

"And the next year?" I struggled to keep my voice level. "You were no longer living your life by other people's expectations."

"Ah, but then a union between an artist and Lady Smithson—"

"What does she have to do with this?" Thomas asked.

"I used her name."

"Ouch." He winced. "I can't imagine she took that well."

"No, she didn't." I mustered a firm tone. "Thomas, this really has nothing to do with you, and while I do appreciate your continuing concern, as you can see, I am perfectly all right."

"Yes, I suppose you are." He heaved a resigned sigh. "I'll wait outside, should you need me."

"Is he in for a long wait?" Hope sounded in Fletcher's voice.

"Forever, I would say." I sighed. "I am sorry, Thomas."

"As am I, Portia." He cast me a resigned smile and took his leave.

I turned my attention back to Fletcher. "You were saying something about being an idiot?"

"I was saying a union between us would have been even more unacceptable last Christmas." He shrugged. "I know how society is, and I know your position is important to you. I couldn't ask you to give it up. For me."

"You could have." I drew a deep breath. "And you should have."

"I can see that now, because you're here." He took another step toward me. "I didn't think you were coming. After all we said to each other, I didn't expect you to be here. But, oddly enough, I still hoped. Even when it was obvious—"

"Weather delayed my ship. There was nothing I could do. I feared, with every minute that passed, that I would miss you. Almost as much as I feared you hadn't come at all. Then when I arrived today . . ." I shook my head in confusion. "How did you know I was here?"

"I left a bag in the carriage, and while arranging transport to return to the villa, I missed the next train to Naples—probably the one you arrived on. Silvestro was returning to the train station with my bag. He passed your carriage headed here. The moment he told me, we raced back here." He paused.

"Yesterday, I discovered Christmas simply isn't Christmas without you. You should know that."

"After we last spoke . . . I thought . . . I didn't know if you wanted me to come." I paused. "Why did you wait so long to call on me in London?"

"I wanted to, desperately, the moment I arrived in London, but there were matters pertaining to my inheritance that demanded my attention, decisions that needed to be made. A few days after my arrival, I attended the queen's garden party at Buckingham Palace. I saw you and Lindsey together. I saw the two of you after that at several other gatherings. It struck me that he was a better match for you than I could ever be. Of all the things you talked about, you never mentioned him, so I assumed your aunt had brought the two of you together after our last Christmas." He blew a long breath. "I thought he could make you happy."

"Thomas is a very good man, and I could be quite content with him." I shook my head. "But it seems I want more than content."

"When I found out you aren't who you said you were— even though I could understand why you lied—I felt betrayed. While I knew we didn't know all the details of our respective lives, all the trappings, as it were, I thought we knew each other." His gaze searched mine. "I thought, given the improbable way we met, that we were, I don't know, meant for each other."

"You should have said something."

"I told you I was a coward." He moved closer, close enough for me to step into his embrace. And, dear Lord, I wanted to. "I was afraid of declaring my feelings for fear you wouldn't feel the same. I was afraid that asking you to give up your position in society for a mere government employee or—God forbid—an artist was asking too much. Then, when I had a title and fortune, everything that would be expected in a match for you—even by your family's standards—I was afraid as well."

"Some of your fears were"—I chose my words with care—"well-founded, I think. Because I was afraid too. I didn't know that I could give up everything in my life that I had always wanted. Or perhaps, always been expected to want."

"Portia—"

"Let me finish." I summoned whatever courage I had. "Before I saw you in London, I had decided to come here for Christmas and tell you how I felt about you. And demand to know your feelings. I was ready to give up everything to be with you."

He cringed. "And I mucked that up."

"You were a bit of an ass, but I could have done better as well. I thought then that we were finished. That what we'd had was no more than the enchantment of the villa."

"Then why are you here?" he said slowly.

"Because the day before I left for Italy, I saw the paintings of an artist by the name of James Florian. You've never told me that you love me, Fletcher." My throat choked with emotion. "But your paintings did."

He stared at me for a long moment. "I've been a fool."

"I believe we've established that."

"Will you allow me to spend the rest of my life trying to make amends?"

"When you say 'me,'"—I struggled to get out the words—"who exactly do you mean?"

Confusion narrowed his eyes. "Me?"

"Which you? The new Earl of Castleton? James Florian, the artist? Or civil servant Fletcher Jamison?"

"All of them." His tone was solemn, but a twinkle sparked in his eyes. "As many, or as few, as you wish, but the earl is probably the most appropriate."

I shook my head. "I doubt the earl is as happy as the artist. I would much prefer you to be happy. I don't think I can be truly happy if you're not."

"Yes, well, about that." The oddest expression of chagrin crossed his face. "It seems I rather enjoy being the earl. With position and wealth come responsibility. My actions affect a myriad of people, people who depend on me. I don't want to disappoint them. This wasn't something I sought and certainly not what I expected, but . . ." He shrugged. "It suits me, and frankly, I find it challenging and invigorating. And I am happy."

"But what about your work? What about Paris?"

"Oh, I have no intentions of giving it up. I suspect James Florian will continue to exhibit." He grinned. "It's one benefit of having lied about a name."

"There is that." I drew a trembling breath. "So, are we discussing marriage?"

"I believe we are."

I stared at him. "Come now, Fletcher, do I have to drag it out of you?"

"Would you?" He cast me a wicked grin.

"I will if you don't—"

He pulled me into his arms. "My darling, Portia. You are my muse and my inspiration and, most of all, my love. I cannot imagine living one more day without you, let alone the rest of my life. Throw your lot in with mine, Portia. Marry me and spend every Christmas until the end of time with me."

My eyes blurred, and I sniffed. "On one condition."

He grinned. "Anything."

"It's obvious, with the furniture missing and the rest covered, and Silvestro and Agostina gone, that the villa has been sold. Isn't there anything you can do to get it back?"

"It hasn't been sold," he said with a reassuring smile. "My great-aunt decided to have her favorite pieces sent to London, and I decided, if I am going to keep the place, it needs a bit of freshening up. As for Silvestro and Agostina, it is Boxing Day. Silvestro left after he dropped me off."

"Then you are not going to sell it?"

"Apparently not. The buyer reconsidered his offer after he understood, even if the villa was sold, I fully intended to continue to spend my Christmases here. And I insisted that be put in any purchase agreement."

I stared. "You told him that?"

"I thought it might be more persuasive than saying I had come to my senses and realized there were too many memories here to let the place go. After all, where else would we spend Christmas?"

"Where else, indeed?" I blinked back tears and smiled up at him.

"Make my Christmas wish come true, Portia, and marry me."

"Your Christmas wish was for me to marry you? Goodness, Fletcher, you didn't need to waste a wish on that. You could have made it happen long ago."

"Actually, my Christmas wish was to spend every Christmas, for the rest of my days, with you."

"I believe I can arrange that."

"And what of your wish? Has it come true?"

"My wish?" I wished to find what Veronica had found with my cousin Sebastian and what Julia had found with her new husband. I wished to find the happiness and the joy and the love. "Why, yes, Fletcher, I believe it has."

With that, I pressed my lips to his and marveled that I had indeed found everything I'd ever hoped for in the arms of a stranger in an enchanted villa overlooking the sea.

For this Christmas and all the Christmases to come.

Postscript

We did indeed spend every Christmas from then on at the Villa Mari Incantati, except in those years when Vesuvius erupted. Even though the scientific community considered most of those eruptions minor, I did not.

I blame a lack of courage on my part, which seems to me quite sensible, and for which I make no apologies.

Discover more by Victoria Alexander

What Happens at Millworth Manor
What Happens at Christmas
Lord Stilwell's Excellent Engagements (novella)
The Importance of Being Wicked (crossover with Wicked Family Secrets)
The Scandalous Adventures of the Sister of the Bride
The Daring Exploits of a Runaway Heiress

Wicked Family Secrets/Hadley-Attwater Family
His Mistress by Christmas
My Wicked Little Lies

Standalone Books & Novellas
Yesterday and Forever (time travel)
The Princess and the Pea (historical)
The Perfect Wife (historical)
Promises to Keep (second chance romance / time travel)
The Emperor's New Clothes (historical)
Shakespeare and the Three Kings (historical novella)
Play it Again, Sam (reincarnation)

Believe (time travel)
One Magic Moment (historical)
Paradise Bay (contemporary)
The Last Love Letter, Secrets of a Perfect Night Anthology (historical novella)

Effington Family & Friends
Regency
The Wedding Bargain
The Husband List
The Marriage Lesson
The Prince's Bride
Her Highness, My Wife
Love with the Proper Husband
The Lady in Question
The Pursuit of Marriage
The Trouble with Charlotte (novella)
When We Meet Again
Victorian (2nd Generation)
A Visit from Sir Nicholas
Let It Be Love

Last Man Standing (connected to Effington Family and Friends)
A Little Bit Wicked
What a Lady Wants
Secrets of a Proper Lady
The Seduction of a Proper Gentleman
Lady Ameilia's Secret Lover (ebook spinoff from What a Lady Wants)

Lost City Series
*stories about the descendents of the characters in The Perfect Wife
The Virgin's Secret
Desires of a Perfect Lady

Wicked Family Secrets/Hadley-Attwater Family
His Mistress by Christmas
My Wicked Little Lies
The Importance of Being Wicked (crossover with Millworth Manor series)

Mistress Trio
The Perfect Mistress
His Mistress by Christmas (crossover with Wicked Family Secrets)
Same Time, Next Christmas

About the Author

Victoria Alexander was an award winning television reporter until she discovered fiction was more fun than real life. The #1 *New York Times* bestseller has written over 33 novels and been published in more than a dozen different countries. Victoria lives in Omaha, Nebraska with a long-suffering husband she kills off in every book and two bearded collies in a house under endless renovation and never ending chaos. She laughs a great deal—she has to.

Check out her website www.victoriaalexander.com and come chat with her on Facebook https://www.facebook.com/VictoriaAlexandersPlace/.

44880027R00163

Made in the USA
Middletown, DE
18 June 2017